PENGUIN CRIME FICTION

THE BLACK SERAPHIM

Michael Gilbert was born in 1912 and educated at Blundell's School and London University. He served in North Africa and Italy during World War II, after which he joined a firm of solicitors, in which he is now a partner. His first novel, *Close Quarters*, was published in 1947; since then he has written many other novels, short stories, plays, and radio and TV scripts. He is a founding member of the Crime Writers' Association. Penguin Books also publishes his *End-Game, The Empty House, The Killing of Katie Steelstock, Mr. Calder and Mr. Behrens*, and *Smallbone Deceased*.

D1043412

THE BLACK SERAPHIM

by
Michael Gilbert

PENGUIN BOOKS

PENGUIN BOOKS
Viking Penguin Inc., 40 West 23rd Street,
New York, New York 10010, U.S.A.
Penguin Books Ltd, Harmondsworth,
Middlesex, England
Penguin Books Australia Ltd, Ringwood,
Victoria, Australia
Penguin Books Canada Limited, 2801 John Street,
Markham, Ontario, Canada L3R 1B4
Penguin Books (N.Z.) Ltd, 182–190 Wairau Road,
Auckland 10, New Zealand

First published in the United States of America by
Harper & Row, Publishers, Inc., 1984
Published in Penguin Books 1985
by arrangement with Harper & Row, Publishers, Inc.

Copyright © Michael Gilbert, 1984
All rights reserved

LIBRARY OF CONGRESS CATALOGING IN PUBLICATION DATA
Gilbert, Michael Francis, 1912–
  The black seraphim.
  I. Title.
[PR6013.I3335B57 1985]   823'.914   84-18911
ISBN 0 14 00.7563 1

Printed in the United States of America by
George Banta Co., Inc., Harrisonburg, Virginia
Set in Palatino

Except in the United States of America,
this book is sold subject to the condition
that it shall not, by way of trade or otherwise,
be lent, re-sold, hired out, or otherwise circulated
without the publisher's prior consent in any form of
binding or cover other than that in which it is
published and without a similar condition
including this condition being imposed
on the subsequent purchaser

*Modern science has
convinced us that nothing
that is obvious is true,
and that everything
that is magical, improbable,
extraordinary, gigantic,
microscopic, heartless, or
outrageous is scientific.*

—GEORGE BERNARD SHAW,
From his Preface to *Saint Joan*

THE BLACK
SERAPHIM

Prologue

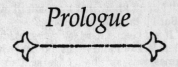

WHEN DR. JAMES PIRIE SCOTLAND FAINTED, he did so in the most dramatic manner, at the conclusion of a lecture on Morbid Anatomy which he was giving to the students of Guy's Hospital. He tumbled off the edge of the rostrum and hit his head on a gallows from which was hanging a fully articulated skeleton.

Twenty medical students, faced with a problem to which there was no answer in their books, proceeded to suggest twenty different courses of action, mostly inappropriate. Fortunately, one of them had the sense to summon the sister on duty, who packed Dr. Scotland off to the nearest private ward.

By the time she had got him there, he had more or less recovered and felt deeply ashamed of himself. Sister Lewthwaite was firm. She said, "That's a nasty cut in your head. It'll need stitches. I'll get the houseman to look at it."

Dr. Scotland put his feet on the floor and said, "Really, Sister. Absolutely stupid of me." He tried to stand up and sat down again abruptly.

"As I thought," said Sister Lewthwaite. "Concussion. If you're going to be sick, the basin's under the bed."

In the end it was the Medical Registrar who pronounced the verdict. He said, "There's nothing organically wrong with you, James. Nature is presenting the bill for six years of overwork. What you need is a month's holiday. Somewhere right away from all this." He dismissed, with a wave of his hand, the grimy stones of South London, which were baking under the September sun. "The isles of Greece, or the mountains of Kashmir. Or if you can't afford that, a cottage in the wildest part of Dartmoor."

"I don't know that I can afford even that," said James sadly. "But I'll think of something."

It *had* been a hard six years; made harder by an almost complete lack of money. His mother, who had been widowed when James was six, had once said to him, "Other people have money. The Scotlands have to get by on brains." And so it had been. A good Secondary Modern School, which had allowed him to specialize in physics, chemistry and biology, followed by a scholarship at Oxford. At the end of his first year, at his tutor's suggestion, he had transferred to the medical school. Here he had discovered a sense of vocation and had worked very hard indeed, winning both the Beaney Prize and the Gull Exhibition in pathology. During his year as a houseman he had continued to read; savage, solitary evenings bent over his books and papers while his contemporaries were drinking beer and making intermittently successful efforts to seduce the nurses.

By now the authorities had their eyes on this earnest young student. A junior registrarship in the Pathology Department had been his for the asking. He had combined the job with tutorial work.

His next move had been to the Poisons Reference Section at New Cross Hospital. Here he had spent a hard but happy year. Much of his time had been spent in considering the toxic properties of everyday things. Of bleaching powders and almond oil and turpentine and white spirits; of the weed-killers and insecticides in people's toolsheds, the kerosene and anti-freeze in their garages, the foxglove and laburnum in their gardens, the yew trees and the nightshade in the hedges.

It was at about this time that he began to have bad nights.

In the earlier years, after a hard day's work, sleep had dropped on him as soon as he had tumbled into bed. Now he seemed to have lost the knack. Sometimes tunes would be running in his head. Hymn tunes mostly. A verse would sing itself a dozen times over. When he went to sleep, the nightmares started. He seemed to be living in a world which was pitch black but shot through with occasional bursts of unwholesome brightness. It was in these bright intervals that he realized that the men and women who thronged about him were all evil. All of them. The half-smile on their faces when they handed you the cup or the glass indicated that they knew there was something unhealthy in it; but you had to drink. Then came the burning sensation in the mouth and throat and he would wake up, his heart beating double time and his forehead damp. Sometimes, but not often, he would be sick.

"At least a month," said the Registrar. "Better two. We'll call it sick leave. On one condition: You take no books with you."

"I must have something to read."

"Not detective stories, then. Too complicated. Straight thrillers, if you like. Cowboy stories. Romances. Or take up fishing. I'm told it's very relaxing."

When the Registrar got home that night and told his wife about it, she said, "He doesn't need relaxing. He needs shaking up. I'm sure he's a very worthy young man, but he's dug himself a groove and buried himself in it. That's all right when you're fifty. Not when you're twenty-four."

"What do you suggest?"

"Something violent and different. You were lucky. You had that call-up in the Infantry."

"Getting up at six o'clock, scrubbing greasy tabletops with cold water."

"It broadened your mind."

Her husband said, "Ugh."

Meanwhile James had been doing some thinking.

In the empty twelve months between leaving school and starting at Oxford he had taken a temporary job teaching at the Choristers' School at Melchester. He had chosen it because his cousin, Lawrence Consett, was headmaster. James had found that he enjoyed teaching, as a change from being taught; and Latin and French and history as a change from physics and chemistry.

"Put you up for a month?" said Lawrence. "No difficulty. To start with, you can share the school cottage with Peter Fleming. You remember Peter? Furbank has broken his ankle, stupid fellow, and won't be back until around the end of the month. After that, there are one or two people I can think of who'd be happy to give you a bed. Our Chapter Clerk—Henry Brookes—was telling me only the other day that he had a spare room now that

3

his old aunt had popped off at last. You could make some arrangement with him for bed and breakfast and get your other meals out."

"That sounds perfect."

"It'll be quiet, of course. But I gather that's what you want."

"Just what the doctor ordered," said James.

One

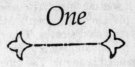

THE BISHOPS WORE CARDBOARD MITERS. The castles had straw hats with ribbons of red and black. The knights carried riding-crops and the kings and queens had paper crowns.

"The white queen is Mrs. Henn-Christie," said Peter Fleming. "Her husband was Archdeacon when you were here before. A little man with a white beard like a goat. He fell off his bicycle and ruptured his spleen. The white king is Canon Maude. He's the one the choristers call Aunt Maude. The black queen is Lady Fallingford and the black king is Archdeacon Pawle."

A piece of sailcloth, painted in sixty-four squares of black and white, had been pegged out on the Theological College lawn. There was a contraption at each end like the folding ladder used by a tennis umpire. A middle-aged clergyman was perched on the nearer one and a much older clergyman on the one at the far end. Both were armed with megaphones.

"King's knight to king four," boomed the middle-aged clergy-man.

A boy stepped two paces forward and one to his right and tapped the occupant of the square on the shoulder. He was grinning as he did so.

"Look at Andrew," said Peter. "He's bagged the head."

The capture of Mr. Consett was greeted with heartless laugh-ter from a line of boy pawns who had already been taken and were squatting on a bench alongside the playing area.

"Of course, this is only a rehearsal," said Peter. "On the day they'll all be wearing proper costumes. Some of them are mag-nificent. The two queens particularly. Mrs. Henn-Christie has promised to wear the pearl tiara which belonged to her great-grandmother."

It was the third week in September, but the sun had lost none of his summer strength. Most of the men who were watching were in shirt sleeves. Two girls, seated together on the far side of the square, were in thin summer dresses. One was a well-rounded brunette. The other was fair and slight.

Peter saw James look in that direction and said, "Watch your step."

"Who are they?"

"The plump one is Penny. She's the head's daughter. She's man-hungry."

"If she's Lawrence Consett's daughter, she's my first cousin once removed."

"Consanguinity won't save you."

"Why didn't I meet her when I was here before?"

"She was away in Switzerland, being finished. The first cozy little chat you have together she'll tell you all about it. It sounded to me like a mixture between a brothel and a school of mountain warfare."

"Queen to king seven," said the old clergyman.

Mrs. Henn-Christie swept forward and abolished a squeaking pawn.

"Check."

"King to queen two," said the middle-aged clergyman hastily. "Who's the other girl?"

"That's Amanda. Dean Forrest's daughter. The Forrests came here about two years ago. Same time as the new Archdeacon."

"Is the Dean here?"

"He wouldn't be likely to attend a function organized by the Archdeacon."

"Why not?"

"They loathe each other's guts."

"Queen's knight to queen six. Check."

"The one on the ladder at the far end is old Canon Lister. I recognize him. And this one must be Canon Humphrey. He came just before I left."

"Francis Humphrey. Canon and Subdean. A very nice man."

"But not a very good chess player."

"Not as good as old Tom Lister."

Canon Humphrey was considering his next move. He did not seem to have much room for maneuver. While he was thinking about it, James looked around. Living chess. That was part of the Melchester tradition. He remembered reading that in the last years of Victoria's reign the great Bishop Townshend had played a game against the Hungarian master Ramek. In that game the kings and queens had been the Marquess and Marchioness of Bridport and Lord and Lady Weldon of Kings Sutton. The meanest pawn had been an esquire of the county.

Characters changed, the scale changed, but, underneath, it was unchanging.

It seemed to be checkmate. Canon Humphrey waved a hand at his opponent and climbed down from his perch. The Archdeacon said, "It's no good, Francis. We're charging people a pound to come in. If Tom's going to beat you in under twenty moves, they won't feel they've had their money's worth."

"Then we'll have to fudge it," said Canon Humphrey. "Hello. Don't I recognize you? You used to teach at the school."

"He's a rising young doctor now," said Peter.

"Splendid. They're giving us tea in the college. Come along."

Tea had been laid out in the refectory. The pawns were already making inroads into the sandwiches. Canon Maude came bouncing in. He was exactly as James remembered him. Large, moist and pink. As soon as he was sighted, the nearest chorister picked up two plates and offered them to him. Canon Maude patted him on the head and said, "Poor little pawn, so soon captured."

"I died in a good cause," said the pawn coolly. "Tomato or cucumber?"

"Would you think I was very greedy if I had one of each?" Another boy offered him a cup of tea. He earned a smile.

"You're being neglected," said a girl's voice behind James. "The boys are such horrid little pigs. They scoff most of the food themselves. Anyone would think we starved them. Andrew, bring those sandwiches here at once."

One of the black knights rescued a plate from a smaller boy and brought it across. He smiled in a friendly way and said, "I recognize you, sir. We were both new together."

"And I wouldn't like to bet on which of us was the more scared," said James. He thought for a moment. "Then you're either Andrew Gould or David Lyon."

"I'm Andrew. This one's David." He indicated his fellow knight.

"You both seem to have grown a lot in the last six years."

"One does," said Andrew. He sounded like a middle-aged man regretting his lost youth.

"Andrew's Bishop's Boy and head of the school now," said Penny. "What about getting us both a cup of tea?"

"See what I can do."

Penny focused friendly brown eyes on James. She seemed to approve of what she saw. She said, "When you were here before, I don't believe we met."

"I did catch one glimpse of you, I think. You had pigtails."

"And a red nose and a squeaky voice."

"I don't remember the red nose."

Andrew returned carrying a cup of tea in either hand. He was closely followed by Lady Fallingford, who cut out James from under Penny's guns with the expertise developed in a hundred social engagements. She said, "Your grandmother Marjorie Lovett was one of my greatest friends. We were at school together, at Oxford. You must come and have tea with me and tell me all about her."

"I didn't know her well," said James. "She died when I was four. I remember her as a little black bundle that jingled when it moved."

Lady Fallingford gave a cackle of laughter. She said, "Monday, then. At half past four. You know where I live. Rivergate Cottages. Just inside the wall. Mine is the one at the far end. You mustn't be late, because we shall all be going on to a recorder session at the Humphreys' afterwards. Now, come along and let me introduce you to Claribel Henn-Christie. Her husband was the last Archdeacon. Happy days they were!"

Since their move had brought them to within easy earshot of the present Archdeacon, James felt that this might have been more tactfully expressed. Lady Fallingford swept him past and introduced him to the spindly lady in a violet frock who was still wearing the white queen's paper crown set at a rakish angle.

"Did you see that?" said Andrew Gould to David Lyon. "Penny thought she'd got her hooks into Dr. Scotland and then Lady F. pinched him."

"Penny's a cow," said David. "Let's go and talk to Masters."

Len Masters, the junior verger, was behind one of the long tables serving tea. The boys admired him because he opened the batting for the Melset Cricket Club and liked him because he did not report them for minor infractions of discipline.

James could see that Penny was waiting to recapture him as soon as Lady Fallingford let him go. He was dangerously *en prise*. He needed a blocking piece. One of the black bishops was chatting up the Dean's daughter. James knew his face well, but the name had escaped him. Think. Brookes, of course. Henry Brookes, the Chapter Clerk. The solid woman beside him was his wife, Dora. A woman of many talents. An arranger of flowers and an excellent cook. The plates of cakes on the table were probably her handiwork. He remembered, too, that she had been at some time a nurse. When the matron had succumbed to an epidemic which was decimating the school, Dora Brookes had stepped in and substituted competently for her.

As soon as Lady Fallingford released him, James sidled across and introduced himself.

"Nice to see you back," said Brookes. "I gather that Lawrence Consett's giving you a bed for the time being. When he has to throw you out, we'll be happy to put you up—did he tell you? We've a spare room now that Alice is gone."

"He did tell me and it's very kind of you."

"Do you know Amanda? Her father is the Dean. It was old Dean Lupton in your time, of course. He retired two years ago and died very soon after."

"I can't think why it was," said James, "that everyone always referred to him as 'poor Dean Lupton.' But they always said it as though it was rather a joke."

"That's because he spent all his time being sorry for himself," said Dora Brookes, in the robust tones of someone who classed illness as a sign of weakness.

"He'd no particular reason to be sad," agreed Brookes. "The Deanery is an excellent house and the stipend is good. Better than Salisbury or Winchester. And he had private means as well."

"*And* he got on with the rest of the Chapter," said Amanda.

James had been examining her covertly. His first reactions were medical. He thought she could have done with more flesh on her bones.

9

"I imagine that's important," he said.

"Most important."

"And not difficult with a bit of give and take," said Brookes.

"That depends on who does the giving and who does the taking. In the old Dean's day it was a lot easier, I believe."

"Oh. Why was that?"

Amanda glanced across the room at the little group by the window. It was composed of theological students and its focal point was Archdeacon Pawle. He seemed to be telling a story. As he spoke, the contours of his plump face shifted, hills changing to valleys, valleys to hills. The only fixed points were two shrewd black eyes.

"Like currants in a suet pudding," said Amanda.

"What are?"

"His eyes, don't you think?"

"My dear!" said Dora Brookes. "You mustn't take any notice of her, Doctor. She says the most terrible things. The fact is, she doesn't like the Archdeacon."

"Who does?" said Amanda.

"A lot of people admire him greatly. He's done wonders for the administration of the Cathedral since he took over from Henn-Christie, who never really thought about money at all. Isn't that right, Henry?"

Her husband, who had clearly been thinking about something quite different, said, "What's that? Yes. Splendid man, very thorough."

"He's not a clergyman," said Amanda. "He's an accountant. When he says his prayers at night—if he does say them—I expect he finishes up, 'And may my profit-and-loss account come out on the right side and my balance sheet balance.'"

Henry Brookes laughed. His wife said, "I'm sure he's a good man at heart."

"If there's any goodness in him," said Amanda, "it's buried deeper than the sixpence in the Christmas pudding."

"Your mind seems to run on food," said James.

"Oh, it does. Sometimes I dream about it. I'm sure that food's the most important thing in most people's lives. Women, anyway. Much more important than sex."

"Amanda, really," said Mrs. Brookes.

"You're a doctor. You understand about these things. I'm right, aren't I?"

"I'm a pathologist. If I was a psychiatrist, I might be able to answer your question."

Amanda said, "Funk," and grinned. The grin exposed a row of gappy teeth and turned an ordinary face into an attractive one. Now that he was close to her, James could see that he had been wrong about her hair. It was not blond. It was long and a very pale auburn.

"Why is it," she said, "that doctors never give you a straight answer to a straight question? Like politicians."

"The same reason in both cases. They don't want to frighten you."

Amanda said, "Oh?" and thought about it. At that moment there was a diversion. A door at the end of the room swung open and a man came limping through. He was six feet tall and carried himself in a way which gave effect to every one of his seventy-two inches. His hair, which was snowy white, hung down on either side of his deeply seamed face. A beaked nose, a mouth drawn tight, as by a purse string, a chin which continued the straight ascetic line of the nose with none of the flabbiness on either side which is normal in men past middle age. It was a face, thought James, which had experienced suffering, but got the better of it.

The crowd parted as he came forward, supporting himself on a rubber-tipped stick. He made straight for Amanda, stooped forward and presented her with a ritual kiss. Amanda accepted it with becoming demureness, managing to wink at James as she did so. She said, "This is Dr. Scotland, Daddy. He used to teach at the school. He's come down here to recuperate."

"And what better place to do so than in the backwater of a cathedral close? Did the game go well?"

"The Archdeacon was mated in sixteen moves."

"Splendid, splendid."

The Dean had made no attempt to lower his voice. If the Archdeacon heard the exchange and the laugh which followed from the little group which had gathered around the Dean, he gave no sign of it. His eyes twinkled as merrily as ever, his bland voice continued its discourse.

The Dean said, "I shall have to drag you away from this delightful entertainment, my dear. We have letters to write." He turned to James. "Amanda is my secretary. In the old days the Dean had a staff of seven. A secretary, a butler, a housekeeper, two maids, a gardener and a coachman. Now Amanda is factotum."

"Not totum, Daddy. Don't forget Rosa."

"True. We have a half-share of Miss Pilcher. We must count our blessings. A terrible woman, but a worker."

He offered his arm to Amanda. The crowd fell back. Two of the choristers competed for the honor of holding the door open. When he had gone, the room seemed half empty.

"I'm on duty at the school until six," said Peter. "After that, I think we might drift down to the town and find a drink."

"An excellent idea," said James. "Let's do just that."

At half past ten that night he was sitting in front of the open window of the school cottage. "What I'd forgotten about," he said, "was the silence."

"When I go back to London for the holidays," said Peter, "it takes me a couple of days to get used to the noise there. Our family house is in St. John's Wood, which is reckoned to be pretty quiet, but this—this is out of the world."

They could just hear, as if it were the humming of distant bees, the cars passing the Bishop's Gate on their way through Melchester to the south. The Cathedral bell beat out the quadruple strokes of the half-hour.

Oh—child—of—God. Be—brave—go—on.

"What did the Dean call it? A backwater?"

"But not, at the moment, a backwater of peace and calm."

"So I gathered. What's the trouble?"

"In the days when I was reluctantly receiving instruction in science, I was taught that there are certain elements which are harmless by themselves—inert is, I believe, the technical description—but if you combine them, you get a mixture which is volatile and explosive."

"The Dean and the Archdeacon."

"Ten out of ten."

"I must say the Archdeacon did look a little bit bloated. A Bishop Bonner, do you think?"

"Bonner?"

"The man who burned a lot of other bishops in Bloody Mary's reign. His cheeks were said to be glutted with the flesh of martyrs."

"Lovely," said Peter. "I'll try that on the boys. Glutted with the flesh of martyrs. They'll enjoy that. They don't care much for the Archdeacon."

"He doesn't seem popular in some quarters. Why is that?"

"His only known vice is gluttony. He lunches frugally, but in the evening he eats and drinks enough for three. Personally, I rather like him."

"Not a very good life, medically speaking, I thought. But that's no reason for unpopularity."

"I agree. Everyone loved Falstaff."

"When I asked Amanda, she said that the Archdeacon was really an accountant."

"I suppose it *is* a fault for a clergyman to think more about money than he does about his soul. But someone's got to do the thinking. A cathedral is a business. It owns a lot of property and employs a lot of people. Someone's got to find the money. It won't drop down like quails and manna from heaven. The old Archdeacon, Henn-Christie, was a sweetie. But I doubt if he could add two and two."

"And is the Dean also a mathematical simpleton?"

"I don't think he's simple in any way at all. He's a tough character. Before he came here, he'd spent most of his life on missionary work in the remoter parts of Africa and India. The boys seem to have got hold of some pretty odd stories about it all. Exaggerated, I don't doubt. But he's certainly a man who'd put sanctity above silver."

"And if it came to a straight fight, how would the Chapter line up?"

"At the moment, the Dean's got the edge. Francis Humphrey, the Subdean, is on his side. And so is Tom Lister. He's the old boy we saw performing this afternoon."

"The chess champion."

"Right. And he's not only good at chess. He's the only real scholar Melchester's got. He reads Greek and Aramaic and Syriac and any other old language you can put your tongue to. You ought to look at his entry in *Who's Who* sometime. Dozens of books on comparative philology and things like that."

"All of which, no doubt, you've read."

"As a matter of fact, I did get hold of one, out of the sixpenny box in the marketplace. Perfect bedside reading. After one page I invariably fell into deep slumber."

James laughed and yawned at the same time. He felt tired, but he was not sure that he was quite ready for sleep.

He said, "All right. That makes it three to one. So what about number four?"

"Number four's Canon Maude. He doesn't count. He's just an old softy."

James laughed and yawned again. He decided that perhaps he was ready for bed. It had been a long day.

As he drifted into sleep, his thoughts kept wandering back to the chessboard. In his imagination the pieces on it grew to more than human size. Black knights and white knights pranced on real horses around the keeps of formidable castles from whose battlements kings and queens looked down.

At one of the slits in the wall stood a girl with hair that was more auburn than blond. It was long hair. It hung down almost to the ground, as though it was inviting James to use it as a rope and climb up it.

By the time the Cathedral clock beat out the strokes of eleven, he was asleep. It was the earliest he had got to sleep for a long time.

Two

AT THE AGE OF FOURTEEN James had imagined, for a few months, that he might become a professional organist. He had a natural ear for music, and a friend who played the services at the local church had encouraged him to practice. At the end of a short flirtation with music, his common sense had shown him the gulf which is fixed between an amateur who can play an instrument and a professional who does play it, and the colorful ambition had been discarded. But he had retained his love for the most solemn and powerful of all musical instruments.

In the year he had spent at Melchester, he had made a friend of the little Canadian sub-organist, Paul Wren. He noted from the service sheet that, though still shown as sub-organist, his name now stood alone, and James assumed that Paul's predecessor, Dr. Tyrrel, had been promoted. As he took his place in the Choir stalls for Matins, he was able to see the back of Paul's head and to catch an occasional glimpse of his face in the mirror beside the console.

The *Jubilate* was Purcell in B flat and the *Te Deum* Vaughan Williams in G. There was no doubt about the mastery of Paul's playing. It spread strong invisible threads from the organ loft to the choir. James thought he had never heard them sing better.

The responses were being intoned by a young clergyman whose face James recognized. He finally placed him as the white bishop. His voice had a strong male clarity, a great improvement on the Vicar Choral of six years before who had bleated like a sheep. The sermon was preached by Canon Maude, who forgot to switch on the microphone in the pulpit. It was only when the head verger managed to turn it on for him that his words became audible. From what they then heard, James thought that they had lost very little.

After the service the officiating clergy and the regular members of the congregation, most of whom had seats in the Choir, trooped through the cloisters and into the Chapter House. Betty Humphrey, the Subdean's wife, Dora Brookes and Julia Consett were pouring a brown liquid from large jugs into plastic mugs. It tasted vaguely like coffee.

Francis Humphrey, catching sight of him, came across and said, "I meant to invite you, but forgot. We've a recorder party tomorrow at six, on the West Canonry lawn, if the weather stays fine."

"Lady Fallingford mentioned it. I was wondering exactly what a recorder party might be."

"Nothing to do with tape recorders, I can assure you. They're sort of wooden flutes. Have you never seen one? My wife and I take the treble and tenor, and Miles Manton, our Cathedral architect, takes the bass. The accompaniment is a viola-da-gamba. What Shakespeare calls a viol de gamboys. Paul plays that and coaches all of us, too."

"He's a remarkable musician. He was only assistant organist when I was here last. I was glad to see that he's got the top job now. What's happened to Dr. Tyrrel?"

"He's gone to Kings. I agree with you about Paul. I only wish it was the universal opinion."

"Isn't it?"

"The Archdeacon doesn't entirely approve."

James noticed that when he said this, Canon Humphrey turned his back on the company. They were in a corner of the room and the clatter of voices screened them.

"Why on earth? The man's a genius."

"Several reasons. The Archdeacon's a traditionalist. His musical taste seems to begin and end with Stanford in B flat. Paul likes to experiment sometimes with something a little more modern. There I support him. There's been plenty of good church music written this century."

"I'm sure you're talking scandal," said Penny Consett. "Otherwise why are you both standing in the corner like a couple of naughty boys?"

"We were talking music, not scandal," said Canon Humphrey. "Dr. Scotland was saying how much he enjoyed Paul's playing."

"Isn't he sweet?" said Penny. "Just like a hamster with a little blond beard. Much nicer than Tyrrel the squirrel."

"You appear to be anthropomorphic," said James.

"Gracious! I hope it isn't catching."

"An anthropomorph is someone who thinks of animals as people and people as animals."

"Most of them are, when you come to think of it. The Archdeacon's exactly like a—"

Canon Humphrey coughed loudly. The Archdeacon, who had surged up behind them with a coffee cup balanced in one hand, said, "Dr. Scotland, isn't it?"

"That's right, sir."

"Come to revisit the scenes of your youth? Not thinking of resuming a scholastic career?"

"Just for a month's holiday."

"An excellent notion." He swung around on Penny. "Tell me. *What* am I exactly like?"

Penny had the grace to blush. Then she said, "We were just saying that most people were like different animals. I was going to say that you were like a grizzly bear."

"Not bad. Not bad at all." His little black eyes twinkled. "Ah. Here comes our organist. None of your modern trash today, I was glad to note, Wren."

"I never play trash," said Paul shortly. He pushed past, toward the coffee table. The Archdeacon looked after him thoughtfully. A grizzly about to pounce? James wondered.

The crowd was thinning out now. James hung around unobtrusively. He wanted a word with Paul and managed to time his exit so that they reached the door together. Paul looked at him blankly for a moment, then smiled.

He said, "James. I hardly recognized you. You look at least twenty years older."

"The *sturm* and *drang* of medical life. Someone was telling me that you'd got a new console."

"Not new. But the old one's been pretty comprehensively rebuilt. It was finished just before Tyrrel left. Would you like to see it?"

"That's what I was hoping you'd say."

17

He followed Paul up the narrow winding stairs into the organ loft: a snug cabin, with curtains shutting it off on three sides and on the fourth the gleaming bank of five manuals and the hundred ivory-headed stops like a hundred little serving maids in mob caps waiting for orders.

James settled down on one end of the bench with a contented sigh and said, "You know, I'd be happy just sitting here all day. It's like being on the bridge of a ship. How I envy you. I saw, by the way, that you'd got the top job now."

"Temporarily."

"Surely not."

"I'm afraid so. The powers that be don't approve of me."

"You mean the Archdeacon? I'd heard something about that."

"He's a bastard," said Paul. "A clever bastard and a busy bastard, but a bastard nonetheless. You know what he's got against me? I've got the wrong letters after my name. I'm not A.R.C.O., I'm A.R.C.C.O."

"That sounds even more impressive."

"Not to him. I'm an associate of the Royal Canadian College of Organists. Get the difference?"

"When you play the way you do, it shouldn't matter if you were a member of the Timbuktu College of Organists."

"I'm not sure that it really does matter all that much. But he uses it as a handle to get at me for other things. You heard what he said just now. None of your modern trash. When we did the Joubert *Te Deum*—and the choir really sang it beautifully—all he said was, 'Joubert—South African, isn't he? Another of your colonial maestros.'"

"Why does he do it?"

"What really sticks in his throat is that my promotion was backed by the Dean."

"No love lost there," agreed James.

"If you searched the ecclesiastical firmament with a powerful telescope," said Paul solemnly, "I doubt you could find two men further poles apart. You probably think I'm biased. Maybe I am. I happen to like the Dean. He's not perfect. Far from it. He's tough and ruthless and devious as all come, but I reckon he puts his faith and his church first. It's led him into some pretty wild places before he came to roost in this hen run."

"So I heard. India and Africa."

"His last posting was in Ethiopia. That's where he got into bad trouble with guerrillas. They broke his leg for him. But he got back at them somehow. There are about six different versions of the story. I'd like to hear the truth sometime."

"I must admit," said James, "that it's hard to visualize Archdeacon Pawle living a missionary life among savage tribesmen."

Paul said, "Let's be fair. If *his* idea of religion is a round of boring tea parties, that's his lookout. No. What I object to is his notion of turning religion into a business proposition. Do you know, he had the nerve to say to me, 'People like to hear the things they're used to. That's what most of them come to church for. If you play all this modern stuff, you'll never bring in the paying customers.' Paying customers. Good God! Just as though a cathedral was a stall in a circus and he was outside beating a drum and shouting, 'Roll up, roll up. You want the old stuff—we've got it!'"

His little beard bristled and he looked so indignant that James couldn't help laughing. He said, "You mustn't take it too seriously, Paul. If he's a musical Philistine, that's his misfortune. Most people in a place like Melchester would be on your side over a thing like that. They appreciate good music."

"Unfortunately, most people don't have a say in the appointment of the Cathedral organist. The Archdeacon does. And he's got a nephew at Worcester who'd like the job."

"And who has all the appropriate letters after his name?"

"That's right."

They sat in silence for a few moments. Then James said, "I suppose you couldn't . . . I mean, people would think it odd if they heard you practicing."

"All right," said Paul resignedly. "What do you want?"

"The Benjamin Britten *Jubilate* with all the twiddly bits."

"You think a little music would have charm to soothe my troubled breast."

"That's just what I did think."

Paul switched on the power and pulled out a few stops, one of which James was delighted to see was labeled CLARIBEL FLUTE. If he ever wrote a novel, he thought, that should be the name of the heroine.

Paul started to play, softly.

O be joyful in the Lord, all ye lands.

The gilt angels on top of the far bank of organ pipes, with their golden trumpets to their lips, seemed to be dancing in time with the music.

> *Serve the Lord with gladness and come before His presence with a song.*

More than half the attraction of the traditional liturgy lay in its music. Perhaps the Archdeacon was right. Perhaps people did come to church just to hear the things they were used to.

> *Be ye sure that the Lord, he is God. It is he that hath made us and not we ourselves.*

That was the Dean speaking. That was the faith that made saints and upheld martyrs. When you had stripped away the overlay of formalism and ceremony and superstition, that was the rock on which the church was built. If you truly believed that, you could go anywhere and dare anything.

In the times that followed, James sometimes found himself looking back at Paul and himself, together in the organ loft, above the empty Cathedral, in the sunshine which streamed through the east window over the high altar and lit up the dark corners of the clerestory.

That afternoon, having lunched in the town, James was coming back into the Close with no idea of how to spend the afternoon when he ran into a flock of blue-and-gold caps, shepherded by Peter.

The pecking order, he observed, was unchanged. A line of senior boys was echeloned on each side of the master who was taking the walk. The two immediately beside him were the black knights, Andrew Gould and David Lyon.

"Come and join us," said Peter. "Stretch your legs. Do you good."

David Lyon made way for him and he fell in beside Peter. He had evidently interrupted a serious debate.

"It's no good fussing about these things," said Peter. "Everyone has to economize these days. That's what inflation does to you."

"This isn't inflation," said David. "It's deflation."

Evidently a student of economics.

"How do you make that out?"

"Three boys in a car don't use up any more petrol than one boy."

"It depends how heavy they are. Three like Piggy . . ." He indicated a fat boy waddling ahead of them. The fat boy turned his head and grinned. James realized that most of the boys had arranged themselves so that they could hear what was being talked about. It was a sort of ambulatory parliament.

"Is this a problem in mathematics?" he said. "Like if two men dig a well in four hours, how long would three men take?"

"It's more practical than that. Last term when we went to away matches, parents who were spectating used to come in the school bus. The—" Peter had been going to say Archdeacon, but changed it at the last moment—"the Finance Committee decided that they ought to pay their own fares, so three of them who had cars got together and offered to take the whole team, *provided* the school paid for their petrol. The Finance Committee is still trying to work out whether they'll save money on it or not."

"What they could do is get Canon Maude to take some in *his* car."

Everyone within earshot seemed to think this was a terrific joke.

"They'd never get there," said Andrew. "He's a terrible driver."

"He'd spend all his time patting them on the head and telling them his corny jokes," said the fat boy.

"We all know who he'd want sitting beside him," said a boy out on the flanks. "He'd want Bottle."

"He couldn't have Bottle. He isn't in the team."

"Who on earth are we talking about?" said James.

Andrew gave a shrill whistle, like a shepherd calling in a sheepdog, and a small boy came trotting back. His hair, James noticed, was almost the same color as Amanda's. He had the guileless face which fills old ladies with sentiment and experienced schoolmasters with suspicion.

"This is Bottle," said Andrew.

"Funny asses."

"Real name Anstruther."

"It's not fair. Just because Aunt Maude—"

"Canon Maude," said Peter.

"Sorry, sir. Canon Maude said I was like a Botticelli cherub and they've been calling me Bottled Cherry ever since."

"All right," said Andrew. "You've said your piece. Back you go. He pretends to be annoyed about it," he explained to James. "But he isn't really. It boosts his personality."

"Inflates his ego," explained David.

Later, as the disorganized army ambled out of the River Gate and into the road leading out of Melchester and into the countryside, the conversation turned to the agreeable topic of murder.

"That's what you do, isn't it?" said the fat boy. "Mr. Fleming told us. You examine dead bodies to find out who killed them."

"You're cutting a few corners there," said James. "I do carry out autopsies—post-mortems—in routine cases. And I've helped the pathologist at Guy's once or twice in criminal cases. Not necessarily murders."

"When you do a—what did you call it?—an autopsy, does that mean cutting the chap open?"

"You have to do that sooner or later, yes."

"Tell us about that."

"Well," said James doubtfully. The boys seemed to be genuinely interested. "It would depend what you were looking for."

"Suppose it was poison."

"Then you'd concentrate first on the abdominal cavity. That's the bit just under your ribs. It's got your stomach in it and one or two other things, like the liver and the kidneys and the spleen."

The fat boy patted himself thoughtfully.

"You'd have to take them out separately to examine them. The stomach is the most important. You tie up each end before you remove it."

"Anyone under thirteen," said Peter, "will withdraw out of earshot."

This had the effect of thickening the crowd around them considerably. Fortunately, they had reached a fairly empty piece of road.

"Then what?" said David.

"Then you cut the lining of the stomach into small pieces and put them into a jar, along with the contents. Probably a number of separate jars, some for the liquids, some for the solid bits. Then you can begin to test for different types of poison. The first thing is to find out if it's acid or alkaline or neutral—"

James forgot after a bit that he wasn't addressing a class of medical students. He was in the middle of Marsh's Test for arsenic when an angry hooting notified them that a motorist wanted to get past.

"For goodness sake," said Peter, who had been listening as interestedly as anyone, "get on the pavement, or we shall have one or two more corpses for Dr. Scotland to examine."

When they got back to the school, Andrew said, "That was a super walk. It's only four o'clock. Why don't we go round again?"

Peter vetoed this and the school dispersed. He said, "I suppose you realize that most of that will go into their next letters home. Come in and join us for tea."

James had tea at the school and his supper at a café in the market square which served meals at a moderate price. At about nine o'clock he strolled across to meet Peter at the Black Lion, which competed with the White Swan for the respectable drinking trade. Peter preferred it because it was the headquarters of the Melchester Rugby Club. The Selection Committee met in a small room at the back on Tuesday evenings through the season.

"Not that anyone ought to be playing rugger in this weather," said Peter. "Die of heat apoplexy. Two pints of bitter, please, Charming."

"The name's Charmian, Mr. Fleming."

"I was using it as a description, love. Not a name."

Charmian sighed. She was an intelligent girl and it sometimes seemed to her that the hardest part of her job was listening to male drinkers trying to be gallant. She didn't mind Peter. He could be amusing, in a schoolmasterly sort of way. But some of the others! And the jokes she had to listen to, all of which she had heard dozens of times before. And the language, particularly toward closing time. Since it was Sunday, closing time would be ten o'clock, thank goodness. She'd soon be tucked up in bed with a cup of cocoa and a book.

"I was up in the organ loft having a gossip with Paul Wren this morning," said James. "Like a lot of people in the Close, he seems to be crossing swords with the Archdeacon. A pity, because I thought the musical part of the service went particularly well."

"It certainly goes better now that we've got a Vicar Choral with a decent voice."

"Agreed. Who is he?"

"Openshaw. Quite a sound type. A bit out of place in a cathedral close. What he really wants to be doing, he told me, is slogging it out in a slum parish. Oh, God! Look who's here now."

The door had been pushed open and two men had come in. James, his mind still running on anthropomorphism, decided that the one in front was a fox. The rufous hair, the sharp nose, even the predatory teeth when he smiled, as he was doing now at Charmian. The man behind had a vaguely military look about him. A lion? A tired and unconvincing lion. Too young to have been in the war. Possibly he had joined the Territorials in order to earn the right to be called the Major by his cronies.

"Two large Scotches, darling," said the first man, "and don't drown them with soda."

The second conclusion which James came to was that both men had been drinking and, while not drunk, were well on the way there.

When he had got his drink and downed a lot of it, the first man looked around and caught sight of Peter. He said, "What ho, the usher. Naughty boy. Shouldn't be down here boozing. Should be tucking the boys up in bed."

Peter said, "About time *you* were tucked up in bed, isn't it, Leo? I only hope you're not driving."

"Are you implying that I am the worse for drink?"

"That's right."

"Then allow me to say that I don't give a twopenny fart what you think."

"Fine," said Peter. "You don't care what I think and I don't care what you think. So suppose we both stop thinking and get on with our drinking."

The second man, who had retired to a seat in the corner, was adopting this excellent advice. James thought, for a moment, that his friend was going to join him. Evidently, however, he considered that it would be more suitable to his dignity if he had the last word. He turned to the girl and said, "You're allowing the place to go downhill, darling. Letting in young tearabouts from the Close. They're wild men, all of them. Before you know where you are, you'll find their Dean coming in here, drinking up all your whiskey."

Charmian thought it safe to laugh at this.

"It's no laughing matter, darling. He's a real baddy. You'd have to keep your blouse buttoned up if *he* was around."

Peter had evidently been meaning to be good, but at this point he lost his temper. He said, addressing his remarks pointedly to James, "You know why this character goes round blackguarding the Dean, don't you?"

James shook his head. He thought there was going to be a fight soon and he had no love for saloon-bar brawls.

"It's because he made Mr. Sandeman look bloody stupid. Has your hat recovered yet, Leo?"

This was clearly a barbed question. Leo Sandeman swung backward and forward, heel to toe, for a few moments, considering his riposte. Then he turned to the girl. "There's one thing to be said for allowing schoolmasters in here, darling. I don't suppose they give *you* a lot of trouble. Not with all those lovely choirboys to occupy their affections, eh? You know the old rhyme? 'His height of desire was a boy in the choir, with a bum like a jelly on springs.'"

James knew the limerick about the young fellow from Kings and had laughed when he first heard it, but there was something particularly unpleasant about it as spoken by Leo Sandeman. It might have been because the speaker had a slight lisp and the words came out as "chelly on shprings."

On this occasion only Sandeman laughed. Even his friend in the corner said nothing. Peter, who had been going red in the face, got slowly to his feet and said, "Just say that little rhyme again."

"Why? Didn't you hear it the first time?"

"I'd like you to say it once more. Then I'm going to punch your nose through the back of your face."

Sandeman took a step back, but was brought up sharply by the bar counter. Charmian said, "Gentlemen, please," but made

25

no attempt to interfere. She thought that a good punch might improve Mr. Sandeman's nose. His friend said, "Stop it, old man. You can't brawl in here."

"Go on," said Peter. "We're all listening."

At this moment there was an interruption. Two more men came into the bar. Both were young. One was large and had red hair. The other had fair hair and was smaller.

The redhead said, "Hullo, Peter. What's this? A fight? Can I join in?"

"No, Bill, you can't."

Sandeman said, "Now you've got two supporters, I suppose you'll be very brave."

"Good heavens!" said the redhead. "If it isn't Leo. What a man for trouble. You want to watch it, or someone will tread on your hat again."

Sandeman said, "Funny man."

"Don't let the odds worry you," said the redhead. "There are six of us here. That makes it three all. I'll fight Gerry. You can take on this character, Philip. I'm afraid I don't know your name, sir."

"Scotland," said James politely.

But the steam had gone out of the situation. The military type who had been sitting quietly got up, took Sandeman by the arm and said, "I think we'll finish our drinks in more agreeable company, Leo. Leave these louts to get on with it."

He went out, followed—not unwillingly, James thought—by Sandeman.

"That's torn it," said the fair-haired boy.

"What's wrong?"

"That was my boss."

"Are you working for Gerry Gloag's outfit?"

"As of last month. As of *next* month, probably not."

"Nonsense, old boy. He can't sack you. *You* didn't do anything. Cheer up. Now that the riffraff have gone, suppose we have a drink. Pull us four foaming pints, Charmian."

"You *are* awful, Mr. Williams."

"I know I am, darling. But it's much too late to do anything about it."

Introductions were effected. James gathered that the redhead was Bill Williams, who worked on the *Melset Journal*, a rival paper to the *Melset Times*. "A stuffy collection at the *Times*," said Bill. "If you want the real news, come to us." The fair-haired boy was Philip Rosewarn. They both played rugby football for the Melset Club, Bill at forward, Philip at scrum half. Philip still seemed to be worried.

"Gloag's so unpredictable," he said. "Most of the time he's the commanding officer being decent to the subalterns, but every now and then he can be an absolute bastard." He drank up some of his beer and added, "I think he's in Sandeman's pocket. They're very thick."

James said, "Who *is* Sandeman? And when and how did he lose his hat?"

Bill Williams said, "He's a councillor. Chairman of the Roads Committee, a trade-union organizer and a shit of the first water. I'll tell you about his hat in a moment. I just want to find out from Philip—" He suddenly sounded both interested and serious. "When you said he was very thick with Gerry Gloag, did you mean anything in particular?"

"Well, Sandeman seems to be round our place a good deal, in office hours. I wondered what was up."

"Perhaps he's buying a house."

"I don't think it's anything simple like that. I happened to go in once when they were together. They had a plan open on the table. Part of it was the Close, I could see that. And the land north of it, the other side of the river. They rolled it up pretty smartly when I walked in."

Williams said something which sounded like "Fletcher's Piece." Then he finished his beer, ordered a final round and regaled them with the story of the Mayor wanting to go to the lavatory in the middle of a mayoral reception.

In the laughter and talk that followed, the story of Leo Sandeman's hat got shelved.

They walked home along the south wall of the Close and through the Bishop's Gate.

"Still shuts sharp at eleven," said Peter. "If you want to get in after that, you have to cross Mullins' palm with silver."

"Or use an alternative entrance."

"That's right. Incidentally, they've put a line of barbed wire along the wall by the south gate, but there's another simple way

27

in along the riverbank. I usually climb straight into the cottage garden."

As they turned into the quiet street which led to the Bishop's Gate, a car slid up behind and a spotlight flicked on. The car slowed and James thought, for a moment, that it was going to stop. Then it accelerated again, passed them and drove off down the street.

"Did you see that?" said Williams.

"What was it all about?"

"That was Detective Sergeant Telfer, a leading light in our local police force. I guess he'd been lurking somewhere near the Lion to see if I'd driven there. Then he'd have stopped me and had me breathalized."

"But why?"

"He doesn't like me. The *Journal* published something rather rude about him. He thought I'd written it. As a matter of fact, he was quite right. I had."

Peter said, "The point is, James, that our two local newspapers, the *Times* and the *Journal*, are at daggers drawn. If one of them blackguards the police, the other supports them and vice versa."

"Civil war," said Bill. "Not always so civil, though."

James said, "War in the Close. War in the town. I'm beginning to wonder if I've come to the right place for a rest cure."

Three

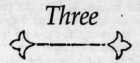

On MONDAY MORNING, after a makeshift breakfast, James strolled out into the Close and made for the High Street Gate. The sun was shining and he felt at peace with the world.

The area inside the gate had been ruled out into ten parking places. Nine of these were already occupied. Two cars were heading for the remaining vacancy. The first car, coming from the direction of the Deanery, was being driven by the Dean's daughter, Amanda. The competitor, coming in from the High Street, was a dark blue official-looking saloon driven by a thick-set young man with a meaty face.

Amanda won the race and slid neatly into the vacant slot. The young man pulled away and parked alongside the pavement opposite. As he was getting out of his car, Mullins, the Close Constable, came out of his cottage and looked at him with disapproval.

"Can't park here, son," he said.

"I'm sorry," said the young man, not looking at all sorry. "But seeing there are no parking spaces vacant, I've got to park somewhere else, right?"

"Plenty of parking places in the town."

"Look, I don't want any argument. I'm here on official business with Archdeacon Pawle."

"Suppose you've got official business with God Almighty, you can't leave your car here."

Splendid, thought James. Church versus State. He wondered who was going to win. Amanda, leaning out of her car window, was listening unashamedly. Possibly it was the presence of an audience which tipped the scale. The young man switched off his engine, applied the parking brake with unnecessary violence, opened his car door and got out.

He said, "You can do what you like about it, Mr. Mullins. That car stays right there."

"Detective Sergeant Telfer, isn't it?" said Mullins placidly.

"Since you know who I am, you've got even less reason for obstructing me in the course of my duty."

"It's not me who's obstructing you," said Mullins mildly. "It's you who's obstructing any of those cars at the end of the line that wants to get out."

The young man said, "Don't bother. I won't be long," and strode off.

"Long enough, I hope," said Mullins and re-entered his cottage.

This was evidently not the end of the drama. Amanda spotted James and said, "Don't go away. This might be fun. Have a seat in the stalls."

James got into the car and sat down beside her. He said, "What happens next?"

"It all depends whether Sam or young Ernie are handy. Mullins will be telephoning them now."

Five peaceful minutes ticked past. Then a tractor came rattling across the Cathedral precinct. Mullins was standing ready. The tractor, which was driven by a middle-aged man with a beard ("Sam Courthope," said Amanda, "a very nice man"), backed up to the car. Two chains were brought out and hooked to the winch on the tractor and the bumper of the car. Mullins leaned into the car to release the hand brake and signaled to Sam, who engaged the winch and lifted the front wheels of the police car clear of the ground.

"Right away," said Mullins and the tractor departed in the direction of the Cathedral with the car bumping behind it.

"Lovely," said James. "Where's he taking it to?"

"He's got a sort of yard where he and the builders keep their stuff. I expect that's where he'll put it."

"Does much of this sort of thing go on?"

"A certain amount. It's got much worse since Daddy took over." As Amanda said this, she showed her teeth in her urchin grin. "One of the things the Corporation doesn't much like is having the Close gates locked at night. You know they had to leave them open during the war because of bombs and fire engines getting in, and they tried to keep it that way when the war ended. There was a terrific argument, but the Cathedral won."

"Why would they object to the gates being shut?"

"They said it was medieval."

"Nothing wrong with being medieval."

Amanda looked at him out of the corner of her eye. She said, "You really think that? Well, so do I. But a lot of people don't. There's a crowd in the town who don't really approve of the Cathedral at all. They pay lip service to it, but in their heart of hearts they think it's an old-fashioned nuisance. They'd like to pull it down and put up a nice modern factory making furniture or fridges. I suppose it's jealousy, really. Town versus Gown. In the old days they used to fight about it. Real fights, with swords and daggers. Now they just sit back and make snide remarks."

"Hold it," said James. "Here comes the law."

The expressions on Detective Sergeant Telfer's face, when he rounded the corner and saw that his car was gone, changed from blank astonishment through dawning comprehension to fury.

"Just like TV, isn't it?" said Amanda happily.

It occurred to James that perhaps a generation brought up on television close-ups might be becoming less ashamed to express their emotions visually.

Telfer stepped up to the Close Constable's cottage, jerked the bell and waited. The tinkling sound died away in the warm air. Nothing else happened. Telfer grabbed the bell pull again and jerked it savagely.

Mullins, who must have come out of his garden gate, rounded the corner, padded up behind Telfer as he had his hand once more on the brass bell pull and said, "Easy with the fittings, son. You don't want it to come away in your hand, do you now? Expensive things to mend."

"What I want," said Telfer, "is my car."

There was more menace in the flat way in which he said it than in any colorful obscenity.

Mullins looked at him thoughtfully. He said, "It isn't here, is it?"

"What have you done with it?"

"I haven't actually what you might call done anything with it. Not myself, that is."

"Where is it?"

"I expect that it has been towed away by the proper authorities in accordance with the instructions of the Dean and Chapter with regard to vehicles illegally parked."

Telfer, who had been red, was now white with fury. "Do you mean to say," he said between his teeth, "that you've had the fucking nerve to have *my* car towed away?"

"I guess that's right."

"Then I want it back and I want it back now."

Mullins put one hand into his side pocket and produced a small notebook and into his top pocket for a pair of reading glasses. He did all this with a massive deliberation which served to stoke Sergeant Telfer's fury to boiling point.

"'Fines for illegal parking,'" he read out. "'First offense, five pounds.'"

The Sergeant took a quick step toward him.

"Go on," breathed Amanda. "Hit him. Two independent witnesses. Hit him just once and we've got you where we want you."

There was an undertone of savage satisfaction in her voice that startled James. For a moment it was touch and go. Then the Sergeant seemed to visualize the pit ahead of him. He swung around on his heel and marched steadily out of the Close into the High Street without looking back.

James let out the breath which he had been holding and said, "I don't know about you, but I could do with a cup of coffee."

"Good idea," said Amanda. "Let's go to the Copper Kettle." She got out of the car. Mullins was still looking at his notebook. He seemed to be abstracted. "Jolly well played, Mullins."

"I'm afraid we may have a bit of bother about that," said Mullins, "but I wasn't going to be trampled on. If he'd been polite, now—"

"Don't worry," said Amanda. "You were only doing your duty. The Dean will back you to the hilt."

Over a cup of coffee in the Copper Kettle, James said to Amanda, "What is the position, really? Does the authority of the police extend to the Close or not?"

Amanda said, "I don't think anyone knows. For crimes and

32

breaches of the peace and things like that, certainly it does. But some things, like traffic control, are left to us."

When James got back to the cottage, he found Peter stretched out in a chair with his heels on the table, smoking.

"Picture of an idle schoolmaster," said James.

"I'm conserving my powers," said Peter. "Difficult days ahead. Finance Committee meeting tomorrow."

"Are you involved in that?"

"We're all involved. Even the Matron has to turn up and account for every cough drop she dishes out." The prospect didn't seem to worry him. He said, "You remember Anstruther."

"Bottle?"

"That's the boy. Aunt Maude has started writing to him."

"Poems?"

"Love letters."

"Good God!" said James.

"It's no joke, really. Luckily, the boy had the sense to hand it straight over to me. I don't think anyone else saw it. I gave it to Lawrence. He nearly had a fit. It was full of stuff about eyes like stars and rose-red lips."

"The man's senile. What's Lawrence going to do?"

"I left him worrying about it."

"If I was him, I'd tell the boy to tear it up."

"And what happens when Anstruther tells his father about it? He's a brigadier general and lives in the town."

"Not easy," agreed James.

"What I guess he'll do is pass the buck to the Archdeacon. He's chairman of the School Governors."

"What will he do?"

"You shall have the next exciting installment this evening."

At three o'clock that afternoon Detective Superintendent Herbert Charles Bracher called, by appointment, on the Dean. He was not the sort of man whom his colleagues, or even his friends, would ever address as Bert or Charlie. He was a tall solemn man with a bush of hair already retreating from his forehead, who stood on his dignity, had an ambitious wife and was said to have money put by. The Dean received him in his

33

study and listened in silence to what he had to say. There was a further silence when the Superintendent had finished.

Finally the Dean spoke. His voice was soft and so deliberate that there seemed to be short intervals between words and longer intervals between sentences.

"First," he said, "I'd like to be a little clearer about the facts. I was aware that there had been pilfering, on a small scale, from houses in the Close. In the summer we live with our front doors open. All sorts of people walk past. Saints and sinners."

The Superintendent said, "Just so, sir."

"The articles which have been stolen have mostly been silver. Trays, cups, inkstands. Things calculated to catch the magpie eye of a sneak thief."

"That's just my point, sir—"

"And now you come and tell me that one of the servants of the Cathedral, the junior verger, Masters, has been seen selling articles of silver to a trader in the market."

"Not just any trader, sir. A man with a bad reputation. We've had our eye on him for some time."

"I see. Then it was one of your men who observed this transaction?"

"Well, no, not actually, sir. But it was reported to us."

"By whom?"

"I'm afraid I can't tell you that, sir."

"Why not?"

"We never reveal the sources of our information."

"But if the matter comes to court, he or she will be called on to give evidence."

"If it comes to court."

The Dean considered this in silence for a full minute while the Superintendent fidgeted. He had never felt comfortable with Dean Forrest. His predecessor had been a great deal easier to deal with. A very agreeable old man. Not a gaunt ruffian like the present incumbent.

"And was this the matter that your Sergeant Telfer came here this morning to discuss with the Archdeacon?"

"Yes, sir."

"Why?"

"I'm not sure I follow you."

"Why was a matter affecting the discipline of the Close discussed with the Archdeacon and not with myself?"

"Well, sir, I suppose in this case it was because—" He broke off, realizing suddenly that he had nearly been trapped into an indiscretion. He changed the end of the sentence smoothly—"because we don't quite appreciate these fine points. We thought that administrative matters would be the concern of the Archdeacon."

"That's a very curious idea, Superintendent. Tell me, if I had information which affected the reputation of your force . . . I say, if—I'm not implying that I have any such information. Would I not then go to the head of your force? To your Chief Constable, Valentine Laporte? I would not discuss it with a sergeant, or even—" the Dean paused delicately—"with a detective superintendent."

"I suppose not, sir. If this was a mistake, I must take the blame for it."

"On general grounds? Or was it perhaps you who suggested that Sergeant Telfer should see the Archdeacon?"

The Superintendent felt himself being forced into a corner. Also he was aware that he was losing his temper and that if he lost it he would put himself at a disadvantage. He said, "On both grounds. And now could I revert to the two points I've already mentioned."

"Two points," said the Dean, placing the tips of his fingers together.

"First, will you ask Masters for an explanation?"

"Certainly not."

"I'm afraid I must insist, sir. If you won't question the man, someone else must. An accusation has been made."

"All that you have told me so far is that an unnamed informant has told you that they saw Masters selling unidentified silver objects in the marketplace. You have no case at all, and unless you can produce some more substantial evidence, I won't have one of the Cathedral servants bothered with it."

"I'm afraid I can't leave it at that, sir."

"If you should ignore my direct instructions and seek to harass Masters in any way, I will make it my business to see that he is legally protected."

The Superintendent hesitated. He was aware that he had no more than suspicions. If the stall-keeper had been anyone but Alf Carney, he wouldn't have given the matter a second thought.

While he was hesitating, the Dean said, "You had a second point?"

"Yes, sir. I had. Sergeant Telfer wants his car back."

"He shall have it. On payment of the stipulated fine. For a first offense, five pounds."

"Aren't you being a little unreasonable, sir?"

"Not in the least. When you were calling on me, I notice you parked your car in my drive. Very reasonable. Why should Sergeant Telfer not have parked his car inside the Archdeacon's gate, instead of leaving it in a position where it blocked three other cars which were legally parked?"

"Being on duty, I expect he thought it would be in order."

"If he thought that, I would suggest a medical check."

"Sir?"

"Because he must be stone deaf. Mullins informs me that he told him not once, but twice that he was breaking Close regulations."

Bracher got up abruptly, put down a five-pound note on the table and said, "If you'll kindly tell me where the car is, I'll have it fetched."

The Dean also got to his feet. He said, "Mullins will show him where the car is. And might I give you a word of advice. Inside the walls of this Close *all* routine matters are regulated by the Church through its constituted authority, the Cathedral Chapter. There is no reason for controversy and friction."

By this time they had reached the front door. The Dean held it open politely. He added, "There are enough troubles in this world, Superintendent, without going out of one's way to look for more."

The Superintendent strode down the path, got into his car and drove off without a word.

Lady Fallingford's cottage was at the far end of a row of cottages along the west wall of the Close. It was rather bigger than the others and had a sizable garden. James found Mrs. Henn-

Christie there, with Francis and Betty Humphrey. Paul Wren, the organist, arrived soon after he did.

"I thought of having tea in the garden," said Lady Fallingford, "but the flies are really intolerable."

"I don't mind flies," said Mrs. Henn-Christie. "It's mosquitoes by night and wasps by day. Toby was stung on the nose yesterday and made a terrible fuss about it."

Toby, James gathered, was a Siamese cat.

Since everybody knew everybody and everybody talked at once, it was not easy for James to ask the question he was dying to ask. A fleeting opportunity occurred when their hostess was distributing second cups of tea. He said, "Can someone please tell me. What exactly *did* happen to Leo Sandeman's hat?"

This produced a laugh and everyone tried to answer the question at once. In the end Mrs. Henn-Christie had to call the meeting to order. She said, "If you all talk at once, the poor young man won't hear any of you. It's your story, Constantia. You tell him."

"He's a terrible little man," said Lady Fallingford. "He does nothing but make trouble for everyone. He's on the Council, you know. He's got some special job. I forget what it is."

"Chairman of the Roads Committee," said Canon Humphrey.

"Is that right? But what he revels in is his other job. He's local boss of Newfu. You've heard of Newfu?"

"I'm afraid not," said James. "It sounds like a health food."

"It's the National Estate Workers Federated Union. They managed to recruit all the men who work on the big estates, particularly the ones that are open to the public. People like the Weldons of Kings Sutton House and the Bridports at Bayford Castle. Last summer they brought them out on strike. I expect you read about it."

"I think I did," said James untruthfully. Among so many strikes this one had hardly caused a ripple.

"The owners had to give in. It was the beginning of their season, and if their workers wouldn't work and pickets blocked the entrance gates, they weren't going to get any visitors at all."

"What was the strike about?"

"What strikes are always about. More money. Lady Weldon said they had to pay so much more that it took away any profit there was. Not that they ever made much. This year they won't be opening the house at all and most of the staff have lost their jobs. So what good was it supposed to have done?"

"Union organizers never think about that," said Betty Humphrey. "Mostly they organize strikes to make themselves feel important."

"Well, anyway," said Lady Fallingford, "the next thing that happened was they tried to rope in the staff here. Sam and young Ernie and the builders. Sam went to see the Dean. He told Sam they were to have nothing to do with it. So, early this summer Newfu tried to blockade the Close."

"They did *what?*"

"It's quite true. They put pickets with banners on all three gates. Can you imagine it?"

"I can indeed," said James. "What happened?"

"The Dean was very angry. Particularly as it was the day of the Diocesan Women's Institute service. They come in, you know, from all over the diocese. Hundreds of them. The Dean took his largest stick and hobbled down to the High Street Gate. People who saw him said he was white with fury. I'm sure he'd have broken a few heads with that stick. Luckily, he didn't have to use it. Because just as he got there, the head of the Women's Institute procession reached the gate. They were good solid women with solid sensible shoes. They'd come a long way and they weren't going to let a miserable little picket stop them. They walked straight over it. Do you know the hymn they sing at their meetings? Blake's 'Jerusalem.'"

"'And did those feet in ancient time,'" hummed Paul Wren happily, "'walk upon England's mountains green?' They certainly walked upon Newfu. Sandeman's hat got knocked off and a very large woman trod on it. The press had been expecting trouble and that young man from the *Melset Journal* was on the spot. The one who plays football."

"Bill Williams."

"That's the man. He got a beautiful photograph of it. It was published in the *Journal* next day."

Mrs. Henn-Christie said, "I thought it was so funny I cut it out and stuck it up in the kitchen. I have a good laugh every time I look at it."

"So what happened to the strike?"

"It fizzled out. The Dean announced that preventing people coming to church was sacrilege. And that sacrilege was a felony, and if the police refused to do anything, the Chapter would institute a private prosecution."

"That wasn't what stopped them," said Canon Humphrey. "Your keen trade-unionist likes being prosecuted. What Sandeman couldn't stand was being laughed at."

"You can't keep a man like that down," said Betty Humphrey. "I'll warrant that he's the man behind this business about Fletcher's Piece."

This produced a brief silence while people thought about Fletcher's Piece. Canon Humphrey said, "Are you sure about that, my dear?"

"I couldn't prove it. But he'd give anything to get his own back on the Cathedral, and it's just the sort of meddling thing he'd be bound to have a finger in. You see if I'm not right."

"I always suspected he might have been one of the people behind the supermarket scheme, too," said Mrs. Henn-Christie. "I'm sure I was swindled. Not that I could prove that, either."

"Come now," said Canon Humphrey. "Just because we don't like the man, we mustn't turn him into a universal villain. There's good in most of us somewhere."

"You're too charitable, Francis," said his wife. She was gathering up her things. "We'll have to be getting along. We've got a lot to do to get things ready for this evening. We're starting at eight o'clock sharp. We're expecting about forty people."

"And you'd better not be late," said Canon Humphrey. "Because we've only got about forty chairs."

With this advice in mind, James had an early supper in the town and was in the West Canonry garden by a quarter to eight. Four music stands and four spindle-legged chairs had been set out on the lawn, which sloped gently down to the river. In the meadow on the other side, brown-and-white cows were grazing. House martins and swifts were dive-bombing the riverbank for insects. It was one of those long late-summer evenings that seem to go on forever.

James recognized many of the people as they arrived, identifying some who had been players in the chess game. The two vergers, who had been the white knights, came together. The senior verger, Grey, with the deportment of a ducal butler, and the young cricketer, Len Masters. Canon Maude had his mother with him. The Archdeacon rolled in, with a train of theological students. Since he was there, James guessed that the Dean would not turn up, and, sure enough, at the last moment Amanda arrived alone. One of the few empty chairs was beside him and he willed her to come and sit in it. For a moment he thought he had lost her to the Consetts, but she ignored Penny's wave, hesitated for a moment by Canon Lister, then came over and joined him. She said, "Peter told me you knew about music. So you can explain what's being played and whether it's good or not. I'm hopeless at things like that."

"If you'd come in at the right time, you'd have got a program." He gave her his. "It's a feast of seventeenth-century chamber music. Purcell, Mattheson, Christopher Sympson and William Brade. And 'Beauty Retire' by Samuel Pepys."

"You mean the man who wrote the diary?"

"He did other things, too."

The players took their seats. Paul Wren had a tuning fork, and the three recorder players each sounded a trial note.

"Like birds starting up the dawn chorus," said Amanda.

James remembered very little of the performance. It was a ritual which depended for most of its charm on the setting and the sense of history which it imposed. Just so a group of pe-ruked and periwigged clerics and their womenfolk must have sat three centuries ago; some enjoying the music, some pretending to enjoy it, some frankly bored. Henry Brookes was smoking cigarette after cigarette, putting the stub carefully in the lid of his cigarette case. Penny Consett was flirting with Peter. Mrs. Henn-Christie was keeping an anxious eye out for mosquitoes. Canon Lister seemed to be asleep. The Archdeacon was motionless, but he was not asleep. His black eyes were open. Penny was right: He really was rather like a bear. Big, deceptively clumsy and slow, but capable of a lightning pounce when the occasion called for it.

The last piece was Purcell's Golden Sonata. The September dusk had closed in, and the faces of the listeners were indistinguishable, but they were all sitting still now, gripped by the liquid simplicity of the playing. As the last notes of the viol died away into silence, they gave a sort of communal sigh of pleasure before breaking into a round of applause. James drifted out into the Close with Amanda beside him.

As they were passing the school cottage, he saw that there was a light in the sitting-room window. He said, "Come into our bachelor retreat and have a cup of coffee."

Amanda said, "Good idea. I'd love a hot drink. We got colder than we realized, sitting out there. It's September, not June."

They found Peter and Bill Williams drinking beer. Both seemed pleased to see Amanda and gave her the only comfortable chair while Peter made coffee for them.

"Instant coffee and powdered milk," he said. "Not what you're accustomed to, I expect."

"I'm not a coffee snob myself," said Amanda, "but a lot of people round here are. Last year, after the Friends of the Cathedral lunch, there were so many snide remarks about our coffee that we've bought a huge machine and this time we're going to dish out the real stuff. It'll cost us the earth."

She was wearing a pair of jeans faded almost to white and a blue roll-necked sweater and fitted easily into the all-male company. "When we were in Ethiopia, we got our supplies up about once every two months. Daddy used to put all the coffee into one of his socks. When we wanted a drink, we used to boil up a saucepan of milk and dip the sock into it and give it a little squeeze. That way we made it last. I must admit it did taste a bit peculiar toward the end."

"What sort of sock?" said Bill Williams.

"Actually, it was an old white cricket sock. Why?"

"If it had been a colored sock, the coffee would have tasted even more peculiar."

They drank for a few moments in silence. Bill said, "I'm told that Fletcher's Piece is rearing its ugly head again."

"Please instruct me," said James. "Who is Fletcher and what is his Piece?"

Amanda said, "It's the field on the other side of the river, opposite where we were sitting just now. Inhabited, at this moment, by cows."

"But if the developers have their wicked way," said Bill, "the cows will be evicted and it will be covered by an extension eastward of Wessex Instrumentation Limited, which is the building you can just see beyond the far hedge. They've been after it for years. It would suit them very well. Access to the road and all the services. Maybe a housing estate as well. The buzz is that the Planning Committee has already informally given them the green light."

"What's stopping them?"

"What's stopping them is that the land belongs to the Cathedral. And they don't somehow fancy having a factory overlooking the gardens of the Deanery and the West Canonry and the Theological College."

"One sees their point," said James. "Who's behind it?"

"We know who's in front of it. It's Gerry Gloag."

"That pseudo-military character we saw in the pub?"

"Maxwell Gloag and Partners, Surveyors and Estate Agents. The biggest in this city, and there aren't many bigger in the county. They've gobbled up a lot of the smaller firms."

"Including Henry Brookes," said Amanda. "They picked him up two years ago. He then retired to what he fondly imagined would be the more peaceful occupation of being Chapter Clerk."

"Was he an estate agent?" said Peter. "I never knew that."

"Not a very good one, I should think. Too nice."

"It's no business for a gentleman," agreed Bill. "Gerry Gloag would cut your throat and smile distantly while he was doing it. He was the man who fronted the supermarket deal, too."

"And swindled Mrs. Henn-Christie," said James.

"So how did you know about *that?*" said Bill.

"They were talking about it at tea."

"I suppose you *could* say they swindled her," said Amanda. "In the sense that they made more money out of it than she did."

"It was the south end of Station Road," said Bill. "It wasn't much of a site, because that road was the main way out of the town to the west and was normally jam-packed with traffic. There were a few old shops in it."

"Five tatty little shops," said Amanda. "With sleeping quarters over them, except no one could sleep in them because of the racket."

"Four of them were empty. Gloag picked them up for peanuts. The only one they had any trouble with was old Mrs.

Piper. She and her family had run their little sweet shop for ages. They had to pay quite a bit to get *her* out, I believe. When they had the lot, Gloag bought the freehold from Mrs. Henn-Christie and sold the whole thing to the supermarket chain."

"So where does the swindle come in?" said James.

"The swindle was that Gloag knew and Mrs. Henn-Christie didn't know that the new by-pass had already been approved. It siphoned all the west-bound traffic out of Station Road, and that turned it into the best shopping site in town."

James thought about it. He said, "If Gloag guessed that the by-pass was coming, it wasn't really a swindle. It was smart business. He outguessed the others."

"He didn't guess," said Bill. "He had inside information. His closest friend is Leo Sandeman, and Leo is chairman of the Roads Committee of the Council."

"That does look a bit dirty. Have you got any proof?"

"No real proof. But I'm certain of one thing: Gloag must have backers. He'd need a fair amount of cash to set up a ramp like that. And he wouldn't be putting his own money into it. He's only an agent."

"And it's the same crowd who are after Fletcher's Piece?"

"That's my guess. They'll make a packet if they get it."

"Over Father's dead body they'll get it," said Amanda.

"Your dad enjoys a fight," agreed Bill.

"I'm afraid he overdoes it sometimes. He had a punch-up with Superintendent Bracher this afternoon. I was eavesdropping from the dining room. Very wrong of me, I suppose."

Everyone agreed that it was very wrong of her and urged her to tell them all about it. When she had done so, Peter said, "If Len Masters is a sneak thief, I'm a rotten judge of character."

"Of course he isn't," said Bill.

"The choristers approve of him," agreed Amanda, "and they're good judges of character. They'd be very upset if they heard about it."

"You're behind the times," said Peter. "They've not only heard about it. They know who the informer was."

"How could they?"

"One of the maids was in the marketplace and saw the whole thing. She told the cook. The cook told the gardener's boy, Charlie, and Charlie told Andrew Gould."

"Beats the African tom-tom, doesn't it?" said Bill. "Who *was* the sneak?"

"Rosa Pilcher. Who else?"

"Rosa," explained Amanda for James' benefit, "is a natural disaster. And, like a natural disaster, she can't be avoided. She does for the Archdeacon and for us and has her finger in half a dozen other pies as well. We only put up with her because we can't get anyone else." She added, with satisfaction, "When I tell Daddy who it was started this Masters business, he'll tear a strip off her."

"If he's too rough, she won't help with the Friends' lunch on Saturday."

"I don't care," said Amanda. "It's time someone told that nasty little toad where she gets off. Time I was going, too. Thanks for the coffee."

"I'll come with you," said James. "I've got a lot more questions to ask. I realize now that when I was here before, I never really got outside the school. I'd no idea that so much was going on all round me."

"Too much," said Amanda as they walked toward the Deanery. She shivered. James looked at her curiously. His first diagnosis had been right. She *was* too thin.

"Who are the Friends? They sound like the Mafia."

"Not quite as bad as that. Though they can be bloody-minded. They're called the Friends of the Cathedral. Most cathedrals have them. They organize things and make money. Quite a lot of money. This Saturday's the big day in their year. We give them a buffet lunch in the Deanery garden. Everyone turns up. It's a terrible scramble. Then there's a service in the Cathedral and a meeting in the Chapter House afterwards. That's when the arguments start. How to spend their funds. The last thing they paid for was the new console for the organ."

"That was a good thing to do."

"If they always spent their money as sensibly as that, they'd be all right. But they don't. Two years ago there was a stand-up fight between the ones who wanted to fit out the Chapter House with full stereo equipment and the ones who wanted a piece of sculpture made of iron girders put up in the West Precinct. Luckily, they canceled each other out and saved their money for the organ."

"It's their money, I suppose, so they can do what they like with it."

"Within reason. It's got to be for the general good of the Cathedral."

"Your father, I take it, would like them to hand it over to him. Then he could decide what *was* for the good of the Cathedral."

Amanda laughed. She said, "You've got him summed up, James. He's a natural despot. He's spent most of his life in places where he *was* the only authority. If there were decisions to be made, *he* had to make them. Under God's guidance, of course."

"I'd like to hear about that properly, please. Do you like walking? I don't mean a stroll round the town. I mean a proper walk."

They had reached the Deanery gate. Amanda stopped with her hand on the top bar and looked at him. Then she said, "Not tomorrow. We've got committees all day. Thursday, perhaps. There's a good walk over Helmet Down and back through Washbury and Bramerton. It's about seven miles."

"Done," said James. "Good night."

He watched Amanda as she strode away up the Deanery path. Nice hips. She'd make a good walker.

The moon, nearly full, had risen early that evening and was already going down behind the Cathedral, throwing a black squat shadow onto the precinct lawn. A small wind had got up and was rustling the leaves of the lime trees.

James felt disinclined for bed. He perched on the precinct wall, got out a cigarette and smoked it slowly.

When he looked up again, the shadow had moved. It was creeping toward him. He had an uncomfortable illusion that if he didn't get away quickly, the Cathedral would fall on top of him.

"Be your age," he said. "Go to bed."

Four

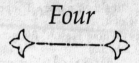

"Having examined the figures," said the Archdeacon, "I have come to the conclusion that it would be cheaper to accept the offer put forward by parents to take the boys to matches in their own cars. We pay for their petrol."

"Not only cheaper," said Dora Brookes. "More comfortable for the boys. Last term two of them were always sick in the coach. It didn't improve their cricket."

"I imagine not. Then that is the last point on the accounts, Headmaster?"

"Nothing else that I know of," said Lawrence Consett, trying to keep the relief out of his voice.

The committee was meeting in the school dining room, about which still hovered the faint smell of school breakfast. In addition to the Archdeacon and Dora Brookes, it consisted of Canon Lister, Anthony Openshaw and Dr. McHarg, who looked after the health of the school and of many of the inhabitants of the Close as well.

"I am sure," the Archdeacon continued with a smile which embraced them all, "that you find me tiresomely insistent on these small economies, but I think you'll agree that in times like the present we have to look carefully at every penny before we spend it. I'd go further. It would be even better if we could not only save money, but actually make a small profit here and there. It's a matter I have been giving thought to in the last few weeks."

The headmaster looked at him suspiciously. What now?

"I have had what seemed to me to be an attractive offer. The Western Operatic Group is doing a season next month at Winchester, Salisbury and Bath. All within easy distance of us here at Melchester. As it happens, three of the works which they have in repertory feature boy singers. *The Queen of Spades*, *The Cunning Little Vixen* and *La Bohème*. The producer tells me that he could use up to eight of our boys in these parts. They would be responsible for any theatrical coaching, of course. And they would pay an honorarium of a hundred pounds for each performance."

There was a moment of silence.

"How many performances?" said Dr. McHarg.

"Four in each town. One matinee and three evening performances."

"What *fun* it would be for them," said Mrs. Brookes. "I'm sure they'd love it. They do adore dressing up."

"Twelve hundred pound," said Dr. McHarg. "Aye, that's a tidy sum. It would almost defray the cost of the bathroom improvements."

"I was thinking of earmarking it for that purpose. It seemed to me an offer we ought to accept. I agree with Mrs. Brookes that the boys should enjoy it. But it was rather in my mind that it would broaden their musical education." He looked round the committee. "Can I take it, then, that you agree?"

"You'll have to take a vote on it," said Canon Lister. "Because I'm against it."

"Why, Tom?"

"The one thing the boys don't need broadening or widening or extending in any direction is their musical education. They get plenty of that here. What needs looking after is their general education. They forfeit nearly two hours to music every morning and an hour every evening. As soon as their voices break, they'll be going on to public schools and their parents will be thinking about scholarships. Some of them are not too well off."

"No doubt their parents will bear in mind that the Cathedral contributes five hundred pounds a year toward their sons' education here," said Dr. McHarg. "They might not grudge a small return for that."

"Well, I'm for it," said Dora Brookes.

"Anthony?"

"I'm with Canon Lister on this," said Openshaw. "It's a matter of trying to cram three half-pints into a pint pot. General education, music, sport. When there aren't enough hours in the day for everything, something has got to go."

"I see," said the Archdeacon smoothly. "That makes us two all. I suppose I should have a casting vote, but I would be unhappy to use it in favor of my own project without rather more support from the committee. I think I shall hand my vote over to the headmaster."

"Good idea," said Canon Lister. "He's the one who has to deal with the parents."

Mr. Consett looked far from happy at the idea of having to give the casting vote. He said, speaking slowly, as though the words were being forced out of him, "Canon Lister mentioned that some of our boys might be sitting scholarships. I'm afraid it isn't as simple as that. To get into any public school a boy has to pass what's called the Common Entrance exam. It used to be just that. A common qualifying exam. If the boy could pass it, he was eligible. It's not like that now. With the competition for places at the leading schools, a boy has to pass high up to get in at all. The whole thing's become competitive."

When he had finished, there was an uncomfortable silence, broken by Canon Lister, who said, "I think that's conclusive, Archdeacon, don't you?"

"Having asked for the headmaster's views," said the Archdeacon, "it would be pointless not to accept them. I will press the scheme no further." There was neither surprise nor resentment in his voice. "If there is no other business, I will declare the meeting closed."

As they were leaving, Mr. Consett said, "There is one matter I'd like to mention, Archdeacon. Not committee business."

"Then perhaps we can discuss it in your study."

When Dora Brookes left the meeting, she walked back to the house next to the Theological College which her husband occupied in his capacity as Chapter Clerk. She found him in the back kitchen, a large, cool, stone-flagged room. Like many of his friends in those days of high prices, he had turned to winemaking; not always with total success.

He said, "You remember that peach wine that didn't quite come off?"

His wife made a face and said, "I shall never forget it."

"It wasn't very nice, was it? What I thought was I might try to turn it into brandy."

"Then we'll drink it ourselves," said his wife firmly. "I'm not going to risk it at a dinner party."

"How did your meeting go?"

"Very well, until right at the end." She explained about the opera company. "I was sorry we had to turn it down."

"How did the Archdeacon take it?"

"He doesn't like not getting his own way. I thought it was courageous of Consett to oppose him. After all, it's the Archdeacon who appoints the headmaster."

"My dear, Lawrence Consett is an excellent headmaster. A first-class scholar and very good with the boys. You don't, surely, imagine that a rebuff in committee would turn the Archdeacon against him."

"I don't know." Dora Brookes' placid face was troubled. "He's an odd man. He doesn't like opposition. I think he'd have made a good managing director or chief accountant or something like that."

"The real trouble," said Brookes, "is that he *isn't* managing director of Melchester Cathedral. That post happens to be filled by someone else." He added, "Someone who also likes getting his own way."

The Archdeacon went directly from the school meeting to the North Canonry and tugged the brass bell pull. The door was opened by Canon Maude's mother. Mrs. Maude was well on into her eighties, a small compact woman, a little deaf, but with all her wits about her. Since Canon Maude was clearly incapable of looking after himself, it was, as everyone observed, providential that his mother was still alive and active.

She said, "I expect it's Mervyn you want," and trotted ahead of him down the long hallway at a speed the Archdeacon could hardly match. "He's in his study. Working on a sermon, he said."

The study overlooked a stretch of lawn running up to the wall which divided the North Canonry garden from the Cathedral School playground. As the Archdeacon came in, Canon Maude swept a copy of the *Times* under a pile of papers and bobbed up to welcome him.

"My dear Raymond. An unexpected pleasure. What can I do for you? Please sit down. You're looking very well. Take a chair. No, that one, please. It's much more comfortable."

Without speaking, the Archdeacon drew an upright chair to the other side of the table, cleared a space by pushing some of the clutter to one side and laid on it a single sheet of deckle-edged notepaper and an opened envelope.

Canon Maude looked at it. His face, which was normally the pink and white of a healthy baby, was now pink all over. A deeper red flush started on his cheekbones and spread upward toward his forehead. He put one hand out as though to pick up the letter, thought better of it and drew it back.

"What's all this, Raymond? What is it?"

"It's a letter."

"A letter?"

"And that is the envelope it came in. Which is addressed, as you can see, to William Anstruther, who is a boy at the choris-ters' school. I understand that it was dropped over the wall of your garden into the playground. Since you wrote the letter yourself, I'm sure you know what's in it."

Canon Maude looked up at the ceiling as though seeking inspiration, but found none there.

"Is it your habit to write love letters to boys?"

"Love letters," said Canon Maude faintly. "Really, Ray-mond."

"I should imagine that is how the court would construe a letter which referred to red-rose lips and velvet eyes and—what was that other expression?" The Archdeacon picked up the let-ter and examined it critically. "Oh, yes. This bit at the end about his sylphlike figure and slim gilt soul."

"What did you mean?" said Canon Maude tremulously. "When you spoke about the court?"

"I meant what I said. Anyone reading this letter would as-sume that you were trying to seduce the boy. If his father, Brigadier Anstruther, saw it, his first instinct would be to come round here with a horsewhip. On further reflection he would probably decide to hand the letter over to the police."

Canon Maude was now as white as he had been red before.

He said, "But he must never see it, Raymond. Never, never, never." His voice rose in a squeak. "I should never have written it. It must be destroyed."

He put a hand out, but the Archdeacon intercepted it, picked up the letter and envelope and restored them to his own pocket.

He said, "Fortunately, the boy had enough sense not to show this to any of his friends. Indeed, I should imagine he was deeply shocked. He took it straight to his form master, Mr. Fleming, who handed it to the headmaster. He gave it to me, after the meeting this morning. By doing so, he laid on me the onus of deciding what to do about it."

Canon Maude said, "Think of the Chapter, Raymond. We must stand by each other."

"I *am* thinking about the Chapter. But I am also thinking about myself. The boy has promised to keep his mouth shut. But if this did get out—if his father heard about it and discovered that I had decided to hush the matter up—my own position would be far from agreeable. You appreciate that?"

"I do, Raymond. I do. I should be eternally grateful."

"Very well. I have decided to take no further step in this matter. But on one condition: That you give me your solemn word that you will never do such a stupid thing again."

"I give you my word, Raymond. I do indeed."

There was a single tear at the corner of each of his eyes.

The Archdeacon rose to his feet. He stood for a moment staring down at Canon Maude, who seemed incapable of moving. He said, "I took particular note of one comment you made, Mervyn." His voice sounded more friendly. "You spoke of the Chapter standing by each other. I'm afraid that's something we're not very good at, just at this moment. Maybe we can do better in future. Please don't trouble your mother. I'll let myself out."

As he padded back, past the High Street Gate, toward his own house, head thrust forward, shoulders hunched, looking more bearlike than ever, the Archdeacon's mind was running down strange channels. "Red-rose lips . . . slim gilt soul. . . ." Canon Maude had not made up those expressions. He had read them somewhere. It was quite unimportant, but it annoyed the Archdeacon that he could not place them.

It was as he turned in at his own gate that he remembered.

Surely, both expressions came from that unfortunate letter which Oscar Wilde had written to Lord Alfred Douglas and which Carson had read out, with such sinister emphasis, at the Old Bailey. The letter had been one of the last nails in Oscar's coffin. Such an odd character. So wise in some ways, so stupid in others. The Archdeacon growled gently to himself as he thought about Oscar Wilde.

The editor of the *Melset Times*, Mr. Arthur Balfour Driffield, was a thin dry man in his early forties. He said to the young lady who stood beside his editorial desk, "There's going to be a meeting of the Cathedral Chapter tomorrow. An informal meeting, called by Archdeacon Pawle, to discuss the question of Fletcher's Piece."

The young lady needed no explanation about this. She and all the staff of the *Melset Times* knew that the paper was supporting the Archdeacon in his attempts to improve the finances of the Cathedral. Driffield had already penned a number of forceful leaders on the subject under such headlines as "The Widow's Mite" and "Charity or Commonsense." The reasons for this policy were clear. Their rival, the *Melset Journal*, had come out in support of the Dean. When the matter had been discussed in the staff room, the view had been expressed that there was more to it than this. Newspaper rivalry was admitted to spark good copy, but the old man seemed to be taking it all a bit personally, they thought.

"We want as much background information as we can get. It's raising a lot of interest and we ought to be able to start people taking sides. Don't tackle the Archdeacon. He won't want to be involved publicly. But there's the lady who does for him."

"Rosa Pilcher."

"That's the one. I'm told you can find her any morning in the Copper Kettle or the Busy Bee. You can probably get something there. And another thing: See what you can find out about Fletcher's Piece. It must have some sort of history. Where did it get its name from? Who was the original Mr. Fletcher? That sort of thing."

The young lady promised to do her best.

Five

◇———◇

"I SUPPOSE THE MEETING is at the Deanery," said Dora Brookes.

"As usual," said her husband. He was looking for the minute book, which had disappeared.

"Will there be a fight?"

"I imagine so. Where did I—?"

"I don't like you getting involved."

"I won't be involved. I'm just there to take notes."

"If things go wrong, you're sure to be blamed."

"I shan't be there at all if I can't find the bloody minute book."

"It's on the hall table."

"I don't know what I should do without you," said Brookes. It was true. He was becoming increasingly reliant on his wife.

In Melchester, as in most cathedrals, there were two Chapters. The Greater Chapter consisted of between forty and fifty clergymen with livings in the diocese. They were appointed by the Bishop as a reward for long and meritorious service in their parishes. The office was largely honorary, but included certain dignities, such as the possession of a stall within the Choir and the right to preach once a year in the Cathedral. As an executive body, the Greater Chapter had few functions and met rarely. When it did meet, it was accommodated in the spacious Chapter House, an octagonal building which could hold two hundred people easily.

All the real power was vested in the Inner Chapter, which consisted of the four Canons Residentiary and was presided over by the Dean. Recently the meetings had been held at the Deanery and it was there that they met that morning, in the beautiful house designed by Christopher Wren, standing at the southeast corner of the Close and overlooking the river.

Men were already busy on the lawn outside, putting up the marquee for the buffet luncheon of the Friends. The sight of it seemed to remind the Archdeacon of something and he made a note on the pad in front of him.

The Dean said, in his most formal voice, "It is at your request that this meeting has been called, Archdeacon. Perhaps you will speak first, then."

The Archdeacon said, with equal formality, "Thank you, Dean. I will be as brief as I can. Maxwell Gloag and Partners have received an offer to buy the whole of our meadowland on the west bank of the river, known popularly as Fletcher's Piece. It is roughly fifteen acres and the sum offered is twelve thousand pounds an acre. A total purchase price of about a hundred and eighty thousand pounds."

Canon Lister said, "At the moment it's farmland."

"Correct, Tom. Mr. Pellett, who farms it, has also had an offer made to him for the surrender of his lease which he is prepared to accept."

"I wasn't thinking of Farmer Pellett. I was thinking of the planning authorities."

"Have they managed to buy them, too?" said the Dean.

"The deal would be conditional on the purchasers being able to obtain planning permission for general industrial development or, failing that, for residential development. I'm given to understand that soundings have already been taken and that one or other of these applications is likely to be successful."

"You talk about purchasers," said the Dean. "Can you be a little more specific? Is the favored purchaser Wessex Instrumentation?"

"Not directly. Gloag tells me he is acting for a syndicate who are prepared to put up the money. Their plan would be to sell part to the Instrumentation company, who badly need room to expand. The remainder would be sold to developers for a housing estate. That might pay them even more handsomely."

"So that if we sell," said Canon Lister, "we have the choice of being overlooked by a factory, or a row of other people's back gardens, or both. I must confess that I don't find the prospect attractive."

The Archdeacon said, "Superficially, Tom, I agree with you. But bear in mind that we have grown used to the almost monastic seclusion of this Close. It is a seclusion which few cathedrals enjoy. St. Paul's stands among office blocks. Winchester has houses and shops all round it. Exeter, Ely and Rochester are planted in the centers of the town and open on all sides to the public. Have we, perhaps, got a little spoiled if we shudder at the thought of a row of new houses on the far side of the river?"

Canon Maude said, "You know, there's something in that."

The Dean looked at him speculatively. Before he could say anything, the Archdeacon had continued, speaking in the calm reasonable voice that Canon Humphrey classified as "good committee." He said, "A hundred and eighty thousand pounds is not, perhaps, an enormous sum of money by modern standards. But consider one point. If one invests money to produce income, one can currently get a return of between twelve and fifteen percent. In our case, as a charity, that is free of tax. If we took the money, I would suggest that we set it aside and allowed it to grow. I have not made an exact computation, but in three years' time it would have increased by approximately a further eighty thousand pounds. This would give us what we have always needed at Melchester and never had: A proper self-supporting fabric fund."

The Dean seemed to have been making some calculations. He said, "And have you also worked out exactly what would have been produced by an investment of thirty pieces of silver at the date of our Lord's death?"

"That's one below the belt," thought Canon Humphrey. "If Raymond blows his top, we *shall* have a merry meeting."

A flush of angry color showed for a moment in the Archdeacon's face, but it was Canon Lister who spoke. He said, "The difficulty about biblical analogies, Dean, is that they are often inconsistent. In a situation like this, the Bible offers us two disparate pieces of advice: 'Lay not up for yourself treasures upon earth, where moth and rust do corrupt,' but on the other hand, 'Render unto Caesar the things that are Caesar's.' I have often wondered how you are supposed to pay the taxes that Caesar demands if you are forbidden to save any of your money."

This intervention had had the desired effect. The Archdeacon's voice and manner were again unruffled.

("It was a close thing, all the same," thought Canon Humphrey.)

"I think, Tom," said the Archdeacon, "that you have, as usual, put your finger on the heart of the problem. Let me remind you that the rent paid by Farmer Pellett is twelve pounds an acre. That adds up to the magnificent sum of a hundred and eighty pounds a year. In fact, it doesn't always come to that because, as landlords, we have certain obligations in the way of fencing and drainage. If we accept this offer, our income, without any deductions at all, would be around twenty-five thousand pounds a year. We stand in the position of trustees of the Cathedral property. Can we allow all the essential repairs and renovations to go by default, for lack of the wherewithal to pay for them, when the necessary cash is being offered to us?"

There was a short silence, broken only by a mumbling noise from Canon Maude, who seemed to be about to say something, but to think better of it.

Canon Humphrey said, "I'd like to be clear about this planning business. Could the planning authorities take the land from us?"

"Henry can probably answer that," said the Dean.

Henry Brookes said, "They have powers of compulsory purchase in certain cases, but I'm sure that they wouldn't, and couldn't, exercise them to take away land that has belonged to the Church for six centuries. It's not on the cards at all."

"So that the planning point is simply whether or not they will give permission for development? Factories and houses?"

"That's right."

"*We* could apply. And put up houses ourselves."

"That seems to be quite an idea," said Canon Maude brightly. "If there's a profit to be made by putting up houses, why shouldn't *we* make it?"

"Because we haven't got the building finance," said the Archdeacon.

"Of course, of course. I'd overlooked that."

The Dean said, "You know this man Gloag, Henry. Wasn't he the one who bought up your business when you retired?"

"That's the man."

"Is he straight?"

Brookes thought about this. Then he said, "Well, he's a businessman."

"That's a Socratic answer, but it doesn't tell me what I want to know. A hundred and eighty thousand pounds is a lot of money. He wouldn't be in this by himself. He must have powerful backers. And be anticipating a handsome profit."

"I expect that's right."

"Would they be the same people who made a killing over Mrs. Henn-Christie's land? You were involved in that."

"I was involved," said Brookes, looking a little uncomfortable. "But only because Mrs. Henn-Christie wouldn't negotiate directly with Gloag. I'd sold up by then, but her family had dealt with my firm for a long time. So she asked me to act as a go-between. There was nothing more to it than that, I assure you."

"My dear Henry," said the Dean, with one of his rare smiles. "No one is suggesting that you were involved financially in that particular deal. But you must have had a good deal to do with Gloag. Perhaps you even know who his backers are?"

"That was something he took great care to keep secret."

"Curious," said the Dean. "I wonder why. After all, making money out of old ladies like Claribel Henn-Christie and unworldly clergymen like us may be unethical, but it's not criminal."

"I did get the impression that the money was local. And I think, from something I wasn't meant to overhear on one occasion, that Driffield might be one of the consortium."

The Archdeacon rotated his big head until he was looking directly at Brookes. He said, "Arthur Driffield? The editor of the *Times?*"

"Actually, he's a bit more than the editor. He owns most of the shares in the company that runs it. His wife has money in it, too."

The Archdeacon said, "I see," and swung his gaze back to the block of paper on the table in front of him. There was a single line of writing on it. He rarely made notes. He was the only member of the Chapter who preached without a written text.

"It would seem, then," said the Dean, "that if we sell our birthright for a mess of pottage, the end result will be to line the pockets of a group of local businessmen. All that we know, or suspect, about them is that they are backed by the *Melset Times* and may be the people who swindled Mrs. Henn-Christie. Is that a fair summing up?"

The Archdeacon said, without troubling to conceal the anger

57

in his voice, "That, Mr. Dean, is about as unfair a summing up as could be imagined, but most of what has been said here this morning has been prejudiced or irrelevant. I would like to put the plain proposition before the meeting. Do we accept Mr. Gloag's offer? I am proposer and I vote for it."

His eyes swung around the table once more, resting on each man in turn.

"I—yes—I *think* I support the proposition," said Canon Maude.

"You must make up your mind, Mervyn," said the Dean gently. "Do you, or don't you?"

Canon Maude said, "I do support the Archdeacon's proposal. Yes, I do. I do."

And looked, thought Canon Humphrey, like a truculent rabbit.

"Those against," said the Dean. "In addition, that is, to myself."

"Against," said Canon Humphrey.

"Against," said Canon Lister.

"Then it would appear," said the Dean, "that your proposal, my dear Raymond, is negatived."

When Brookes got home, his wife said, "You look as if you've had a hard morning. I'll get you a cup of coffee."

A cup of coffee was her panacea for most of life's ills.

When she had gone, Brookes sat for a minute staring down at the blank page of the minute book. Then he took out his pen and wrote, after the date, "Special Meeting of the Chapter. Present: Dean Matthew Forrest; Francis Humphrey, Subdean; Raymond Pawle, Archdeacon; Thomas Parmoor Lister, D.D., Canon; Mervyn Maude, Canon and Precentor. In attendance: Henry Graham Brookes, Clerk to the Chapter."

During the long pause that followed he could hear his wife bustling about in the kitchen. What could he write next? How could he hope to reduce to official prose the things which had been said, the positions adopted, the battle stations taken up.

Brookes was not the most intelligent of men, but he was no fool. He could see the storm cones which had been hoisted, could hear the breakers ahead, could see them smashing on the rocks in tattered sheets of foam.

When his wife came back, she found him still staring at the

blank page. She said, "Was it as bad as you thought it was going to be?"

"Worse," said Brookes. "Much worse."

The Melchester Cycling Club was a curious institution. It had been founded toward the end of the previous century, when its members had dressed in natty bicycling outfits and had actually ridden bicycles. It was now an exclusive drinking and gaming club with a self-perpetuating committee. Most of its members owned expensive cars. To be elected to it was a token of your admission into the commercial and professional caucus which dominated the life of the Borough. The keys to entry were success and the money that success brought with it.

In the high-stakes rubber of bridge which had just finished in the small card room, Leo Sandeman was partnering Gerry Gloag against Arthur Driffield of the *Melset Times* and Grant Adey. Adey was a big man with the loose comfortable frame of someone who had once been an athlete in youth and was still capable of physical effort. The combination of white hair and black eyebrows gave an impression of good-tempered authority to his face. Not a man to cross unnecessarily.

"Six no trumps and lucky to make it," he said. "Both finesses right."

Sandeman had taken out his wallet and was laying a number of notes on the table. They settled up after each rubber. He said, "Cut for partners, or revenge?"

"Neither," said Driffield. "I've got work to do. Not like you lazy layabouts. My Friday editorial. One of my people has got hold of some useful background stuff about Fletcher's Piece. Who do you think Fletcher was?"

"A nineteenth-century industrialist," said Sandeman.

"A thirteenth-century pig farmer," said Adey.

"Both wrong. There never was such a person. It was called Fletcher's Piece because it was the site of an arrow-making establishment and arrow-makers, as you all no doubt know, were called fletchers."

"Interesting," said Gloag. "But how are you going to use it?"

"But obviously. If it was once a center of industry, why not again? Reviving an old tradition. Cathedral folk are nuts on tradition."

"I suppose making transistors could be said to be the modern equivalent of making arrows."

"Arthur can prove anything if he gives his mind to it," said Adey. "Do you remember his editorial on why Welshmen don't wear kilts?"

"I've got a bit of news for you," said Sandeman. "Straight from the front line. I don't see how you can use it, though. They had a Chapter meeting today and the Archdeacon swung one of the votes his way. The voting went two-three. One more convert and we're home and dry."

The other three considered this in silence while Adey collected and shuffled the cards they had been playing with. Then he said, "That's right. You can't use it. But it's bloody interesting."

Six

✧————✧

A LITTLE EARLIER on that same Wednesday evening, Peter said to James, "If you're at a loose end, would you like to come slumming with Roger and me?"

"O.K. Why slumming?"

"Theological College students aren't supposed to spend their evenings boozing. Saturday night after rugger is winked at. Other nights are discouraged. So we don't go to the Lion or the Swan, where the upper crust do their drinking. We cross the tracks. There are a lot of nice little pubs up that end of the town."

"Do I have to sew up my pockets and leave my gold watch at home?"

"They're perfectly respectable. Just not so up-market."

In the area of small streets behind the railway station they found the Wheatsheaf, the Three Tons and the Market Tavern. The only difference between these and the Black Lion was that the beer was cheaper and the company was, on the whole, better behaved. The older men sat at corner tables and played dominoes. The young ones played shove ha'penny. Roger talked to anyone who would talk to him and managed to do so without undue familiarity, but without appearing to be stuffy. James thought that he would make a good parish priest. Maybe a compulsory round of pub-crawling ought to be included in the curriculum of all theological colleges.

The Market Tavern, which they came to last, was the largest of the three and was the only one with room in it for a dart board. The licensee, Mr. Samuel Garnett, obligingly made a fourth at doubles, but he was so evidently better than the three of them that they abandoned the game and went back to the bar to talk.

Mr. Garnett said, "Having a bit of an argument about Fletcher's Piece, I hear."

"We certainly are," said Peter, "but I didn't know it was public property."

"Been a lot about it in the papers. Speaking for myself, I'd say leave it alone. Don't want change for the sake of change."

A man with a white beard said, "It's not change for the sake of change, Sam. It's change for the sake of progress."

"Progress never did us much good, not that I can see."

"This is different. Sell that field to the Wessex, they double their factory, right? Double their factory, they take on twice the people, right?"

A small man with a bent nose said, "That's all very well, Mr. Pierce, but suppose they don't sell it to the factory. Suppose they put up houses. What happens then? People who've got houses buy the new ones and other people buy their houses. That doesn't solve the unemployment problem. It just moves people around."

"And puts money into the hands of the house agents."

"And the lawyers," said a bitter-looking woman in black. A tall man who seemed to be her husband observed that anything anyone did put money into lawyers' hands sooner or later. Take divorce.

But Mr. Pierce was not prepared to take divorce. His beard gave him authority and he reclaimed the floor. "Whatever gets put up," he said, "factory or houses or any other sort of building, what I say is that it's a valuable piece of land and the Church hasn't got no right to hold on to it and keep cows on it when they might sell it and raise a tidy sum of money. If they don't want money, why do they pass the plate round at services?"

"Everyone wants money," said the small man with the bent nose.

At this point the argument became general. The progressives, led by Mr. Pierce, slightly outnumbering the traditionalist party supported by the landlord. James had wandered away toward the window. On a shelf above the empty fireplace were two cups which looked as though they might be real silver. He thought that Mr. Garnett must have an unusually trustworthy clientele.

Outside it was already dark and that corner of the bar was lit by electric lanterns fixed to the wall on either side of the fireplace. The light gleamed from the polished surface of the cups. Not only polished, thought James, scoured. It looked as though someone had been scraping them with a very rough burnisher.

He put a hand up and shifted one of the cups slightly. Then the true explanation struck him. Originally the cups had carried an inscription, but it had not been cut too deeply and it had been smoothed off with abrasive; but not entirely obliterated. The small movement of the cup and the angle at which the light fell on it enabled James to read it without difficulty, and when he had done so, he stood quite still for a moment wondering what to do next.

MELCHESTER CRICKET CLUB—BATTING CUP and, underneath, the year followed by the name LEONARD MASTERS.

He was saved trouble by the small man with the bent nose, who had moved up behind him. He said, "Pity we had to rough 'em up, wannit?"

"I was thinking the same," said James.

"Gotter think of Len's feelings. Comes in here sometimes himself. Wooden want everyone to know he'd been pushed for money."

"Then these *are* Masters' cricket cups?"

"That's right. Nice pieces of silver. Worth more if they hadn't had all that writing on them, of course."

Mr. Garnett had walked over with Peter and Roger. He said, "You admiring my new flower vases, sir. I bought 'em from Alf Carney here. I expect he swindled me. He swindles most people."

Mr. Carney accepted this as a compliment. He said, "I was telling this gentleman . . . You come from the Close, don't you? Then you'd know Len Masters, of course. I was telling him how I bought them."

Light was beginning to dawn.

"At your stall in the market?"

"That's right. Poor old Len. Came sidling up with the cups in a suitcase and slid 'em out as if he'd stolen 'em. I said, 'No need

63

to be ashamed, old friend. Better men than you've popped their family silver.' I gave him a fair price for 'em."

"How much?" said Mr. Garnett.

"Well—"

"Half as much as you sold them to me for, I don't mind betting."

"You see how it is," said Mr. Carney. "You're as bad as the police. Give a dog a bad name and kick him every time he barks."

"I think it's time we had some more beer," said Roger firmly.

Later, as they were walking home, he said, "I feel rather bad about this. It seems to be one of the things you have to accept in a Cathedral organization, that its employees are inadequately paid."

"And take the balance in sanctity," suggested Peter.

"That may be right if you're talking about the clergy. I'm talking about the lay staff. Vergers are only commissionaires, and you wouldn't get a commissionaire in an office block for twice what we pay Masters. If we'd paid him a bit more, he wouldn't have had to sell those cups. It must have been terribly embarrassing for him, too. I remember once, when I was more than usually hard up, I tried to pawn a gold watch I'd inherited from my godfather. It took me half an hour to work up my courage even to go into the shop."

"It's worse than embarrassing in this case," said James. "Of course, you don't know about Rosa Pilcher—"

Roger listened in silence. At the end he said, "We'll have to tell someone about this."

"Better not be you," said Peter. "They'll want to know where you met this Carney character."

"I don't mind doing it," said James. "But who do I tell?"

They had almost reached the outskirts of the Close before Roger and Peter spoke, almost simultaneously. Roger said, "Tell the Dean." Peter said, "Have a word with Brookes first."

By this time it was past eleven and the Close gate was shut. This did not worry them. There were a number of recognized methods of entry. They made off down the road which skirted the north wall, climbed over a gate into the premises of a nursery garden, over a fence at the far end and out into Fletcher's Piece. They sat down on the riverbank opposite the school building, removed their shoes and socks and rolled up their trousers.

Roger said, "This is a bit tricky. Why don't you come down to the college? It's a lot easier down there."

"It's quite all right," said Peter, stepping into the brown water which was chuckling along under the moon, "provided you know where to put your feet."

As he said this, he put a foot in the wrong place and sat down.

"I see what you mean," said James. "Why not try the other crossing?"

"In view of the fact," said Peter—he was sitting up to his waist in the water and seemed quite happy—"in view of the fact that I couldn't possibly get any wetter, I think I'll push on."

"I'm getting too old for midnight bathing," said James. "We'll use the easy way."

They negotiated the lower crossing without difficulty, climbed the wall into the garden of the Theological College and sat down on a seat, alongside a summerhouse, to dry their legs with their handkerchiefs and resume their socks and shoes. It took James back, more vividly than anything had done yet.

"Was it really six years ago when I did this last?" he said. "It seems more like six weeks."

"You'll find," said a voice from the darkness of the summerhouse, "that time moves even more quickly as you grow older. Dr. Scotland, isn't it?"

At the first word Roger had vanished, slipping off up the grass path toward the college. James, having been identified, thought it more dignified to stand his ground.

"An unexpected pleasure," continued the voice, which he now recognized as belonging to Canon Lister. "No doubt you waded across the river as an alternative to rousing Mullins from his virtuous slumbers?"

"My recollection, sir, was that Mullins had no objection to being roused if you recompensed him adequately. When I was here last, the price was ten pence up to midnight and twenty pence thereafter, but I believe that it has now doubled, or even trebled."

"It is the age of inflation. Why not sit down for a few minutes? I find this corner of the garden particularly attractive on a fine summer night. Sidney Smith, do you remember, said that *his*

65

idea of heaven was eating *pâté de foie gras* to the sound of trumpets. A little vulgar? You agree. Now, *my* idea of heaven is sitting in a garden on a summer evening listening to the sound of running water."

The air was heady with the stored smell of wallflowers and night-scented stock.

"It's really peaceful," said James. "And I must apologize for interrupting you."

"Peaceful," said Canon Lister wistfully. "Yes. A few moments of peace are very precious. They say that the onlooker sees most of the game. It's not a very happy game that's being played here at the moment, Doctor. It will not have taken you long to detect that."

"No," said James. It was clear that the Canon needed a confidant. It was a perfect night. He was happy to oblige him.

"But you mustn't make the mistake of supposing that what we have here is a simple case of the good against the bad. It's more complex than that. It's a case of two different versions of the good in conflict with each other. Raymond Pawle has done more for the Cathedral foundation in the two years he has been here than his predecessor did in twenty years. I will give you an example. Do you know what I mean by an ecclesiastical trust?"

"More or less. But rather less than more."

"Some benefactor leaves money to the Cathedral. But attaches strings to it. The money must be kept separate and used for specific purposes. The capital is in the hands of trustees. There were a number of these trusts in existence. They seemed to produce surprisingly little income. The Archdeacon started by investigating them. In two cases the reason was inefficiency, in one case something close to fraud. A local solicitor was involved. He had so arranged matters that nine-tenths of the income went to him, as administrator. It took the threat of a lawsuit to clear it up. When he had cleansed those Augean stables, he turned his attention to our own affairs. He started by reorganizing the finances of the school and gave poor Lawrence Consett a rough passage. After that—" James could detect that Canon Lister was smiling—"he turned the searchlight onto the Theological College. I employ an admirable accountant. No blood was spilled. His next objective, no doubt, will be the general Cathedral accounts. I expect he'll tread on a few toes there, too."

"Couldn't these investigations be carried out without causing offense? I don't mean that dishonest solicitor you were talking about. Clearly, he had to use a big stick on him. But in the other cases—"

"If you are blessed, or cursed, with an analytical mind and are faced with a problem, you tend to overlook personal considerations. I expect you find much the same thing in your own case."

"In my case?"

"I understood that you were a forensic pathologist. That means, does it not, that you have to give evidence in court of your findings in the laboratory?"

"Not much of our work is done in the laboratory, actually. That's the field of the scientist and the chemist. Our job starts at the scene of the crime and usually finishes in the mortuary."

"But you have to apply scientific reasoning to your investigations?"

"Oh, certainly."

"And do you never find that that is difficult? I mean, applying logic and reason to the most illogical and unreasonable of all actions: the killing of one human being by another."

"We only have to find out how the victim died. Not why he was killed."

"But discovery of the method must have some bearing on the motive. You cannot entirely exclude the human factor."

"In what way?"

There was a moment of silence before Canon Lister spoke again. He said, "Suppose that your examination of the scientific evidence made it fairly plain both how a murder had been committed and by whom. And suppose you found yourself sympathizing with the murderer. Would you let your personal feelings influence your findings?"

"I would try not to let them do so."

"Then you regard scientific truth as sacrosanct?"

"In its own sphere, yes. You must strive to arrive at the truth."

"Whoever it hurts?"

"Yes. Whoever it hurts."

"And you really think that human problems can be solved like an equation in algebra?"

"I think," said James, "with respect, that non-scientists have a very odd idea of how scientists actually work. It isn't an algebraic process at all. In some ways it isn't even a logical process. A scientist starts by making a presumption. Then he tries to disprove it. He considers every possible alternative explanation, and as he discards them, one by one, the shape of what is left begins to appear."

"That means that when you start on an inquiry, you can see the end, but you don't know by what path you're going to arrive at it."

"Not exactly. You do follow a sort of path. Hacking down the brambles which block it, and diving up dozens of side paths until they peter out and force you back to your original track."

"And at the end of it all?"

"At the end you hope to arrive at a small piece of firm ground. A trustworthy point of departure for further exploration."

"As long as you don't arrive at an imposing-looking building labeled 'The Pavilion of Truth' and when you go through the door you find it's one of those constructions on a film lot, all front and no back, there's nothing behind it at all. You step out onto a piece of wasteland, full of nettles and rusty tins and the messes left by passing dogs."

There was so much bitterness in Canon Lister's voice that James felt unable to say anything. He suddenly felt very tired. The Canon must have sensed this because he said, in his former cheerful voice, "Forgive me. You would rather be in bed than listening to the views of a tiresome old man. It has been a pleasure to talk to someone with such intelligent prejudices. Sleep well."

As James rose to go, the Canon added, "If you happen to see Roger Blakeway, set his mind at rest. I entirely failed to identify him. That's an example, you see, of personal consideration diluting the purity of truth."

As James padded away up the grass path, he could hear Canon Lister chuckling to himself.

Seven

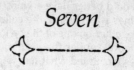

On Thursday morning James went around to see Henry Brookes. He had to have a word with him anyway, since the dilatory Furbank had announced his return and Friday was to be his last night at the school cottage.

The Chapter Clerk's mind seemed to be on other things. He said, "Well, I'm very glad to hear that Masters is clear of suspicion. The whole thing was a storm in a teacup and I'll tell the Dean. But he's got a lot to cope with just now. Of course, you won't have heard. Canon Lister passed away last night."

James found himself staring at Brookes, his face stiff with surprise. He said, "Last night?"

"It may have been in the early hours of this morning. One of the students found him, in the summerhouse."

"But—" said James. "Good Lord!"

"You sound surprised? He was eighty-four."

"But I was with him last night. It must have been after midnight when I left him. I never realized—"

He was trying to adjust himself to the thought that someone who had been talking to him in such a friendly and sensible way a few hours before should now be—where? What had he found at the end of *his* path?

Brookes said, "It's always a shock when someone goes suddenly like that. Did he seem to be himself?"

"Completely. I'd no idea there was anything wrong. If I had, I might have persuaded him to come indoors."

"Do you suppose he'd have been any happier dying in his bed?"

"No," said James. "I don't." He was thinking of the smell of the flowers and the sound of the running water.

"You'd better have a word with Dr. McHarg."

James was passing the college as the doctor came out. They sat together on one of the benches opposite the west front of the Cathedral, under the gaze of the twelve stone apostles, while James recounted what had happened on the previous evening.

Dr. McHarg was not a great talker. He listened in silence, only interjecting an occasional grunt which seemed equally to express surprise or sympathy. At the end he said, "The exact time of death is of no great signeeficance in this case, but I should surmise that he died at about the turn of the night. Say, one o'clock in the morning."

"Of heart failure?"

"Cardiac arrest will no doubt be what is stated on his death certificate. If I was to be pairfectly honest, I should put 'of old age.' Old men are like cars. When they have run their appointed mileage, they stop."

"Did he have any idea that this might be going to happen?"

"It could be. He called me in a few days ago. I knew there was nothing I could do, and he knew it too. We talked about roses." The doctor added, "It was fortunate he did call me in, though. It means I can sign his certificate without any nonsensical autopsy."

"Do I gather that you don't approve of pathologists?"

Dr. McHarg regarded him with the ghost of a twinkle in his eye. He said, "You mustn't derive general propositions from parteecular instances. I happen to think nothing of the pathologist from South Wessex who would have made the examination if one had to be made. Dr. Brian Barkworth—" McHarg leaned heavily on the double letter B—"was a student at Guy's with me. He had very little knowledge at the time he qualified, and such knowledge as he did have has been dimeenishing steadily over the past forty years. Speaking for myself, I wouldna trust him to do an autopsy on a dead field mouse."

"Guy's has produced one good pathologist."

"You'll be meaning Dr. Summerson. I'd agree with that. I haird him lecture recently on odontological identification. A lucid mind. I must be off. One of the boys is reported to have a stomachache. When I was a boy, stomachaches were treated with gregory powder. I mind the filthy taste yet. Maybe that was why we didna complain about stomachaches. That's a guid example of preventative medicine for you.''

Dr. McHarg stumped off.

When James got back to the school cottage, he found Bill Williams waiting for him. His face was red and it was clear that he was upset. He said, "Look here, I want you to help me.''

"Do what I can," said James cautiously. "What's up?''

"That shit Gloag has given Phil Rosewarn his tickets.''

James had to think for a moment. Then he remembered the scene in the bar of the Black Lion. He said, "Why on earth? Philip wasn't involved in that.''

"He wasn't involved, but he heard what happened. *And* he's a friend of mine. That was enough to damn him.''

"Surely he can't just turn him out. He'd have to give some reason.''

"He doesn't have to give reasons. Phil was taken on for a trial period. All Gloag's got to say is that he isn't up to the work. Which is bloody nonsense. I happen to know that he's done some damn good work.''

"So what do you propose to do about it?''

Bill had calmed down a little by now. He sat on the edge of the table, swinging his legs. He said, "We can't make Gloag take Phil back. That's for sure. But we can make him wish he'd never sacked him. I had a word with our editor, Edwin Fisher. The *Times*, as you may have noticed, is running the Fletcher's Piece business and supporting the Archdeacon. I understand they've got a thundering editorial coming out on it tomorrow. Heavy type and biblical quotations. The obvious thing would be to come out on the other side, but Fisher says, 'No. Don't chase other people's hares for them. Start one of your own.' What we're going to do is exhume an old one.''

"Your metaphors are getting a bit mixed. If it's a dead hare, you can't chase it.''

"Certainly we can. This is a drag hunt. We draw a piece of stinking meat across the track and the hounds all set off on a different trail.''

"All right. Where do I come into it?''

"It struck me you were just the chap to help. You know the people and you've got lots of time.''

"Don't break it to me gently."

"I want you to find out exactly what Gloag and his pals paid Mrs. Henn-Christie for her property and what they paid Mrs. Piper to get out."

"From which I gather that you're reviving the supermarket affair."

"Right."

"And Mrs. Piper, I seem to recall, is the old lady who had the only remaining shop. Where do I find her?"

"She used the compensation money to open another little shop. On the other side of the road outside Bishop's Gate. Then you will help? That's very sporting of you."

"I'll think about it," said James.

Bill evidently took this as signifying assent. He said, "That's splendid. I've got to dash." He sprinted off down the path and James heard his motorcycle roaring into life. He then began to wonder just what he had undertaken and how he could set about it. He needed a plausible excuse for calling, and a reason for discussing their private financial affairs with one old lady he hardly knew and another he did not know at all.

He tried out some possible openings.

"I must apologize for presuming on such a slight acquaintance—" or perhaps, "Money, I know, is an embarrassing topic—"

He was still thinking about this when there was a knock on the door. When he opened it, he found Mrs. Henn-Christie standing there. She said, "I do hope you'll excuse me for presuming on having met you socially, Dr. Scotland, but I'm worried and I think you may be able to help me."

"Come in."

"Thank you. You're sure I'm not interrupting something?"

"Not a bit. Won't you sit down?"

"I'd have gone to Dr. McHarg, but I'm certain he'd have been off-putting. He's so—what should I say?—abrupt."

"He has got a certain Scottish brusqueness. But I'm sure he'd listen sympathetically to anything you told him. After all, he is your doctor and there's some ethical difficulty—"

Mrs. Henn-Christie was not to be diverted. She said, "This isn't a medical problem. And it isn't my problem. It's Canon Maude. He thinks he's going mad."

James was lacking in experience, but he had been a doctor long enough not to say anything silly. He said, "Are you sure?"

"Not sure that he is, no. But sure that he thinks he is. He told me so."

"I should say that's an encouraging sign."

"Oh, why?"

"There are two things to remember about people who really are insane. The first is that they have no idea about it themselves. In the ordinary way when someone says, 'I think I'm going mad,' he means that he finds himself forgetting things he ought to remember or behaving illogically. If he really *was* mad, he wouldn't have noticed anything wrong."

"I suppose not," said Mrs. Henn-Christie doubtfully. "What's the other thing?"

"That's even simpler. A madman is no longer capable of doing his job properly. You've seen Canon Maude in Cathedral. Does he still seem to be functioning all right?"

"Yes. I suppose he is. He took Evensong yesterday and he did it all right. We never get a large congregation at weekday services, so we all sit up in the Choir and I should certainly have noticed if there'd been anything wrong. In fact, I remember thinking that he read the lesson rather better than usual. It was the one about Elijah slaying four hundred and fifty of the prophets of Baal by the brook Kishon."

The thought brought a glint into Mrs. Henn-Christie's eye. James seized the opportunity deftly. He said, "I often think it's a pity we can't use such direct methods with the prophets of Baal today. You were telling me at tea about that man Gloag—"

Five minutes later he had the whole story.

"Two thousand pounds was his first offer. Can you believe it? Well, I mayn't know a lot about land values, but I wasn't falling for that. I had a word with Henry Brookes. I wanted him to handle it for me. He'd sold his practice, but I knew he kept an eye on the market and at least he's honest. He said, 'Don't take a penny less than five thousand.'"

"And that's what you got?"

"In the end. Of course, it turned out to be worth a great deal more, but I'm not blaming Henry for that. He didn't know the traffic was going to be diverted. That's what made all the difference."

"Did it occur to you to consult your solicitor?"

"No. Ought I to have done?"

"I imagine he's a local man. He'd have his ear to the ground."

Mrs. Henn-Christie thought about this. She said, "If I'd gone to anyone, it would have been Elliot Macindoe. He's good, but he's expensive. I didn't see any reason to involve him. It was just a matter of fixing the price and being paid the money."

James agreed with her, uttered a few more comforting words about Canon Maude and went in search of Mrs. Piper. He found her in the room behind her small shop and she needed neither excuse nor encouragement.

"That Gloag," she said, "he must have thought I was soft in the head."

She did not look soft. She looked cheerful and spry.

"You'd hardly credit it, but he came right into the shop—not this one, the shop I had in Station Road—forty years I'd been there—and offered me two hundred pounds to clear out. Slapped it down on the counter, just as if he'd been buying twenty cigarettes."

"And what did you say?"

"What did I say? I said, 'You must be joking.' He said he wasn't joking. The place was going to be pulled down and two hundred pounds was better than nothing at all. I told him he was wasting his time. When he saw I meant what I said, he raised the price a bit. Creeping up, like, by fifty and a hundred pounds a time until he got to five hundred. 'That's my last offer,' he said, banging his fist on the counter. Quite angry he was by this time and shouting. 'I'm staying here until you accept it.' He'd brought a bit of paper with him he wanted me to sign. 'You're *not* staying here,' I said. 'This is a shop and unless you're planning to buy a box of boiled sweets or maybe a packet of Gold Flake, there's only one place for you and that's out in the street.' 'I'm not going until you sign,' he said, 'not if I have to stay here all day. Let's make it five hundred and fifty.' Well, luckily, my son was home on leave. He's a physical instructor in the Army. He'd heard the shouting and banging and came in from the back room and said, 'What's up, Ma?' And I said, 'I asked this gentleman, quite polite, to leave the shop and he won't go.' 'Oh, won't he?' says my son, looking him up and down. That was all he said. 'Oh, won't he?'"

Mrs. Piper gave a throaty chuckle as she recalled the scene. "And he went."

"With his tail between his legs. But, of course, that wasn't the end of it. He started writing letters. I didn't answer them. I took them round to Mr. Macindoe."

"That'd be Elliot Macindoe?"

"That's right. Porter, Pallance and Macindoe. They look after the Cathedral business. A very nice firm. Mr. Macindoe said, 'You've got him over a barrel, Mrs. Piper. You leave it to me.' A bit later he came to see me. Right into the shop. A very nice gentleman, Mr. Macindoe. He said, 'What'd you say to four thousand pounds? It'd be enough to buy you the lease of a little property in East Street, behind the Cathedral, and pay your moving expenses and something over.' 'You handle it for me, Mr. Macindoe,' I said, 'and then I know it'll be done proper.' And so it was."

James thanked Mrs. Piper warmly, admired a photograph of her son, who looked capable of dealing with any number of Gloags, bought a packet of cigarettes and walked back to the Close. As he walked, he was doing sums. If the Gloag gang paid £5,000 for the freehold and £4,000 to the redoubtable Mrs. Piper and maybe another £1,000 in expenses, that involved an outlay of £10,000. Nothing, really, split between a group of businessmen. If they sold the plot, as rumor had it, to the supermarket for a figure near £100,000, that would have given them an ample float for their next venture, Fletcher's Piece. And every inducement to push ahead with it. Success breeds success.

By this time he had reached the Close and was walking up the broad path which ran between the school playing field and the flank of the Cathedral. The single bell had started tolling for morning service. A file of choristers in their cloaks and square black caps swung out of the school building and across into the diagonal path leading to the north door. They stared steadily ahead of themselves. James watched them until the porch had swallowed them. Here came Canon Humphrey, hurrying from the West Canonry, to take the service, followed by a group of theological students from the college and two old ladies. A normal weekday congregation.

Two hawks were circling the base of the spire, volplaning down the wind currents set up by the mass of the building.

James was watching them so closely that he nearly collided with Amanda, who said severely, "Bird-watching. At your age."

"Aren't hawks lovely?"

"The pigeons don't think so. You haven't forgotten that we're going for a walk this afternoon. Half past two start."

"I hadn't forgotten," said James.

He hadn't forgotten. He had been thinking about it a good deal.

The next person he met was Dora Brookes, coming through the High Street Gate encumbered with the results of her shopping. He relieved her of one of the bags and fell in beside her. She said, "I like to do most of the week's shopping on Thursday if I can. By Friday the shops are beginning to get crowded, and on Saturdays, of course, they're impossible. It's very kind of you. I do hope I'm not taking you out of your way."

"I haven't got a way," said James. "I'm a drone, not a worker."

"Henry was telling me that you'd been overdoing things and had been ordered to have a layoff. I only wish I could get him to do the same. When he had his estate-agent business—particularly toward the end, when things were all going wrong—I got very worried about him. He was smoking too much and he used to come home in the evenings looking like nothing on earth and collapse into a chair. I had to coax him to eat a bit of supper and pack him off to bed. Not that it did much good, because he used to lie awake half the night. He didn't tell me how serious things were, because he didn't want to worry me. Bless the man, if he'd told me, it would have been much easier for both of us. Then, about two years ago it was, Gloag came along with his offer. It wasn't very generous, but it cleared off the old debts and let him get out just the right side of the ledger. And when I was wondering what we were going to live on, this job came along and I thought all our troubles were over." Mrs. Brookes laughed, but not bitterly. "And so they were, for a time. There now, I've taken you right out of your way. Would you care to come in and have a cup of coffee?"

James said he would like to do this. It was not that he was fond of coffee, but he thought that anything he could learn about the troubles in the Close might be valuable and Mrs. Brookes was clearly itching to talk.

As soon as they were settled down with their coffee, she went on from exactly the point at which she had left off. "First it was Archdeacon Henn-Christie dying. Henry never had any trouble with him. 'He does his job, I do mine,' he used to say. Then Dean Lupton retiring. He died soon after. All within two or three months. And there we were, all of a sudden, in a real old tangle." Mrs. Brookes spread her hands as though she was demonstrating a piece of knitting that had gone astray. "We got Dean Forrest and Archdeacon Pawle. Mind you, I'm not saying that one's all wrong and the other all right. They're both strong-minded men. Left to themselves, they might get on quite well. It was having them both here together that was so difficult. And it won't be any easier now that Tom Lister has gone. They both respected him. There's to be a Chapter tomorrow to rearrange the duties until they can get a replacement."

James had been thinking about this. He said, "Who does elect the Canons?"

"The Canons Residentiary? They're appointed by the Queen."

"No doubt. But don't tell me she has a little notebook and opens it and says, 'We must give Canon Buggins a turn at Melchester.'"

Mrs. Brookes laughed and said, "I don't entirely understand it myself, but I believe it's the Dean who puts up the names to some committee in London and they advise the Queen."

"The Dean does it? Not the Bishop?"

"Certainly not the Bishop. He never interferes in Cathedral matters. Anyway, he's in Australia."

"But it's not something that's done quickly."

"When Canon Carstairs died, it was six months before we got Canon Humphrey."

"I see," said James thoughtfully. "Not like the Army."

"Not a bit like the Army. We've been talking so much you've let your coffee get cold. I'll get you another cup."

Eight

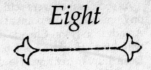

"I$_{T'S}$ THE SORT OF ENGLAND I used to dream about when we were in India," said Amanda. "Green fields and bosomy trees and little villages hidden among them with the church spire peeping out like a giraffe in a pampas clump."

From where they were sitting, on the top of Helmet Down, a fair slice of southern England was spread below them. Not dramatic, thought James, but old and tidy and secure.

"It looks peaceful," he said. "But I expect that underneath the surface all the basic passions are running hot. Progressives against conservatives, men against women, the old against the young."

"Talking about running hot," said Amanda, "I thought you were going to blow up on that last uphill stretch. You can't be fit. It must be all that desk work. Didn't you get any exercise at all?"

"There wasn't time for much. I used to play a little squash."

"Fine. There's an Army court we've got the use of. We could have a game."

"I haven't got any clothes. Or a racquet."

"Don't be feeble. Peter can lend you the clothes. You're about the same size."

"You'll be too good for me."

"Then you'll get a lot of exercise, won't you?"

"I suppose so," said James. He was changing his mind about Amanda. He had thought she was thin. Now he realized that thin wasn't the right word. Thinness implied weakness. There was nothing weak about her. She had led him up that last steep bit like a chamois. There was strength in the shoulders too.

What was the expression people used about boxers? That they'd strip well. He was certain she would strip well.

"Why is it," said Amanda, "that doctors look at you as though you were a prime piece of beef hanging up in a butcher's shop?"

"Sorry. Professional interest in the human frame," said James. "Actually, I was admiring that jersey you're wearing."

It was a pale blue sweat-shirt embroidered in front with the words NORTHWESTERN UNIVERSITY.

"I stole it from my brother. He's the real athlete of the family. Low hurdles. An international prospect—"

"Is that how he got to Northwestern?"

"Certainly. We could never have afforded it otherwise. He got what's called an athletics grant. English universities don't approve of that sort of thing. I can't see why. They give people scholarships because they're brainy and hope they'll bring credit on the university by writing learned theses and things. Why shouldn't you bring just as much credit by jumping further or running faster than anyone else in the world?"

"The Ancient Greeks would have approved of that. Was your father an athlete too?"

"The thing he was really good at was fencing."

"He would have been a difficult man to beat," agreed James. He visualized the Dean as a young man, tall, with strong arms and wrists, ruthlessly dedicated to finding and exploiting the weak spots in an opponent's technique. He said, "You promised to tell me the real story of what happened to your father in his last mission in Africa."

There was a pause, measured in minutes more than in seconds, before Amanda said, "Did I?"

This was followed by another long pause.

"It's not a very nice story. You're not easily shocked, are you?"

"Not easily," said James, but as he said it, he was conscious of a feeling of disquiet.

"Then don't interrupt me. And don't look at me. Our mission was on the plateau between the Ilubabor and the Keta Mountains, near the boundary line between Abyssinia and the Southern Sudan. The nearest town was Jimma, about eighty miles away, and from there to Addis Ababa was another hundred miles by quite a good road. Our supplies used to come up from there. When we first arrived, I thought it was the nicest place we'd been in. It was February and everything was green. Mimosa and pine trees and giant sycamores and all sorts of fruit trees—oranges and peaches and tamarinds and figs. The people of the plateau were friendly and a lot more sympathetic than some of the ones we'd lived among before, in Central Africa and India. After all, they'd been Christians longer than we had. It was a primitive sort of Christianity, but it gave Father a basis to work on. There was a nice convert called Jobo who helped with the services, and three or four servants. One of them was quite a good cook. I was sixteen at the time and had a pony which I rode when we visited the villages. It all seemed too good to be true. I think our first hint of trouble was when Jobo told us about our predecessors. We'd known, in a general way, that there'd been two missionaries there before us and that one of them had died and the second had left rather quickly. What we didn't know was that the first one had committed suicide. Not in any dramatic sort of way. He just wandered off into the hills in mid-June—that's the hottest of the hot weather—without any water or food or even a hat on his head and after a time he lay down and died. The natives found what the foxes had left of him. They're not like English foxes. They're gray and nearly twice as big. More like wolves, really. We used to hear them barking at night. The second man stood it for about six months and then came back to Addis and advised them to abandon the mission. He had been told about men who came across the border from the Sudan and terrorized the villagers. Gangas, the villagers called them. At the first hint of them they'd abandon the village and hide out in the hills until they'd gone. Father took all this with a pinch of salt. We'd been in dangerous places before and the dangers had mostly proved to be exaggerated. It would have been better if he had listened."

When Amanda stopped talking, the sounds of the English countryside reasserted themselves. There were grasshoppers in the dry grass. A flock of starlings passed overhead like a dark cloud, formed, re-formed and swept away.

"I was in the kitchen, trying to find out what had happened to all the servants, when the Gangas arrived. There were five of them, almost naked. They were carrying machetes and iron-wood clubs. Jobo was arguing with them, telling them to go away, I suppose. They cut him to pieces. The first blow nearly took his head off. Then they started cutting off his arms and legs. They were like boys playing a game. Then Father came out. He must have heard the noise. He just stood looking down at what was left of Jobo. The man nearest to him took a swipe at him with his club and broke his leg. They'd have killed him, of course, but at that moment they caught sight of me in the window. They all swung round and came crowding into the kitchen. The only thing I could do was back into the corner and crouch down. I think my legs had given way under me. That was when they saw something more interesting than a sixteen-year-old girl. There were a dozen lumps of raw meat on the dresser. They grabbed them and started stuffing them into their mouths. The blood was running down their chins and dripping onto their naked bodies. They fought each other for the odd piece. I suppose they must have been starving. Father, who had dragged himself to the doorway, stood watching them. As long as I live, I shall never forget the look on his face. A few moments later the five men were all rolling on the floor in agony, jerking and twisting. They died quite soon. The meat was bait, for the foxes. There was cyanide in each lump. I don't remember much after that. The servants who had run away came back. They buried the Gangas. They could have driven Father into Jimma, where there was a hospital, but he wouldn't let them. He showed them how to set and splint his leg. It wasn't a sensible thing to do and it made a lot of trouble later. Something went wrong with the leg bone. It had to be broken and re-set. He was nearly a year in and out of hospital when we got back to England. I think he welcomed the pain. It was a penance for what he'd done. He could have stopped them, you see. He knew enough of their language to shout out, 'Poison!' But he didn't. He let them die. If he'd had to do it to save the Church, it would have been justified. It wasn't justified to save me. I told you *not* to look at me."

James said, "Sorry." He knew that she was crying, although she was making no noise about it. He watched two boys on bicycles racing each other on the road at the foot of the down.

Their shouts came distantly up to him. When Amanda spoke again, she seemed to be back on balance.

She said, "Now you know what a dangerous man he is."

"Not an easy member for a Cathedral community to accommodate," agreed James.

"Oh, he got on well enough with most of them. Tom Lister was a great stand-by. Is it true you were talking to him on the night he died?"

"Quite true."

"What a perfect way to go. Like a candle being blown out when it's time for bed. I wonder if he knew it was going to happen."

"I think he must have done."

"What did you talk about?"

"He said that scientists were so dangerous that they ought to be locked up in their own laboratories."

"James," said Amanda, "you do like me, don't you?" Before he could say anything, she went on, "Because if you do, you mustn't talk to me as though I was ten years old."

"I'm sorry. It was quite a long discussion." He tried to collect his thoughts. "What Tom seemed to feel was that scientists were all right when they were doing their proper job, which was, I suppose, inventing useful things like anesthetics and anti-biotics, but when they went too far and meddled with things they weren't meant to meddle with, they were stepping out of their proper ground and that was when they hurt people more than they helped them. I didn't agree. I said that a scientist must always go the whole way and damn the consequences."

"Then you were wrong and Tom was right."

"You really think that?"

"Certainly. Do you believe in God?"

Faced with this sudden and practically unanswerable question, James took refuge in silence.

"Before you say something stupid, let me tell you what I *don't* mean. I'm not asking if you believe that there's an old man with a white beard waiting to say hello when you go aloft, or that if you live respectably down here on the ground floor, you earn yourself a stay in a golden penthouse afterward."

"I'm with Omar on that," agreed James. "'For this is truth,

though all the rest be lies. The rose that once is blown forever dies.' "

"Right. But what I *do* mean is that all this—" Amanda lay back on her elbows and looked down at the patchwork of fields below them—"all this can't just be blind chance. Someone must have thought it out. The world and all the weird and wonderful creatures in it. The dolphins, who knew all about radar before we imagined we'd invented it, and the swallows that come every year, without maps or compasses, from a particular house in North Africa to a particular house in Melchester, and the ants who organize themselves like an army, and hummingbirds, and the creatures who live so deep down in the sea that no one has ever set eyes on them, to say nothing of the balance of elements that allows the world to exist at all. Don't tell me it's all a fluke."

"Darwin—" said James.

"Oh, Darwin. All he explained was why some giraffes have longer necks than others. He doesn't get near the real point that some intelligence, so much more intelligent than we are that we can't even begin to understand it, *must* have thought it all out. Ever since people have started to think, they've realized that an intelligence like that *must* exist. Mostly they've been prepared to be thankful and enjoy their luck. It's only scientists who probe and peer. It's so—so impertinent. And dangerous, because they never know when to stop. And what happens at the end of the day? They produce a baby out of a test tube and think they've done something terribly clever."

James had listened in silence to the altars of his faith being trampled on. What he would have said was never put to the test, since a lady, who had approached Helmet Down from the rear, arrived at this moment with an English setter which fell on Amanda and started to lick her face.

"Good walk?" said Peter.

"Smashing."

"You look stiff."

"I am stiff."

"I'm telling you, don't let that girl get you onto a squash court. She'll run you off your feet."

"Thanks for the warning."

"What did you find to talk about?"

"Everything under the sun," said James. "What about a drink? I could just hobble as far as the Black Lion."

"Not tonight. Thursdays and Fridays are no-booze and early-bed nights. We've got a needle match on Saturday against Salisbury. They always put out a good side."

"In that case," said James, "since I didn't get much lunch and no tea at all, I think I'll stand myself a proper evening meal for once."

He was not sorry to be alone. He didn't want to talk about Amanda. He wanted to think about her. The elaborate four-course dinner at the Black Lion, with decorous intervals between the courses, gave him plenty of time to do this.

For a start, how old was she? If she had been sixteen or seventeen at the time of the Ganga episode and had come back to England soon after that, and her father had been in and out of hospital for a year and had been at Melchester for the best part of two years, that made her about twenty. She looked older than that, but, living the sort of life she did, she'd have grown up quickly. That last episode must have been traumatic. Clearly, it was not for general publication, since all that he had heard before had been vague rumors. From remarks dropped during the school walk he gathered that there were at least three versions current among the boys, the most widely believed being that the Dean had a wooden leg in place of one cut off and eaten by cannibals.

"Red currant jelly with it, sir?"

"Thank you," said James, "I think I'd rather have mint sauce."

Why had she confided in him? A number of explanations occurred to him, some more flattering than others. She was a serious girl. No doubt about that. With very definite ideas about life—and death. She was also, probably, still a virgin. Though damned nearly not. Damned nearly deflowered and dead. He visualized her father watching silently while his enemies destroyed themselves. What had she said about that? If he had done such a thing for his Church, it would have been justified. But not to save his own daughter. He had regarded *that* as a sin which merited penance. That was a hard, bitter philosophy.

"Will you take the sweet, sir?

"Will you take the sweet, sir?"

"I'll have the raspberries."

"With some cream?"

"Yes, I'd like some cream."

By the time he had finished his second cup of coffee, he was alone in the dining room and the waiters were beginning to lay the tables for breakfast. He paid his bill and strolled out into the street. It was a black, heavy night. The moon and stars were hidden by an overcast sky. Not a night when sleep would come easily. He decided to make a gentle detour to the south of the town to stretch his legs. By the time this leisurely circuit had brought him to the River Gate, it was shut. The Bishop's Gate would be shut too. He would have to circle the Close wall widdershins to reach the High Street Gate. By the time he got there, it was a few minutes short of eleven and he was surprised to find the Close Constable absent from his post. Mullins was usually waiting inside the gate to count in the late-comers and close the gate as soon as the last of his flock was inside.

A short-cut across the school playing field brought James to the north front of the Cathedral. Here he stopped. There was a light showing, shining out through the clerestory window. It was a single light and he guessed that it must come from the organ loft. A moment later this was confirmed. He heard the sound of the organ being played. It could only be Paul Wren. Paul had, he knew, a private key of the cloister door and sometimes practiced in the evenings, but not often at eleven o'clock at night. He decided to investigate.

The cloisters, which formed an open square at the southwest corner of the Cathedral, were in deep shadow. James felt his way along. As he reached the far end, something moved in the blackness. James threw up an arm in an instinctive gesture of defense, then lowered it again. It was Mullins. James said, "Does he often do this?"

"Never before," said Mullins. "I thought I'd better come along and have a look. Ten to one he'll forget to lock the door when he goes. Then it's me that gets into trouble."

When he opened the door, a very faint reflection of the light from the organ loft emphasized the vast emptiness of the Cathedral. The organist was improvising, starting one cadence and breaking off into another, using the softest stops, in little runs and trills.

"Odd sort of music," said Mullins.

"He isn't playing. He's talking to the organ and the organ's answering him back."

"Then I hope it soon tells him to go to bed."

At this moment the music reached a sort of resolution and stopped. The light in the organ loft went out. The next thing they saw was the pinpoint of a torch coming toward them along the transept. It was Paul Wren and he was not hurrying. He could hardly have avoided seeing the two men by the door, but he gave no sign of having done so and walked slowly past them. They watched the light of his torch bobbing down under the cloister arches and disappearing at the far end.

Mullins said, "Just like as if he was saying goodbye to his girlfriend and didn't want to leave." He added, "And he *didn't* lock the door. I told you he wouldn't."

Nine

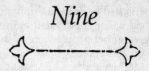

"THE SIMPLEST ARRANGEMENT," said the Dean, "will be for each of you to take a month in residence in turn until we get a new Canon installed. Then, if you find that more convenient, we can revert to four three-monthly tours of duty. That will mean that you finish October, Archdeacon. Mervyn takes November and you take December, Francis."

"Which means that I get Christmas," said Canon Humphrey. "Thank you very much."

"We may have a new Canon by then."

"Not a chance. When Canon Carstairs died, it took them four months to choose me and another two months before I was installed."

"I have already alerted the secretary of the Appointments Committee. We can only hope they'll be a bit quicker this time." The Dean consulted some notes he had made. "Tom's funeral will be on Tuesday week. We couldn't fix it sooner because the Archbishop had expressed a wish to officiate. He was a great admirer of Tom's."

"We shall have to alert the stewards," said Canon Humphrey. "It will be a packed Cathedral. We don't want a repetition of the sort of trouble we had when the Queen came down."

"Tickets only," said the Archdeacon.

"I'll consult the chief steward," said the Dean shortly. "I don't like turning a service into a theatrical performance. Next point, the college. We shall have to put someone in charge there temporarily."

"Openshaw," suggested the Archdeacon.

"He should be able to handle it," agreed Canon Humphrey.

"As a stopgap, then." The Dean looked at Canon Maude,

who had been sitting unhappily at the far end of the table and had so far contributed nothing to their discussions. Becoming aware that people were looking at him, he said, "Yes, yes. Of course I agree."

"Then perhaps you would record that, Henry. Now, is there anything more?"

"Two things," said the Archdeacon. "I have been in correspondence with Bernard Lovett. As you know, he is at the moment assistant organist at Worcester. He is a medalist of the Royal College and was chosen to play at the Three Choirs Festival this summer. I have always thought that he would be just the man for us here. Two days ago I heard that he was agreeable—in principle. The details would have to be worked out, of course."

"Where does that leave Paul Wren?" said Canon Humphrey.

"I'm sure he would be very happy to work under such a distinguished man. If not, he could always apply for a post elsewhere."

The Dean said, "I don't agree with that."

"I'm not happy about it either," said Canon Humphrey. "I think Paul is a fine musician and has a remarkable rapport with the choir. Several people have told me that they've never heard them sing better."

"But surely," said the Archdeacon, "a cathedral like Melchester cannot be content with anything less than an associate of our own Royal College." He looked across at Canon Maude, who jerked himself back into the proceedings and said, "Yes. Of course. I agree with that."

"Since we seem to be equally divided," said the Dean, "we shall have to postpone a decision. If Wren gets a firm offer of a top job elsewhere, it might be different."

"Even then I should be against it," said Canon Humphrey. "The man's a genius."

"With some of the defects of a genius," said the Archdeacon. "I'm afraid he's a little unbalanced."

The Dean said, "I think we must leave it there for the time being. You had a second point, Archdeacon?"

"There is one other matter. And if it had not been both urgent and important, I should not have raised it at a moment like this. Yesterday I received a letter from Gerald Gloag—"

"Really, Archdeacon. Do you think—?"

"I think I had better read it to you. It refers to his earlier letter making us the offer of a hundred and eighty thousand pounds for Fletcher's Piece. It says, 'You will appreciate that men who are prepared to raise money on this scale cannot allow it to stand idle. The consortium concerned is pursuing a number of projects, of which Fletcher's Piece is only one. I have to tell you, therefore, that they must have agreement, if only in principle, by the end of next week or the offer will be withdrawn.'"

The Dean's face had set like stone. He said, "And do you require our comments on this letter?"

"If you please."

"Then the first thing I would say is that I find it extremely distasteful that you should have raised the matter at all. We are all aware that Tom Lister was opposed to this project. Is it your suggestion that, now that he is dead, we should immediately reopen it in order to get a different decision from the Chapter?"

"I am simply suggesting that the letter needs an answer."

"Then let the answer be short and simple. We note that the consortium intends to withdraw their offer. We are content that they should do so."

The Archdeacon, who had managed so far to keep his temper, said, "Might I suggest that it merits our serious consideration. The rights and wrongs of the matter are already the subject of public comment."

"Public comment!" said the Dean. "If you mean that piece of juvenile nonsense which purported to be a leading article in today's number of the *Melset Times*, I think we could safely ignore it."

"I read it, too," said Canon Humphrey. "And it did strike me that Arthur Driffield seemed curiously well informed about our deliberations."

"The same point had, of course, occurred to me," said the Dean. "I did not intend to raise it, but since you have done so, may I say that I hope—" he refrained so pointedly from looking at the Archdeacon that he could hardly have made his meaning clearer—"I hope that the confidentiality which we have always enjoyed in our meetings has not been breached."

There was an awkward silence. The Archdeacon said, "If that was aimed at me, Dean, it is wide of the mark. I have had no communication of any sort with Driffield. On the other hand, I have never made any secret of my views on Cathedral finances. As you know, I have only just been able to begin my detailed investigation of the main Cathedral accounts, some of which are so complex that I begin to suspect that my predecessors deliberately got them into a state in which no one could understand them."

"I'm afraid," said Canon Humphrey pacifically, "that Henn-Christie's mind was more on things eternal than things temporal."

"However, it did not need a close investigation to unearth one point. We are living beyond our means. In commercial terms, we are running a bankrupt company. And doing so without informing our shareholders."

"Your conclusions," said the Dean, "might have been more acceptable if your investigations had been made in a more impartial spirit."

"I don't know what that means."

"I mean that ever since you came to Melchester, you have been looking for trouble and hoping to find it."

"I resent that."

"You have cast aspersions on a number of people who are no longer here. But we *are* here and are well able to defend ourselves."

"I was not aware that I was aspersing anyone. I have simply been doing my duty as a man of business."

"Then let me suggest that you stop thinking of yourself as a businessman and start, for a change, to think of yourself as a priest."

"The two offices are not incompatible."

"Christ thought so. He threw the moneylenders out of the Temple."

Canon Humphrey said, in a voice of obvious distress, "Gentlemen—Matthew, Raymond—I must beg you to stop. This does nothing to assist."

Brookes, who had been staring in a bemused manner at the minute book, said, "Am I to make a record of this?"

"Certainly not," said the Archdeacon. "It was an informal discussion. I would like to suggest that we revert to business. I have made a suggestion which I will now put, if I may, as a formal proposal. That we accept, in principle, and subject to discussion of details, the offer put to us in Gerald Gloag's letter."

There was a further silence, broken at last by Brookes, who said, with a belated recollection of company procedure, "Are there any amendments to that proposal?"

The Dean said, "Perhaps I might suggest an amendment."

The pendulum had swung. He seemed suddenly to be in an excellent humor.

"I would suggest that we say to Mr. Gloag that if he will tell us the names of the purchasers who are behind him, we *might* consider the matter further. After all, we ought to know who we're dealing with."

"Reasonable," said Canon Humphrey.

"Then can I take a vote on that amendment?" said Brookes. "You, Mr. Dean, and Canon Humphrey in favor."

"If we do answer in those terms," said the Archdeacon, "the offer will almost certainly be withdrawn. I oppose the amendment." As he said this, he looked across at Canon Maude, who emerged from the trance that was gripping him and said, "I support the Archdeacon."

"In that case," said Brookes, feeling easier now that the proper routine of the meeting had reasserted itself, "the amendment fails and I must now record your votes on the Archdeacon's original proposal. In favor—you, Mr. Archdeacon, and, I take it, Canon Maude."

Canon Maude nodded.

"Against—you, Mr. Dean, and Canon Humphrey. In that case, the votes being equal, the proposal also fails."

"Splendid," said the Dean. "An excellent example of democracy in action. And now, if there is no further business—"

The Archdeacon said, "I'm afraid that the matter cannot be disposed of quite so lightly."

There was a note in his voice which made Canon Humphrey look up. He wondered what the Archdeacon was up to. The Dean seemed unperturbed. He said, "You must follow the rules of procedure, Archdeacon. Since neither my amendment nor your proposal received a majority of votes, both fall to the ground and we are back where we started."

"Not quite." The Archdeacon opened the black-covered book

which he had placed on the table at the start of the meeting. Brookes had assumed it to be a Bible, but he now saw that it was a copy, which the Archdeacon must have taken from the Chapter House library, of the Canons and Regulations of the Cathedral Establishment.

"This matter is dealt with under the Rules of Protocol and Procedure. Rule Eleven, 'Where the members of the Inner Chapter are equally divided on a matter of importance and concern to the welfare of the Cathedral body and the matter cannot therefore be decided by them, it shall be referred for decision, with the least possible delay, to a meeting of the Greater Chapter.'"

The silence which followed this pronouncement was broken by the Dean, who leaned back in his chair and laughed heartily and with what seemed to be genuine amusement.

"My dear Archdeacon," he said and was convulsed again with laughter. "My dear Archdeacon—"

"You find it funny."

"You must be joking. How do you imagine that fifty unworldly country clergymen can decide a matter like this?" He chuckled again. "I was reading the other day that Bishop King of Lincoln once said that the clergy of *his* diocese could be divided into three categories: those who had gone out of their minds, those who were about to go out of their minds and those who had no minds to go out of."

"I'm sure that the members of the Greater Chapter will appreciate that," said the Archdeacon smoothly.

"Ah, but remember. Everything said at our meetings is confidential."

"Naturally," said the Archdeacon.

"Will you have to do it?" said Dora Brookes.

"If the Archdeacon formally instructs me to summon a meeting of the Greater Chapter, I shall be bound to do so. The canons of the Cathedral are quite clear on the matter."

"And if you do?"

"They will almost certainly support the Archdeacon. For a start, you can be sure that he'll manage to pass on that joke of the Dean's."

"It wasn't very tactful."

"It certainly wasn't. But quite apart from that, I think they'll be in favor of the Archdeacon's plan. From the financial point of view, there's a lot of sense in it. And it won't worry *them* if we have a factory or a housing estate on our doorstep. They won't have to live with it."

When the last of the Canons had gone, the Dean got swiftly to his feet, opened the long windows, as if to let in some fresh air, and hobbled out and down the grass path that led to the lawn at the foot of the garden. At this point the river curved and the current had cut into the far bank, forming a ledge under which lived a trout of formidable size, a cannibal who fed on the small fish that flicked in and out of the weeds in the clear green water. No fly or bait would tempt him. The Dean had spent many hours watching the old villain.

He supposed that if a factory was built on Fletcher's Piece, the effluent would quickly kill off all the fish. In thinking in this way he was not thinking for himself alone, but for all his predecessors and all his successors. For more than five hundred years Deans of Melchester had sat in the garden where he was sitting, had enjoyed the tranquillity and seclusion which it offered, had thought through the problems and perplexities of their office.

Suppose that journalist was right. Suppose that there had once been a hut or hovel there, from which had come the storm of arrows which had cut the French chivalry to pieces at Crécy and Poitiers. What possible comparison was there between such a place and a brick monstrosity which manufactured transistors? The Dean was a traditionalist. One of his first moves had been to have the telephone removed from the Deanery. If people wished to communicate with him, they could write a letter or call, as people had done for hundreds of years. Another thing he had done was to ban transistors from the Close. Was that particular enemy now coming in from the rear? In the sacred name of progress. Progress which seemed to bring little with it but dirt, dissatisfaction and mindless uproar.

The Dean stumped back to the house.

Rosa Pilcher was at work in the study with a duster. She was a small woman with a sharp nose and large brown eyes which seemed to be set unnaturally wide apart. Like a horse's eyes, thought the Dean. Made to see things on both sides of her face at once.

She divided her working hours between the Deanery and the Archdeaconry. The Dean had inherited her with the house. He had often wished he could get rid of her, but a substitute was hard to come by.

He said, "I wanted a word with you."

Rosa folded her duster neatly and said, "Yes, sir."

"Why did you accuse Masters of theft?"

Rosa stood up like a grenadier to this assault. Only a faint flush at the top of her sallow cheeks showed that it had gone home. She said, "I accused Masters of thieving? I never—"

"Don't add untruthfulness to your other sins."

"Sins? Who's talking about sins? *I* never took the silver."

"So you do know what I'm talking about."

"I see what's in front of my eyes. I saw him sneaking it out of his bag and passing it across to Alf Carney, and everyone knows what sort of man *he* is."

"And it didn't occur to you to make any inquiries before accusing a servant of the Cathedral of theft? It didn't occur to you that the silver might belong to Masters?"

"How would he get hold of silver?"

"They were cups that he got hold of by his skill and prowess on the cricket field."

"Oh. Is that his story?"

"It's not his story. It's the story of the man who bought them. The cups have been seen by a number of people. There's no question that what I have told you is the truth."

Rosa said, "Oh," again, but this time with less confidence.

"I've two things to say to you. The first is, don't make accusations unless you're sure of your facts. Do you understand?"

Rosa gave a bob of her head which might have indicated that she understood.

"The second is more important. If you have any complaint to make about a member of the Cathedral staff, make it to me, not to the Archdeacon."

"Yes, sir. I understand. Can I go now?"

The Dean was on the point of saying, "Yes. And don't come back," when he remembered, in the nick of time, the Deanery party for the Friends of the Cathedral at which Rosa's assistance would be vital. But as soon as he could find a substitute, that woman would have to go.

From his office, late that evening, Gloag telephoned Leo Sandeman. He said, "It looks as though we're winning. We've not passed the post yet, but we're on the run-in."

"Did the Archdeacon swing it?"

"The vote was two all. That means it goes to the Greater Chapter."

"Who the hell are they?"

"A lot of dozy clergymen in the sticks. The betting is they'll support the Archdeacon. He's almost the only member of the big five they know."

"He's the one who gets around," agreed Sandeman. "I met him down in Westport the day before yesterday, doing a stint in the docks. When do the backwoodsmen meet?"

"They haven't been officially notified yet. But probably not for about a fortnight."

"I think we could extend the option until then."

"I think we might," said Gloag with a grin.

James was dreaming.

It was not the old, hopeless sort of nightmare which had hag-ridden him lately. He had left those behind in London. But it was extraordinarily vivid. He was in the organ loft, looking down along the nave toward the great west door, wide open to admit the crowd of people who were pressing through it. He was not in the least surprised to observe the Medical Registrar from Guy's and with him Archdeacon Henn-Christie.

"And look there," said Paul Wren. "If that isn't old Dean Lupton himself."

This did seem a little odd since he was walking arm in arm with the present Dean. James said, "Surely not."

"Of course it is," said Paul. "Look quickly, or he may disappear." So strongly did he feel about this that he shook James by the arm. James woke to find Peter standing beside his bed.

"Sorry," he said, "but there's a bit of a panic on. Amanda said to call you. Better put on a sweater or something."

James swung his legs over the side of the bed. He was still half asleep. He said, "Sweater? Wassup?"

"And shoes. We've got to go out. But hurry." He clattered off downstairs, and James, pausing only to push his feet into a pair of sandals and pull a sweater over his head, ran down after him. By the time he reached the front door, he was wide awake. Amanda was standing there. She, too, had clearly dressed in a hurry. She said, "Come along. I'll tell you as we go," and led the way at a brisk pace past the dark front of the school building.

"It's Canon Maude," she said. "You know his old mother. Eighty plus, but a game old girl. She knocked us up at the Deanery five minutes ago. Father's gone along. He told me to fetch you in case a doctor was wanted."

By this time they had reached the door of the North Canonry. It was open and the light was on in the hall. The Dean, in a long gray dressing gown, was leaning forward, one hand on his stick, the other on Mrs. Maude's shoulder as he listened to what she had to say. As the others came up, he looked around and said, "Splendid. I'm so glad you could get here." He might have been welcoming late-comers to a party. If James had known him better, he would have realized that this particular tone of voice meant that the situation was serious.

"Canon Maude has locked himself into his study. From a note which his mother found, it seems that he meant to take his own life." As the Dean spoke, he was leading the way toward the door at the end of the passage. "We have tried shouting, but he seems to have blocked the gap under the door and he can't or won't answer."

James stooped toward the keyhole. The smell was unmistakable.

He said, "Is there some way in at the back?"

"From the garden, yes. But the windows have been shuttered on the inside."

"Then we shall have to break down this door."

"Can we help?"

"You can help best, sir, by taking Mrs. Maude and your daughter right out of the house. Or if you won't do that—" he noted the obstinate look in the Dean's eyes—"take them into the dining room and shut the door. And don't let anyone stand directly in front of the windows. Actually, it would be best of all if you could induce the women to get under the dining-room table."

"I see," said the Dean. "Then you think—"

"I think that we are in just as much danger as Canon Maude. It depends what pressure has been built up and what friction we set up when we break down the door."

"Very well," said the Dean. Both his charges seemed prepared to argue, but he shepherded them into the dining room and shut the door.

"Now what?" said Peter.

"Now we break the door down. I think we could handle that bench between us. But we'd better pad the end." He got a cushion out of the drawing room and lashed it to the end of the bench with one of the curtain cords. "Turn the light out. And leave the front door wide open."

They stood in front of the study door and swung their homemade battering ram. It was a heavy bench, but the door was a stout one. They were both sweating now.

"One more good one and aim for the lock."

The door gave inward as the lock tore away from the hasp. The gas rolled out in a cloud. Peter ignored the figure of Canon Maude slumped over his desk. First he turned off the control tap of the big gas cylinder, then gently eased open first the shutters and then the windows. The through draft to the open front door had already started to clear the room.

"Give me a hand and we'll take the old boy into the drawing room. Try not to knock anything over while we're doing it."

They carried Canon Maude between them, a hand under each arm. He was red in the face and breathing heavily, but seemed to be coming around.

"Silly old buffer," said James. "I suppose he didn't know the difference between coal gas and methane."

"One of the defects of a classical education," said Peter. He was looking at Canon Maude, who had started to mutter to himself. "All the same, even if he couldn't poison himself, he might have suffocated if he'd stayed in there long enough, I suppose."

"The danger was detonation, not suffocation. Once he'd built up a concentration in the room, the slightest spark, even the heat of a light bulb, would have set off an explosion which would have taken out this house and the houses on either side and started a fire as well. I saw the results once in Woolwich and wouldn't much care to see it in Melchester Close. There, I think it should be safe enough now."

He opened the dining-room door. The Dean was sitting at the head of the table. He had found a book of Canon Maude's which interested him and was reading it. Amanda and old Mrs. Maude were sitting together on a sofa.

"I thought I told you to get under the table."

"We suggested it," said Amanda. "But Mrs. Maude wouldn't hear of it. She said she'd been in London during the blitz and had slept through every single night of it."

The Dean looked up from his book and said, "I assume that the excitement is over. Could you explain what happened?"

When James had explained, the Dean said, "Yes. I see," and closed his book carefully. "I'd better have a word with Mervyn, and all you young people had better get back to bed. Thank you for helping."

James said, "We'd better put that gas cylinder back in the kitchen where it belongs and hitch it up to the stove." They found Mrs. Maude in the study, pottering around the room, tidying things up. James took the cylinder and carried it out. It was quite light. It would have been a lot heavier when it was full, he thought. "I wonder how the old boy managed it. He must have been fairly desperate."

"And why did he bother to move it at all?" said Peter. "He could just as well have done it in the kitchen."

"Suicides get odd ideas," said James. "I expect the study was his favorite room. He didn't want to die among a lot of pots and pans. He wanted his books round him."

As they moved out into the hall and passed the dining room, they heard Canon Maude say, "I'm a silly old man, Dean. I'd be better dead." And the Dean's voice in reply. They were too far away to catch the words, but the tone was not sympathetic. It was rough and austere, a cold douche of water quenching Canon Maude's apologies.

As they reached the front door, Mrs. Maude came pattering after them. She seized James by the arm and said, in the sing-song voice of the deaf, "He's a wicked man."

Curiously, James had no doubt who the wicked man was.

"He was here earlier this week. Talking to Mervyn, upsetting him. Making him do things he didn't want to. He's a wicked

man. Someone must stop him. You understand me, don't you?"
She gave his arm a shake.

"I understand you," said James, disengaging himself gently.
The old woman looked at him doubtfully, then turned around,
went in and shut the door.

As James and Peter walked back to the cottage, the first faint
dawn of Saturday was coming up into the sky.

Ten

"It's not just the cathedral people," said Amanda. "All the nobs from the town turn up as well."

She had come around after breakfast to thank James for his help the night before and to gossip.

"Which nobs in particular?"

"People like Val Laporte, the Chief Constable. And Grant Adey. He's chairman of the Council. And a lot of little noblets like Sandeman and Gloag. And of course Arthur Driffield is bound to be there with his notebook, gathering material for another of his slashing editorials."

"It sounds as though you're in for a lively time."

"Friends of the Cathedral," said Amanda bitterly. "I sometimes think Enemies of the Cathedral would be a better name for them. They turn up in droves, eat us out of house and home, go across to the Cathedral and pledge themselves to peace and amity and other Christian ideals, and follow that up with their annual meeting, which always seems to degenerate into a slanging match."

"Always?"

"Ever since we've been here, anyway. The trouble is they've really got more money than the Chapter. I don't mean they've got a bigger income, but they haven't got any real expenses. They don't even pay for the meal they have here. They might do that, don't you think?"

"It would be a gesture."

"All they do is argue about what money they're going to give and what it's to be used for. Sometimes it's sensible, like when they paid for rebuilding the console of the organ. Sometimes it's crazy, like filling the precincts with modernistic statues. When they've finished arguing about what they're going to do with their money, they start telling the Chapter what it ought to do with *its* money."

"Fletcher's Piece?"

"Right. They'll all have read the gospel according to Arthur Driffield and be armed with poison darts to stick into Daddy. Lucky he's got a tough skin. I'll have to go now. Those bloody tables take two hours to lay and two hours to clean up."

"And I've got to pack up my stuff. I'm moving in with Aunt Alice."

Amanda looked blank.

"Alan Furbank is coming back this afternoon. I've been offered a bedroom by the Brookeses. Aunt Alice was Henry's mother's sister. She died last year."

"I remember her. She was a complete freak. She wore a gray toupee about a yard high and spent her time smoking cigarettes in a long holder and complaining about her stomach."

"I expect the two things were not unconnected," said James.

It turned out to be a pleasant enough room, tucked away on the top story at the back of the Chapter Clerk's house. It was still faintly redolent of Aunt Alice. James traced this to its source when, in the course of stowing away his own few clothes, he opened a cupboard at the back which was still full of her belongings. Like many old ladies, she seemed, in her last years, to have become a hoarder. He counted thirty-two tablets of soap and sixty rolls of lavatory paper stacked neatly on a shelf with six Bibles, four prayerbooks and a set of Dr. Spurgeon's *Sermons.* Two shelves were devoted to hats, bonnets and reticules. On the floor were several pairs of surprisingly small and dainty shoes and a pair of buttoned boots with long wooden boot trees.

James stood for a few moments in front of the cupboard, absorbing the smell of lavender, mixed with others less easily identifiable, and trying to re-create Aunt Alice from the things she had left behind her when she set out on her last journey. He thought that it must have been a happy close to her long life, in this quiet and sunny room. Her ghost would not disturb his sleep.

"Mixed crowd you get at these functions," said Laporte.

"Very mixed," agreed Canon Humphrey.

Valentine Laporte, Chief Constable of Melchester, was one of the few remaining holders of that office who had been appointed from the Army and not from the ranks of the police. He was a soldier and he looked like a soldier. His most arresting feature was a bold mustache, under cover of which lived a ready smile.

"I suppose most of them will have read Driffield's stuff and use it to take pot shots at the Cathedral establishment."

"I'm afraid they will," said Canon Humphrey sadly. "Do you think we could rely on you to create a diversion?"

"Flank attack, you mean? Something about the new service book? Or the creeping menace of Roman Catholicism?"

"The new service book, for preference. They'll all have something to say about *that*."

The side curtains of the big marquee had been fully rolled up, but the heat under the sun-baked canvas was considerable. The buffet lunch had been served without too many mishaps. Mrs. Henn-Christie had dropped a strawberry ice on Gerald Gloag's foot, and Lady Fallingford's Irish setter, who had infiltrated the party, had eaten six liver-sausage sandwiches before he was ejected. He was being sick in the Dean's herbaceous border.

"Par for the course, really," said Amanda. "Two years ago they set fire to the marquee. They all seem to be fairly happy, don't you think?"

"Most of them," said James. "That tall thin man in the corner doesn't look very happy, though. He's spent most of his time glowering at the Archdeacon."

Amanda said, "He's a solicitor. I think his name's Gibbon or Gilborne. He was the man the Archdeacon went for over one of the Cathedral trusts and nearly got him struck off the roll."

"He looks as if he'd be happy to strike the Archdeacon off. Isn't it hot in here? What happens next?"

"Coffee and move over to Cathedral. I shan't be coming to the service. I shall have to help with the washing up."

"Can I lend a hand?"

"No. You go and pray for peace and quiet. There's that dog trying to get in again. He must have a one-way stomach. Hoof him out."

Penny Consett had detached Paul Wren from a country clergyman who wanted to talk to him about organ music and was busy impressing her personality on him.

"I've always thought how difficult it must be for you to do everything by yourself," she said. "I mean, all those stops and gadgets. Wouldn't it be helpful if you had someone to turn for you?"

"Turn?"

"Turn the pages."

"You're thinking of concert pianists. It's nothing like that. I know most of the music, anyway. And what I don't know I make up."

"Wonderful," said Penny soulfully. "Have another ice."

Arthur Driffield had succeeded, at long last, in attracting the attention of the Archdeacon, who had been deep in discussion with Openshaw and one of the theological students for most of the lunch. He said, "I hear that Fletcher's Piece is being handed over to the Greater Chapter for decision."

The Archdeacon made a half-turn toward him, stared at him for a long moment and said, "Oh?"

Unrebuffed, Driffield said, "Am I right about that?"

"No."

"Well, I certainly understood that was so."

"No decision has yet been made."

"But if you can't decide the matter between the four of you, surely it'll have to go to the Greater Chapter."

The Archdeacon said, "No comment," turned away again and said to Canon Humphrey, "Reverting to that point about outside courses for students, Francis. I'd agree in principle, but we shall have to watch the cost."

Driffield looked thoughtfully at the broad clerical back which had been presented to him.

On his way back from evicting Lady Fallingford's dog, James found her talking to an impressive-looking character with white hair and a slash of black eyebrows.

She said, "Thank you, Doctor. He's usually very well behaved, but he can't resist liver. Do you know Mr. Adey? We all have to remember to be polite to him. He's chairman of the Council."

Grant Adey smiled. Lady Fallingford, immediately forgetting

her good intentions, said, "I was just telling him that I thought he had behaved in a very dilatory manner over implementing the provisions of the Wild Life and Countryside Act."

"Not my pigeon. I delegate all that sort of thing to a rural-affairs committee."

"You can't get out of something by delegating it."

"*I* can," said Adey. "And if it's something I know nothing about, I take care not to get put on that committee."

"As chairman of the Council," retorted Lady Fallingford, "you are ex-officio chairman of *all* committees."

At this point James detected a signal from Amanda and detached himself.

"Coffee coming up," she said, "and then we can get rid of them." She moved behind the serving table, where Dora Brookes and Julia Consett were already installed. The coffee appeared from the annex in a huge jug carried by Rosa and was distributed into four smaller jugs, one in front of the servers and a spare one at the end.

"We'll need some more handers-out," said Henry Brookes. "Len and I can't do it all. You can help, Paul." The organist detached himself gratefully from Penny. "And you two boys. It's time you earned your keep."

"Real coffee," said Amanda. "Not ready-made. A wild extravagance and unappreciated by most of the people here." She was dispensing the coffee into a neat row of cups in front of her.

"I don't drink it myself now," said the Dean to Mrs. Henn-Christie. "But to some, I know, coffee is the best part of the meal."

There was one thing to be said for the Cathedral, thought James. It was cooler than the marquee. He had found himself a seat on the north side of the Choir which gave him a good view of the proceedings.

The Church establishment had turned out in full fig. The Dean and the Canons in copes and bands, the Vicars Choral and the students from the Theological College, the vergers in their vestments, bearing their silver staves of office. His eyes passed upward from them to the choristers, whose heads seemed oddly detached from their bodies by their stiff white ruffs, to the lay clerks behind them, and above them again to a line of diocesan clergy who had come in for the service, robed and stoled, each occupying a canonical stall; and upward again to where, among the fretted beams and the gilt angels, the organist perched in his eyrie.

Paul had played them in with a soft voluntary, an invitation to worship in the minor key. When he glanced at his service sheet, James saw that they were to follow the traditional liturgy. The hymns were old favorites. And surely it had been the Dean who had selected the ninety-first psalm.

> *Thou shalt not be afraid for any terror by night:*
> *nor for the arrow that flieth by day;*

(There were certainly plenty of arrows flying about, some of them barbed and poisoned.)

> *For the pestilence that walketh in darkness:*
> *nor for the sickness that destroyeth in the noonday.*
> *A thousand shall fall beside thee, and ten thousand*
> *at thy right hand: but it shall not come nigh thee.*

An old friend of his father, who had survived three years of war in the trenches, had once told him that this verse was a talisman and that he had made a habit of whispering it to himself as he climbed the parapet and advanced into the storm of the German machine guns.

The first lesson was read, competently, by Grant Adey. The second, rather badly, by Canon Maude. What could have driven him to try to end his own life? Why had he said he would be better dead? And what had the Archdeacon got to do with it?

The hymn before the sermon was the Old Hundredth:

> *All people that on earth do dwell,*
> *Sing to the Lord with cheerful voice.*

The packed congregation was obeying this injunction with enthusiasm. As the last verse began, the senior verger approached the Dean, who was on his knees. He rose slowly and hobbled after Mr. Grey to the pulpit. When he turned to mount the steps, James caught a glimpse of his face. He looked tired, the result no doubt of loss of sleep the night before, but there was a glint in his eyes and a fighting cock to his head. Like an old warhorse, he had scented the battle from afar. The congregation may have suspected something, for when he began to speak, the silence was absolute.

He said, "I take my text from the hymn you have just been singing. It's a fine hymn and I'm sure you enjoyed it. But did you think about the words as well as the tune? 'His truth at all times firmly stood.' Truth. It's not such a popular word today. People think more of tolerance, accommodation and compromise. But truth was the light by which our forefathers steered. It was their belief that if you did something crooked, something untrue, to gain an advantage—" a tiny pause in which he seemed to be searching the congregation for a particular face—"then that prize was not worth having. The falsity of the means had destroyed the end." He paused again. "When we assemble here for our annual civic service, we say, 'Give grace to those who occupy positions of authority, that they may fulfill their responsibilities with wisdom and equity and in the fear of God. Grant that true faith and honest dealing may be the standard of our common life.'"

"Well, that was straight from the shoulder," thought James. He missed the next few sentences, having become aware of a disturbance in the seats inside the Choir screen. The next moment, Grey was touching him on the arm. He said, "Could you come, Doctor, please? It's the Archdeacon. They're taking him to the vestry."

James saw that the head verger was seriously troubled. As they took the short-cut through the choir robing room, he said, "What is it, Grey? Has the Archdeacon fainted?"

"It seems to be something worse than that. Through here, sir."

As soon as he got into the vestry, James saw that the Archdeacon was very ill indeed. He had been placed in a chair and Masters was standing beside him. He had got hold of a glass of water, but seemed uncertain what to do with it. The Archdeacon put up a hand, took the glass from him, swallowing some of the water and spilling the rest. Then he keeled over and was sick. As he righted himself, James could see that he was in pain. His breathing was deep and rapid and the pupils of his eyes were contracted.

"Can't we do something for him?" said Grey in tones of distress.

"Yes," said James. "We can." He was trying to remember the lessons which had been drummed into him at medical school. Don't panic. Take time to note the symptoms. The right remedy given after thought is better than the wrong remedy given in haste.

The two things which had to be controlled were the convulsions which had now started, alternate contraction and relaxation, deep and frightening, and the abdominal pain. He took an old service sheet off the table and scribbled on it two words: "Diazepam" and "Dibenzyline." He said to Masters, "There's a telephone in the Cathedral office. Get hold of Dr. McHarg and ask him to bring the things I've written down there, or something similar. You won't have to spell it out. He'll know what's wanted. Hurry." Masters sped off.

After that there was nothing to do but wait. The tremors had now become persistent, and when he got a hand to the Archdeacon's wrist, he could feel that the pulse was rapid and irregular, like an engine which had lost its governing mechanism and was racing and faulting at the same time.

Outside, the service was proceeding on its appointed way. Once Grey, who was holding on to himself with an effort, said, "Shouldn't I clear some of this up? It's not pleasant."

James said, "No. Leave it."

"They'll be coming in here after the service."

"No one must come in here. They'll have to use the robing room. Is there a key to this door?"

"I could get one."

"Then get it now. I think that's the last hymn starting."

Grey seemed glad to escape. He arrived back at the same time as Dr. McHarg, who came in carrying a small bag. He said, "I got your message. No Dibenzyline, but I've got some Diparcol which might help."

Then he looked at the Archdeacon, who was slumped forward in his chair, put a finger under his jawbone and said, "Too late, I'm afraid."

James said, "I think the service is ending. Could you and Grey explain to them what has happened? I'll stay here. You'd better lock the door behind you."

He sounded so flat and tired that McHarg looked at him curiously. He said, "Not your fault, my boy. You did what you could. We'd better get on with it."

When they had gone, James moved a chair across to the window, opened it wide and sat staring at the grass in the center of the cloisters, drawing in gulps of air and feeling his own heart steady down.

He thought, "If I was a proper doctor and not just a sucking pathologist, I wouldn't let a thing like that worry me."

Through the open window he could hear the organ voluntary which closed the service. This was no soft invitation to prayer. This was a pagan chant, a chant of triumph. Bass-bourdon and diapason were rioting together. The tuba and the trompette militaire were an army on the march, a triumphant army returning home bearing its spoils with it; while high over all, the flutes and the horns skittered and squealed in infernal glee.

"'For the pestilence that walketh in darkness,'" said James to himself. "'For the sickness that destroyeth in the noonday.'"

Eleven

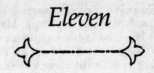

THE ROOM WAS CLEAN AND BLEAK AND COLD. The smell of formaldehyde battled with the smell of corruption. Dr. Brian Barkworth, in his white butcher's overall, was giving a final edge to a knife, using a small oilstone which he kept in his top pocket.

"A hearty eater, I should guess," he said, glancing down at the body of the Archdeacon on the slab in front of him with as little interest as a butcher would have looked at a side of beef.

"I believe so," said James shortly. In the absence of Dr. Barkworth's regular assistant, he had volunteered to act as notetaker and had already decided that he disliked the doctor. This was nothing to do with his attitude toward the dead, which was professional and to be expected. His dislike was instinctive and probably quite unfair.

Dr. Barkworth made the first incisions with practiced speed, exchanged the knife for a saw and started to cut away the rib cage.

"Can you tell me," he said, "had he been in contact with anyone down here lately?"

James thought about it. He said, "I think I was told that he had been visiting in the port area. It was part of his pastoral duty."

"Ye-e-s. I thought he might have been."

Dr. Barkworth had worked one of the lungs free and was holding it in his hand.

"A beautiful color. You can see that he spent most of *his* life in nice clean country vicarages. I had a docker in here not long ago. His lungs were so black with coal dust I wondered how he managed to breathe at all. Ah! I thought as much. Look there."

He poked a rubber-covered finger into the lung. "And there. Just what I was expecting. Massive edema."

The fluid in the lung tissue was apparent to the naked eye.

"I don't think we have to look very much further." The satisfaction in Dr. Barkworth's voice was apparent. It was clear that he had made his diagnosis before he started the autopsy.

"I suppose," said James deferentially, "that we ought to have some of the other organs."

"That's just like you youngsters from the London hospitals. You want to prove everything three times over. When there's a clear case, why blur the edges?"

"Professional caution, I suppose," said James apologetically. He didn't feel like apologizing, but realized that he was in no position to command.

"I suppose you'll be suggesting next that we open the skull and take a look at his brain."

James would indeed have liked to suggest it, but saw that it was going to be counter-productive. He said, with a smile, "I'd be happy with less than that."

Dr. Barkworth glanced at his watch. James thought that he was weighing the claims of a game of golf against the carrying out of a routine procedure which he had decided was unnecessary. Routine won. He sighed and picked up his knife again.

He said, "Will you be satisfied with heart, liver and kidneys?"

"That would be splendid," said James. "And I can do the sections, if that would help."

"As long as you don't want the brain," said Dr. Barkworth. "Most of the time it doesn't prove a damn thing. When you've transcribed your notes, could you write me out a short report? I'll have to bring the Health Authorities in on this. We don't want an epidemic starting up. Though how they're going to stop it, God knows."

"They'd have to isolate that area of the docks, I suppose."

"That's *their* job, not mine," said Dr. Barkworth. He sounded more cheerful. It was someone else's job.

James got back to the Close at nine o'clock. He had snatched a meal on the way, and he was feeling spiritually empty and mentally depressed. It was a relief to sink back into the homely comfort of the Brookeses' drawing room.

It was the sort of room, he thought, that should have been lit by oil lamps. It was full of odd items of old furniture, many of them shabby but most of them good. Handed down, James guessed, from generation to generation. There was a mixed lot of dim family portraits and framed samplers on the walls, and on the shelf over the fireplace, among the photographs and china dogs, a pair of *famille rose* bowls.

James, who knew something about china, was examining them when Dora Brookes came in with two cups of coffee. She said, "Aren't they lovely? Henry gave them to me on one of the few occasions that he pulled off a really good property deal. I'm afraid he wasn't cut out for commercial life. That's why I was so pleased when we found our niche here. All the same—" she looked at her watch—"they seem to be working him overtime tonight. The Dean called an emergency meeting for seven o'clock, which gave Henry just time to bolt half his supper."

"I imagine they've got a good deal to talk about," agreed James. "First Tom Lister and now the Archdeacon."

"Yes," said Dora. There was a question she wanted to ask, but felt some hesitation about asking it. "They'll be very short-handed until they can get two new Canons installed." She stopped and listened. "I think that's him now. I'll get another cup of coffee."

The Chapter Clerk came in carrying a bundle of papers which he dumped on a side table. He looked tired. He said, "I'm not going to bother about business any more tonight. The Dean's taken it all in his stride. He's a wonderful man. I suppose the sort of life he's led has made him more accustomed to crises than most of us."

Dora put her head around the door to say, "Do you want the rest of your supper?"

"Certainly not. A cup of coffee and then bed."

"The Dean and Canon Humphrey are carrying on on their own, then?" said James.

"With Canon Maude."

"Yes, of course. I'd forgotten Canon Maude."

"People tend to forget him," said Brookes with a smile. "But I think he's being as helpful as he can. It will mean double shifts of duty, of course, but some of the minor Canons will be brought in to help with the services."

"I was wondering what would happen," said James. "I'm sure it won't arise, but suppose, for instance, the Dean and Francis Humphrey were involved in a car smash so that there was no one left really capable of running things."

"Oddly enough, that was one of the matters we were discussing. The diocesan clergy could handle the services, but someone would have to be appointed as administrator to look after the financial side. The difficult question is who would make the appointment. The Archbishop would be the logical person, but I suggested that it might be the Bishop, in his capacity as Visitor of the Cathedral."

"A somewhat irregular visitor," said James. "He never seems to be here."

"He's a splendid person," said Brookes loyally, "but he does spend a good deal of his time in travel round the Dominions."

"If he'd spent more of his time in the diocese," said his wife, coming back with the coffee, "the Archdeacon wouldn't have had to do so much of the pastoral visiting. What has been fixed about the funeral?"

"The Archbishop has agreed that it would be appropriate to hold a joint service, followed by interment in the cloisters. That would be in accordance with tradition, you know. For many years now—unless, of course, there were objections from the family—Deans and Canons have been buried there."

James visualized the limited space available in the center of the cloisters and was about to say something when Brookes, reading his thoughts, said, "Naturally, it is only the ashes that are interred nowadays. The bodies are cremated first."

His wife said, "Was anything else arranged?"

"A number of routine matters, yes. The Dean is taking over the administrative functions of the Archdeacon for the time being. In which case I think we can regard any question of summoning the Greater Chapter to discuss the sale of Fletcher's Piece as a dead letter."

"Excellent," said Dora. "What about our friends, the Friends of the Cathedral?"

The Saturday meeting had been abortive. The Dean had announced the death of the Archdeacon and had said that he felt certain that it would be the wish of all concerned that the meeting should be adjourned. One or two people had looked as though they would have liked to say something, but the Dean had cut short the meeting by leaving the Chapter House.

"The meeting stands adjourned."

"Indefinitely, I hope," said Dora and picked up a piece of embroidery. It had been occupying her spare moments for the last two years. Brookes sipped his coffee. Silence fell. It was a silence which contained a question which, as James realized, both of them were now longing to ask.

In the end it was Brookes who took the plunge. He put down his empty cup and said diffidently, "I wouldn't want you to tell us anything if it was confidential or anything like that, but *did* your post-mortem examination give any possible explanation— any indication—of the cause of the Archdeacon's death?"

Dora's needle had stopped moving through the tapestry.

James said, "First I ought to explain that it wasn't *my* post-mortem. I was only there as a spectator. However, I don't see any reason why you shouldn't know what will be public knowledge soon enough, though you'd better not say anything until Dr. Barkworth's report is out. It's his view that the Archdeacon died of influenza."

"Flu!" said Brookes. "But surely that's most unusual. I mean—it was so rapid."

"When you talk about it as flu," said James, "I agree that it sounds fairly harmless. In ninety-nine cases out of a hundred, all you're talking about is a bad cold, with perhaps a bit of fever on top of it. But in the hundredth case, virus influenza can be quick and very deadly. You get a heavy discharge of fluid into the lungs and—to put the matter simply—you drown. We had a case last winter. A woman brought her children up from the country to take them to the zoo. She was perfectly all right until she got back to London Bridge station, when she collapsed. They got her into the emergency ward at Guy's. She died that night."

Dora said, "I can remember my father—he was a warrant officer in the R.A.M.C.—talking about that epidemic they called Spanish flu. It killed hundreds of thousands of soldiers just after the end of the Great War. More than died in the trenches, they said. He told me that a man would come on parade in the morning completely fit and be dead before lights-out."

"But," said Brookes, "this is terrible. How did it start? However did the Archdeacon come to catch it?"

"There doesn't seem to be much doubt about that. There have been three cases already, two of them sailors in a ship which had come from Singapore and one of them a docker who'd been unloading the ship. The Archdeacon had been down at Westport visiting the Dockland Settlement and talking to the men."

"Then it could be the start of a serious epidemic?"

"If you mean another Spanish flu epidemic, no. We're armed with anti-biotics which weren't available in 1918. In any event, forewarned is forearmed. The Medical Officer of Health has been alerted and he may be able to isolate the outbreak."

Dora said, "I'll make you one prediction: People are going to feel sorry for some of the things they've been saying about the Archdeacon. He was a man who didn't shirk his job. In fact, you might say that he died doing it."

"I'm afraid it won't change the Dean's opinion of him," said Brookes sadly.

Lately James had been sleeping well. That night he knew that sleep would not come easily. His mind was far too active. The instinct which guides a doctor, more surely than reason, told him that something was wrong. Certainly there had been fluid in the lungs. Certainly that suggested virus influenza. But there were a lot of things that didn't fit into that diagnosis. However, was it any concern of his? He was not the doctor in charge of the case. He would not have to sign the death certificate. In fact, he had no official status in the matter at all. He felt an unaccountable desire to talk the whole thing over with Amanda. She had a clear and dispassionate way of looking at things. Even if he didn't always agree with her conclusions.

The Cathedral clock had struck two by the time he reached this point in his thinking and fell asleep.

Twelve

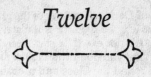

Next morning James walked over to the Deanery. He reached it as Penny Consett was coming out.

She said, "If you're looking for Amanda, you're out of luck. She's gone to Winchester."

"Shopping?"

"I expect she'll do some shopping, but it's duty, really. She tries to go over most weeks to visit Nanny Hawkes. Not *her* nanny. Her father's. She's nearly a hundred, and as tiresome as they come. I went over with Amanda once and the old witch spent half the time complaining and the other half telling us what a nasty little boy Matthew had been."

It took a moment for him to realize that she was talking about the Dean. It was difficult to think of him as a nasty little boy called Matthew.

Penny had fixed him with an artless blue eye. She said, "I don't mind betting that if Amanda had been here, you'd have suggested that you went out and had a cup of coffee. Right? Well, as she isn't here, suppose you suggest it to me."

James was on the point of inventing a plausible excuse when it occurred to him that Peter had been wrong. Penny wasn't a man-snatcher. She was simply young and friendly. He said, "Let's do that. Where shall we go?"

"One thing Melchester isn't short of is coffee shops. Let's try the Busy Bee."

Since it was eleven o'clock, the Busy Bee was living up to its name, but they managed to find themselves a table. Unlike the Brookeses, Penny expended no finesse in getting to the point. She said, "You did the post-mortem on the Archdeacon, didn't you? Don't tell me any of the gruesome details, but did you find out why he died, or is it a state secret?"

"It's not exactly a state secret, no."

"But you don't want to tell me because you think I'd repeat it all round the Close and probably get it wrong."

"That's right," said James.

"Well, I don't mind, because, whatever the answer is, I'm sure it's much duller than what I was hearing at breakfast."

James tried not to look startled. He said, "Hearing from who?"

"The boys, of course."

"And what is their view of the matter?"

"You sounded a bit stuffy when you said that."

"I'm sorry."

"They are quite certain that the Dean and Amanda organized the whole thing between them. The Dean put a drop of something in the Archdeacon's coffee and Amanda handed it to him."

"I see. And have they any grounds for this startling idea?"

"Naturally. The Dean has spent half his life in darkest Africa and India. He'd be certain to have come across one of those poisons unknown to science that you read about in books."

At this point the coffee arrived and the interruption allowed James to get his breath back. He said, "Do they actually believe this story?"

"It's difficult to say. Quite often, of course, they make up stories which sound exciting, but they don't really believe them. This time I'm not sure. Mind you, this isn't an anti-Dean platform. They much preferred him to the Archdeacon."

"Of course they did. He's a romantic character. The virtues of the Archdeacon would have been less likely to appeal to them."

"I suppose he had some virtues, or are you just saying that because he's dead?"

"Certainly he had virtues. The main one was that he did his job. It's all very well people telling us what nice men Dean Lupton and Archdeacon Henn-Christie were. If they'd been in charge of things a few years longer, the Cathedral would have been bankrupt."

"I suppose so," said Penny doubtfully. "Oh, God! Here she comes."

James had his back to the room and was wedged so tightly behind the table that it was difficult to turn around. He said, "Who?"

"That nasty little creep Rosa."

"Rosa Pilcher?"

"That's right. She's pure poison. Amanda loathes her. And the Dean hasn't got much use for her either."

"Then why do they employ her?"

"If they could get anyone else, they wouldn't. For God's sake! Look at that get-up! She might be the Archdeacon's widow."

Rosa was in elaborate mourning. Her dress was black, her shoes and stockings were black and her hat had a black veil, thrown half back, under which a pair of malevolent eyes peeped out.

It looked as though she was heading for their table, but at the last moment she saw two of her cronies and diverted her course toward them.

"Do you think she saw us?" said James.

"Of course she did. She's got panoramic vision. Like a horse. She's not only seen us, she's already turning the information over in her nasty little mind to see whether she can make something out of it."

"You mean I've compromised you?"

"That's right," said Penny.

She didn't seem to be worried.

"I expect you're giving Raymond Pawle a splendid obituary in your column," said Sandeman. He managed to say this in a way which suggested, at the same time, that he didn't care one way or the other about the Archdeacon now that he had been thoughtless enough to die and could, therefore, be no further use to them; and that he didn't think much of the *Melset Times* either.

"I've already written it," said Driffield.

"A handsome funeral oration?" suggested Gloag.

"Plus a few facts. Did you know that before he was ordained, he actually qualified as an accountant?"

"All clergymen should be trained as something else first," said Gloag. "Broaden their minds. One heart."

Driffield said, "What were *you* trained as, Gerry?"

"I broadened my mind by joining Her Majesty's Territorial Forces," said Gloag with dignity. "Are you saying anything?"

"On these cards? Certainly not. No bid."

"In that case," said Sandeman, "I shall venture to bid three no trumps."

The cards lay badly and this went two down. While the score was being entered, Sandeman said, "I suppose we shall have to back-pedal a bit on Fletcher's Piece now. A pity when we were almost past the post."

"Always be another time," said Driffield.

"It all depends," said Gloag, "on who they get. If the new Canons are business people as well as being clergymen—men like the Archdeacon—they should be able to recognize a bargain when it's handed to them on a plate."

"Not much chance of that," said Sandeman. "The Dean will make certain he gets the sort of people who'll see things *his* way."

"Who chooses new Canons?" said Gloag.

Sandeman stopped shuffling the cards. He said, "I never thought about that. Who does choose them, Arthur? You know about that sort of thing."

"I don't know," said Driffield. "But I can find out. If you shuffle those cards much more, you'll shuffle the spots right off them."

This time Driffield tried four hearts, a gross overbid which he managed to make, partly by luck and partly because Sandeman's mind seemed to be on other things. This concluded the rubber. While they were settling up, Driffield said to his partner, a tall man with a bushy head of hair who had so far joined very little in the conversation, "You weren't in Cathedral on Saturday, were you, Bert?"

Detective Superintendent Herbert Bracher agreed that he hadn't been in Cathedral. He'd been busy interrogating a suspected shop-breaker.

"You missed something."

"You mean the Archdeacon's death?"

"I didn't, actually. I meant the Dean's sermon. He was firing on all six cylinders."

"I thought it was disgraceful," said Sandeman. "In fact, I wasn't at all sure that it wasn't actually libelous."

"Slanderous," said Driffield. "You can only be libelous in writing."

"Insulting, anyway. I asked Macindoe if there wasn't something we could do about it."

"Sue the Dean for slander, you mean?"

"Something like that."

"What did Mac say?"

"He didn't seem to think much of the idea."

Bracher said, "I'm off."

"If you see Grant in the bar," said Gloag, "you might send him along. It's time I won some money off him for a change."

When Bracher had gone, the three men pushed their chairs back and stretched their legs. They seemed rather more at ease in his absence. Driffield said, "By the way, who's that young doctor who's hanging round in the Close? I seem to have seen him before."

"He's some relation of Consett's," said Sandeman. "He taught at the school for a few terms about six years ago. Why?"

"One of my people was in old Mrs. Piper's shop and heard them nattering away in the back room. He seemed to be asking her a lot of questions about the time she was turned out of her other shop. I wondered why he'd have been interested in that."

"He and Fleming—that other master at the school—are both very thick with Bill Williams," said Sandeman. "You remember we ran into them in pub that night, Gerry."

Gloag grunted. He remembered it with displeasure.

Sandeman said, "You don't think the *Journal* might be planning to reopen the supermarket deal?"

"There's nothing to reopen," said Gloag. "It was a perfectly straightforward property deal. It cost us a little more than we expected and we made a fair profit. Why should we worry if they do reopen it?"

Sandeman and Driffield agreed that there was absolutely nothing to worry about.

Another quartet of bridge players was discussing the Archdeacon's death. It was the afternoon of Wednesday and the passing of four days had allowed the first shock waves to subside a little. Lady Fallingford, Julia Consett and Betty Humphrey had assembled in Mrs. Henn-Christie's drawing room for their regular weekly game; but so far the packs of cards lay unopened on the table.

Important matters were occupying their attention.

"Poor Betty," said Lady Fallingford. "I don't imagine you see a lot of Francis these days. He must be horribly overworked."

"To be fair," said Mrs. Henn-Christie, "I suppose we're only beginning to realize, now that he's gone, what a load of work the Archdeacon really did carry on his own shoulders."

A respectful silence greeted this observation. Betty Humphrey said, "Actually, it's the Dean I'm most sorry for. He has to do three men's work. Canon Maude, I am told, has retired to bed. His mother says it's gastric trouble, but I think it's simple feebleness."

"His mother's a better man than he is," agreed Lady Fallingford.

Julia Consett said, "Is it true that the Bishop has been asked to cut short his visit to Australia and fly home?"

"He ought never to have gone," said Lady Fallingford.

This was felt to be harsh.

"He couldn't have known that all this was going to happen."

"That's not the point. He's got enough work to do here without flying about all over the world."

"I'm not sure," said Mrs. Henn-Christie, "that the Bishop coming back is necessarily going to make things all that much easier for the Dean. They never really saw eye to eye, you know. In fact, I'm inclined to think that one of the reasons he does make these lengthy foreign excursions is to steer clear of the infighting that went on. You remember the trouble that blew up over the last ordination service."

The ladies thought about this. Julia made a half-hearted effort to open the cards, but there was a matter on the agenda more engrossing than the habits of the Bishop. Mrs. Henn-Christie opened it by saying, "I understand the cremation service is fixed for next Monday at twelve. I imagine it will be a private affair. Family only."

"Who *are* the family?"

"There's a married sister. She's coming down from Nottingham, with her husband."

"It won't be a very large congregation."

"I know someone who'll be there," said Mrs. Henn-Christie, speaking the thought that was in all their minds.

"You mean Rosa."

"She really is carrying on in the *most* peculiar way."

"That get-up!"

"*Totally* unsuitable."

"I understand she's been putting it about, now, that she was a distant relative of the Archdeacon."

"And that he's left her all his money."

"I don't know about the money," said Mrs. Henn-Christie. "People do make very odd wills. You remember Lord Weldon's grandfather. He left the untailed parts of his estate to his cook. Fortunately, they decided that he was mad when he did it. But I absolutely refuse to believe that Pilcher woman is any connection of Raymond's, however many times removed. After all, the Pawles were a perfectly respectable Lincolnshire family."

"I seem to remember," said Lady Fallingford, "that when Rosa first came here—it must have been more than thirty years ago—she was housemaid in the West Canonry. That was in Canon Fox's time."

"I think the money part of it might be true," said Julia, "because I understand that she's made an offer for Tony Openshaw's cottage. If he's confirmed in office as assistant head of the Theological College, he'll have accommodation there."

The ladies looked at each other.

"You mean," said Lady Fallingford, "that she proposes to install herself as a member of the Close community and a lady of leisure?"

"She'll have plenty of leisure," said Julia. "Because she won't be working at the Deanery any more. There was some trouble about Len Masters, which led to the Dean giving her the rough edge of his tongue. And anyway Amanda told me that she'd rather do everything herself than have that woman in the house a moment longer."

"She may buy that cottage," said Lady Fallingford, "and she may call herself Miss Pilcher, but one thing I promise you: I'm not asking her to tea."

That evening Peter came around with Alan Furbank and collected James for their evening visit to the Black Lion. Alan hobbled along quite briskly, his left foot encased in a lump of plaster.

"I didn't break my ankle," he said. "It's the Achilles tendon. I did it a bit of no good trying to turn too quickly on the squash court. Do you play?"

"I played a bit at the hospital."

"You ought to have a game with Amanda. She's hot stuff. She knocked spots off me."

"You wouldn't need to be good at squash to knock spots off Alan," said Peter.

"It's more than you can do."

The three young men were passing the school, wrangling happily, when Peter caught sight of a light in an upstairs room in Canon Maude's house. This put him in mind of something. He said, "I'd guess that the boys know about that silly letter. Everyone in the top form, at least."

"How on earth—"

"If you mean how did they find out, I don't know. I imagine Anstruther told someone, who told someone else. But if you mean how do I know, I can tell you that. When Alan was taking the top form in history, he made some joke about Bottle and his admirer. Last term it would have been good for a laugh. This time it fell into a pit of stony silence."

"Just as if I'd made a bad joke about the Queen and found out too late that she was in the audience," said Alan.

"How very odd," said James.

"It's not odd, really. It's just that they no longer think it's funny."

"If they all know about it, it's going to be public knowledge pretty soon."

"I'm not sure. If boys decide not to talk about something, the Mafia could take lessons from them."

"Even so, it might slip out when they're at home. Anstruther's father is a soldier, isn't he?"

"He's G.S.O. at Southern Command. Luckily, he's by way of being a friend of the Dean's. If anything did come to his ears, he'd probably consult the Dean first and he might be able to smooth it down."

"It was a fairly bold decision of the Archdeacon's, all the

same," said Alan. "Because if anything did come out, he was the one who was going to be carrying the can."

"He wasn't afraid of responsibility," said Peter. "In fact, I don't think there were many things he was afraid of."

It occurred to James that the rehabilitation of the Archdeacon was already under way.

Thirteen

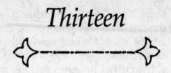

Nᴇxᴛ ᴍᴏʀɴɪɴɢ ᴊᴀᴍᴇs ᴅɪsᴄᴏᴠᴇʀᴇᴅ that the Archdeacon's re-habilitation was not universal. As he was making for the Deanery in search of Amanda, he spotted Paul Wren hurrying across the precinct lawn.

Paul had a piece of paper in his hand, which he waved when he saw James. James waited for him to come up. The organist was smiling broadly.

James said, "You look as if you've been left a legacy."

"Better than that," said Paul and pushed the paper into his hand. It was the weekly service sheet, which came out each Thursday. James cast an eye down it without, at first, noticing anything unusual. Then he spotted it, at the bottom of the paper. "Canon in Residence: Canon Humphrey. Organist: Paul Wren."

"Organist. Does this mean that you've got the top job?"

"Certainly. The Dean confirmed it to me yesterday. He's told Lovett that the job's no longer open."

"That's splendid."

"It *is* splendid. The only fly in the ointment is that Arch-deacon Raymond Pawle is no longer with us. So I'm denied the pleasure of telling him that his nasty little intrigue has failed."

James felt slightly shocked and must have looked it, because Paul said, "I know what you're thinking, but I refuse to change my opinion about him simply because he's dead. When he was alive, I said he was a bastard, and I still think he was a bastard. The only difference is that he's a dead bastard and can't harm me now."

"I suppose that's one way of looking at it," said James. "I

didn't really know the man well enough to form an opinion. Congratulations anyway."

The door of the Deanery was opened by the Dean. He was in his shirtsleeves. He said, "As you will see, I am my own butler and footman. Also my own cook and parlor maid." He sounded unusually cheerful.

"Then Rosa has finally ditched you?"

"On the contrary. We ditched *her*. I told her that there were enough sorrows in life without her adding to them by creeping round the house looking like a black beetle. She took umbrage and departed. Does that strike you as odd? Umbrage, I mean. It appears that you can take it, but not give it. If it's Amanda you're looking for, you'll find her in the herbaceous border."

This was literally true. The herbaceous border was a deep one which ran along the western side of the garden, and the only part of Amanda that was visible was the top of her head, a golden chrysanthemum among a wilderness of flowers and shrubs. As she emerged, he saw that she was wearing her normal off-duty uniform of sweat-shirt and jeans. The mud patches on them suggested that she had been doing most of her work on her knees.

"Hello," she said. "Have you come to help? I can find another fork."

"I know nothing about plants. I should dig up all the wrong things."

"Excuses, excuses. Have you seen Daddy pretending to be a butler?"

"He told me that he was cook and parlor maid as well."

"He was showing off. You must have noticed that he likes to dramatize everything. Actually, all he does is answer the door and make his own bed. Mind you, he *can* cook. Once in India, when I had malaria and there was no one else around, he cooked for both of us for a fortnight. Quite ambitious things like pilaus and fritters, all done on an old oil stove. When I eat fritters nowadays, I always imagine they're going to taste slightly of paraffin. But we can't stand here talking all day. If you won't dig, you can mow the lawn."

"Couldn't we just talk?"

"After you've mowed the lawn."

By the time he had finished mowing the lawn, Amanda had developed another project. She said, "I really have got to get on with things in the house now, but I should be through by lunchtime. Would you like that game of squash?"

"If I can borrow the kit."

"Peter and Alan will lend you what you want. If you come round at about half past two, I'll drive us out. Brigadier Anstruther lets me use one of the Army courts in the afternoon."

"I'll be there," said James.

As he made his way to the Deanery after lunch, carrying a rugger shirt and shorts of Peter's and gym shoes and a squash racquet belonging to Alan Furbank, he was wondering whether Amanda was really any good at the game. When he had said that he "played a bit," that was the sort of statement one made in conversation. In fact, squash was the only game he had ever played with real enthusiasm. As a chronic overworker, he had found it convenient. He could compress a day's exercise into thirty minutes on the court and get back to his books, without any of the rigmarole and waste of time which seemed to attend other sporting activities. Possessed of long arms, strong wrists and a good eye, he had quickly become proficient and had often been brought in as fourth or fifth string for Guy's in their Cumberland Cup matches. He remembered George Towcester, who played first string, grumbling at him, "Do you realize, James, that if you gave half the time and attention to squash that you give to your rotten pathology, you could be a county player?"

Good old George. Now a G.P. in deepest Devonshire.

"Excellent," said Amanda. "You've got the stuff. Climb in."

Southern Command District Headquarters was a solid establishment which had been put up before the war. There were two squash courts, both of them good ones. As James stepped onto the springy wooden floor, he experienced the tingling and exhilaration with which he always started a game. He felt certain that it was going to be a memorable one.

Amanda was already on the court. He remembered one of the students at Guy's saying about the object of his current interest, "She's the sort of girl who looks best in least." Amanda in a sleeveless aertex vest and a short white skirt looked better than he had ever seen her before. She was certainly not fat, but equally she was not thin. There must be an appropriate adjective to describe a proper proportion of flesh to bone.

"Come in, shut the door and stop analyzing me," said Amanda.

"I was admiring your legs. I think it's the first time I've seen them out of these hideous jeans girls seem to affect these days."

"We didn't come here to admire each other's legs," said Amanda coldly. She was holding the ball in one hand. Now she gave her racquet a sharp flick and dispatched the ball down the right-hand wall. James picked it neatly off the wall and returned it.

They knocked up for a few minutes, assessing each other's game. James thought that Amanda would prove a worthy opponent. He remembered what she had said about her father, that his specialty had been fencing. He guessed that she would play squash as though it were a fencing match—fast thrust and sudden riposte, supple wrists and quick reactions, but perhaps without the patience or the tactical skill for a long rally.

To start with, either politeness or overconfidence made him stand too far back and this gave Amanda the freedom of the front court. She won the first game fairly easily, and the second with more difficulty when James abandoned courtesy and started to crowd her, after which he took the next two games.

It was like a dance, he thought. Not the modern style, which was a parody of the real thing, but an old-fashioned dance, with mutual give and take, the accommodation of body to body and step to step. Halfway through the fifth game, in the middle of a rally, he realized how deeply he was in love with Amanda. At the first opportunity, he was going to ask her to marry him.

This shook him so much that he hit what should have been a winning shot tamely onto the tin.

Amanda said, "You're not going to ease up and let me win, I hope."

"No, no. Nothing like that. It was just that I suddenly thought of something."

"You shouldn't think of less important things when you're playing squash."

"Actually, it *was* rather important. But I'll keep my mind on the game now."

He did so and finally ran out a close winner. As they were leaving the court, she put one hand on his arm and said, "That was the best game I've had for years, James."

If two officers in squash kit had not chosen that moment to appear in the gallery, he would have put his free arm around her and told her everything that was in his mind.

"Afterward, when we're in the car," he thought.

When they got into the car, Amanda said, "Now you can tell me."

James took a deep breath and said, "I've been wanting to tell you—"

"About the post-mortem."

"Oh, that."

The death of the Archdeacon seemed infinitely unimportant.

"You did find out how he died, didn't you? Penny says you did, but you're not supposed to tell anyone until the official report comes out. Is that right?"

"I suppose it is, more or less."

"But you'll tell *me*."

"I don't mind telling you as long as you keep it to yourself until the report comes out."

As he started to speak, he realized that the casualness of Amanda's voice and manner was a pose. She was as taut as a fiddle string.

"Dr. Barkworth is going to say that in his opinion, based on his post-mortem findings, the Archdeacon died of virulent influenza, probably caught by contact with sailors in the dock area."

He drew the sentence out to its fullest extent to give Amanda time to relax. He heard her breath going out in a long sigh.

He said, "There was some evidence to support his diagnosis." Tension again.

"You mean there could be other explanations?"

"There can always be more than one explanation of even quite straightforward symptoms."

"I told you once before not to treat me like an idiot child. Just what was wrong with Dr. Barkworth's diagnosis?"

"It was pathologically correct, but it didn't take account of the symptoms."

"You mean what happened in the vestry when he was dying."

"Yes. It wasn't very pleasant."

"I'll take your word for it." She started the car and they drove in silence for a few minutes. Then she said, "Did Dr. Barkworth ask you about these symptoms?"

"No. He was quite satisfied with what he found. He didn't want to go outside his own diagnosis."

"Did you tell him you disagreed with him?"

"No. In fact, he was in such a hurry to get off that, if I hadn't insisted, I don't believe he'd have taken any samples, except from the lungs."

"I see," said Amanda thoughtfully. "So what *did* you do?"

"I made sections of the heart, the liver and the kidneys. And took some blood samples."

"What did you expect to find?"

"I didn't expect to find anything. It was the sort of routine step one always does take."

"Who examines these—what did you call them?—sections?"

"They'll go to the Home Office Central Research Establishment at Aldermaston."

"And a lot of nosy little scientists will poke and pry at them and decide that Dr. Barkworth was wrong and the Archdeacon died of something quite different."

There was so much bitterness in Amanda's voice that James hesitated. He knew what dangerous ground he was on. To a different sort of girl he might have said, "Oh, I don't suppose so. It was just a routine precaution," and changed the subject. It would not serve in this case. She wanted the truth. He said, slowly, "Even if I hadn't done what I did, I'm pretty certain that someone would have taken those samples sooner or later. The local health authority could have ordered it. Or the coroner."

"Coroner?"

"If there had to be an inquest."

"Why should there be an inquest?"

"Well—"

"If people believed what Dr. Barkworth said, there wouldn't be an inquest."

"I'm not sure about that," said James unhappily.

"Oh, why?"

"Brookes was telling me that it's the tradition here that

Canons are buried in the cloisters. That means the body has to be cremated first."

"So?"

"There are a lot of formalities to be gone through before that can be done. Normally, there has to be a certificate signed by two doctors, though actually we could have got over that if Dr. Barkworth had been willing to sign a certificate after he'd done the post-mortem."

"Why wasn't he?"

"I think he wanted to shift the responsibility onto someone else."

"You mean he wasn't really sure?"

"It was a plausible diagnosis and he sounded quite confident at the time, but he may have changed his mind when he'd had time to think about it."

"Time to think about what the scientists might find in the specimens you'd been conscientious enough to send them."

James shifted uncomfortably in his seat. He said, "Something like that. Yes."

"I see. So what happens now?"

"The cremation authorities will need a death certificate. It would have been signed by the Archdeacon's regular doctor if he'd attended him in his last illness. Otherwise there have to be two doctors."

"Then Dr. McHarg *can* do it."

"I'm not sure."

"For goodness sake, why not? He *was* his regular doctor."

"But he didn't actually attend him in his last illness. Unless he's prepared to stretch a point and say that he was there when the Archdeacon died."

"If he can do it, I'm sure he will. He's not the sort of man to let a few stupid regulations stand in the way of doing the right thing."

"Not a sort of man like me, you mean?"

"If you want my honest opinion, yes. I think you're being extraordinarily fussy about something that seems absolutely straightforward. Of course, I'm not an expert."

By this time they had reached the twisting road which led into Melchester from the north and Amanda had to concentrate on her driving. He wanted to say something to propitiate the desirable and angry girl beside him, but couldn't think of any words.

They were turning into the Close now. As they drew up in front of the Chapter Clerk's gate, Amanda said, "If Dr. McHarg decided that he could sign that certificate, you wouldn't have any reason for interfering, would you?"

"I shouldn't dream of interfering."

"I'm glad of that." There was a moment of silence. "I'm sorry if I sounded a bit rude back there. I didn't really mean to."

"That's quite all right," said James. It was a half-hearted declaration of truce. A suspension of actual warfare. But he wanted much more than that. Interfere? Of course he wasn't going to interfere. Did she imagine that he was going to rush around to Dr. McHarg and tell him that he mustn't sign a death certificate? The idea was nonsensical.

Any decision he might have made on the matter was preempted. Dr. McHarg had come to see him.

He found him sitting in the drawing room talking to Henry Brookes and sampling a glass of his homemade wine. When James appeared, Henry got up and said, "I guess you want to talk. I'll get on with my brewing."

"Make more of this stuff," said McHarg. "It's top-class."

"It's the only batch that came out well. The last lot developed acidity. I didn't throw it away. I managed to distill quite a passable cooking brandy out of it."

When they were alone, McHarg said, "You can guess why I'm here."

"You've been asked for a certificate."

"Aye. And I think I'll very likely sign it. But before I do so, I'd like to ask you a few questions. In confidence, you understand. I'm speaking as one doctor to another."

James' heart sank. One doctor to another. In confidence. The shade of Hippocrates was heavy in the room.

"You were with the Archdeacon, poor man, in his last minutes and I mind your message to me—" McHarg extracted a crumpled piece of paper from his pocket—"was to bring Diazepam and Dibenzyline."

James nodded. He knew what was coming.

"Diazepam being a barbiturate, I surmise that would be to control the convulsions. Were they severe?"

"Spasmodic to start with. Toward the end, very deep and persistent."

Dr. McHarg turned the information over in his mind, considering its implications, before he spoke again.

"The Dibenzyline would be to control the diarrhea and vomiting."

"Yes."

"Did you obsairve any other symptoms?"

"There was clearly a great deal of abdominal pain. And the breathing was labored and difficult, particularly toward the end."

"That was to be expected, of course. It would be the effect of saturation in the lung tissues and would be consistent with virus influenza. Nothing else?"

James hesitated. Hippocrates gave him a nudge.

"I did notice," he said slowly, "that the pupils of the eyes were contracted."

"Did you now?" said McHarg. "That would be an uncommon result of influenza. Forbye there might be an explanation for it."

He lumbered to his feet and said, "I'll have to think it through. There's a sairtin amount of hurry. The cremation is fixed for Monday, I understand."

From the hall he shouted goodnight to the Chapter Clerk, who appeared a few minutes later with a bottle and two glasses.

"My last year's peach wine," he said. "I think you'll find it palatable."

James sipped it cautiously and found it very good indeed. He had two glasses of it and they finished the bottle at dinner.

That night he slept well. It might have been the peach wine, or it might have been the thought that it wasn't he who had to sign the Archdeacon's death certificate.

Fourteen

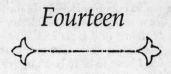

"IT'S THAT WOMAN AGAIN," said Sergeant Telfer.

Superintendent Bracher looked up from a batch of dockets he was sorting and said, "Which woman?"

"The Pilcher woman. You managed to sidestep her last time."

"I've got a lot on my plate just now. Couldn't you head her off?"

"I think she'd make trouble if we did it again."

Bracher knew what trouble meant. It would be a letter to the Chief Constable and interdepartmental minutes and more time wasted. It might be quicker to see her and get it over.

"Push her in," he said.

Five minutes later he wished he had been firmer. The woman seemed to him to be unhinged, rambling along about Chapter meetings. What could she possibly know about Chapter meetings? And what concern was it of the police?

He said, "I'm afraid, ma'am, that these things are outside my field. If you have some complaint about the way matters are conducted at the Cathedral, you should complain to the Dean. It isn't really a police matter."

"Are you telling me that murder isn't a police matter?"

Bracher stared at her. He said, "Who has been murdered?"

"The Archdeacon."

"I understand that he died of influenza."

"He did not die of influenza. He was poisoned."

"Would you care to tell me who by?"

"By the Dean, of course."

His first diagnosis had been correct. The woman *was* mad. The next thing was how to get rid of her with as little disturbance as possible. He said, in the tones of one humoring a child, "Come along now, Miss Pilcher, why would he do that?"

"I thought I'd explained."

"Explain it again. But you mustn't be too long about it, because I have to be in court in five minutes' time."

"It won't take five minutes to explain, if you'll listen properly. The Archdeacon wanted to sell the land on the other side of the river. Fletcher's Piece, it's called. Canon Maude supported him. The Dean and Canon Humphrey were against him. So there was a deadlock."

"A goalless draw," said Bracher brightly.

"Because it was a deadlock, they would have had to summon the Greater Chapter, who would have voted with the Archdeacon."

"And to prevent that, the Dean killed the Archdeacon."

"I can tell from the way you say it that you don't believe it," said Rosa. "But it's true, nonetheless."

"You must admit it's a little hard to believe," said Bracher with a smile. He got to his feet, hoping that Rosa would do the same so that he could maneuver her out of the room. She sat tight. Bracher noted the look on her face and sighed.

She said, "You'd believe it easily enough, Superintendent, if you knew the Dean as well as I do. He's a devil."

Elliot Macindoe, senior partner in the firm of Porter, Pallance and Macindoe, was a very experienced solicitor. One of the conclusions he had reached in a lifetime of practice was that no marriage could endure unless one of the parties was positive and the other negative. If both were positive, the marriage would wear itself out. If both were negative, it would perish of inanition. By this yardstick he found Mr. and Mrs. Fairbrass a satisfactory couple.

Mrs. Fairbrass, who had been a Miss Pawle, was the late Archdeacon's sister. She had all of his drive and initiative, backed by a formidable femininity. Mr. Fairbrass was a large silent Yorkshireman, the longest of whose utterances so far had been "Aye."

"Am I right in assuming," said Mrs. Fairbrass, "that Raymond made me his sole executor or, to be correct, I should say executrix?"

134

"Correct," said Macindoe. "I did at one time suggest a bank executor to help you, but he told me that he had every confidence in your business ability."

"And he in yours," said Mrs. Fairbrass graciously.

"I have had a copy of the will made for you. It is quite short. There are the usual clauses for getting in the assets and paying the debts and the duty. The whole of his estate is then divided into three equal parts. The first part goes to you. He didn't leave you more because he knew that you were comfortably situated." As he said this, he looked at Mr. Fairbrass, who nodded to indicate that he knew what brass was and had plenty of it.

"The second part goes to the Clergy Stipend Fund."

"He always maintained that parish clergymen were scandalously underpaid. The third share?"

"He describes this in his will as being designed to help people who had been helpful to him. I shall need your assistance in identifying some of them."

Macindoe looked down at the document in front of him.

"The money was to have been equally divided between six people. Mr. and Mrs. Edward Webb."

"They were a couple who looked after Raymond in his first living at Andover. I heard, incidentally, that they had died in a coach accident when on holiday in Spain."

"I'm sorry. The next is Eliza Gibbons."

"Ah, yes. She was Raymond's old nurse. Gathered a year or two ago."

"Then we have Thomas Corrie."

"Tom Corrie," said Mrs. Fairbrass thoughtfully. "Now, who was Tom Corrie? Of course, yes. He was gardener and handyman when Raymond was at Lincoln. I had a sort of feeling, however—"

"Dead," said Mr. Fairbrass.

"Are you sure, dear?"

"Stroke."

"I think you're right. Who is next?"

"The next one was to have been the Reverend Desmond Pitt. But in a codicil made a few years later the Reverend Pitt's name was struck out."

"I'm not surprised," said Mrs. Fairbrass. "I should have been surprised if it had been left in. He was my brother's curate when

135

he was at Lincoln. A man of considerable promise. Sadly not fulfilled. His carnal nature got the better of him."

"His carnal nature?"

"Choirboys," said Mr. Fairbrass.

"Oh, I see. Yes."

"You said six, Mr. Macindoe."

"The sixth beneficiary is certainly alive and with us. She is his housekeeper, a Miss Rosa Pilcher. She was in here yesterday inquiring about the terms of the will. I imagine the Archdeacon had told her she might be a beneficiary."

Mrs. Fairbrass had been working things out.

She said, "Are you telling us, Mr. Macindoe, that Miss Pilcher—not in fact his housekeeper, but merely a woman who worked part time in his house—is on equal terms with us?"

"It would seem so."

"How much?" said Mr. Fairbrass.

"I have only been able to make a rough calculation so far. A lot of his money was invested in property, and that is more difficult to value than stocks and shares. But I should have said that after all debts and duties have been paid, it will amount to around a hundred and twenty thousand pounds."

"So Miss Pilcher will get forty thousand."

"Yes. But you have to remember that when he made his will, some seven years ago, his estate was more modest. Property values have risen dramatically lately. At that time he would have been worth between fifty and sixty thousand pounds and he imagined that he was dividing one third of it between six people. That would have amounted to quite a modest legacy of about three thousand pounds each."

"No doubt," said Mrs. Fairbrass. "But, whatever his will says, I'm certain he didn't mean her to have forty thousand."

"People often fail to express their true intentions when they make their wills," said Macindoe sadly.

"Slush," said Edwin Fisher.

"Driffield at his worst," agreed Bill Williams. They were reading the Archdeacon's obituary notice in the *Melset Times*. It was set in a thick black border with the headline in Gothic script. "I didn't feel strongly about the man either way, but 'A noble man of God gone to his rest' seems an exaggerated way of describing a businesslike Archdeacon who died of flu."

"Are you sure of that?"

"Very businesslike, by all accounts."

"I meant, is it certain he died of flu?"

"They wouldn't be cremating him on Monday unless that had been established."

"I suppose not." Fisher sounded depressed. It was a two-horse race between the *Times* and the *Journal*, and the *Journal* had been slipping a little. He said, "Our figures were down again last week."

"Don't worry," said Bill. "I think I'm on to something that will give us a real shot in the arm. Nothing to do with the quarrels in the Close. That sort of thing became a dead letter when the Archdeacon died. This is live stuff. Piping hot."

Fisher looked at his young subordinate suspiciously. He said, "Whose toes are you planning to tread on now?"

"Several people," said Bill, "and all of them eminent in the life of this city."

On Monday morning Valentine Laporte, Chief Constable of Melchester, woke with severe toothache. Good woman that she was, his wife ordered him to stay in bed, brought him a warm bottle to lay against his cheek, a cup of coffee and some milky porridge and made an appointment with the dentist for ten-thirty.

By half past eleven, feeling much happier and minus one molar, Laporte was at his desk. The first thing he saw was a note, timed nine o'clock: "Dr. Gadney rang." A second note, timed 10.45 a.m., said: "Dr. Gadney rang again."

Who the devil was Dr. Gadney? Well, if he wanted him all that badly, no doubt he would ring a third time.

Some of his euphoria had diminished by now. The remainder disappeared when he recognized the handwriting on the envelope on top of the pile.

This was the third letter he had had in the past week from Miss Pilcher. The first two had been complaints about his police officers, who had treated her discourteously. This one was less easy to understand. It seemed to suggest that things had been going on in the Close which the police ought to investigate; things which had led to the death of Archdeacon Pawle; things which the ecclesiastical establishment was trying to cover up.

"A mischievous woman," decided Laporte. "If she doesn't watch out, she'll land herself with a thumping suit for libel." It was at this point that he spotted the official-looking envelope carrying the superscription of the Home Office Central Research Establishment at Aldermaston. He opened it and extracted the two documents which it contained.

The first was a letter from the director, Dr. Gadney, addressed to him personally. It said, "Dear Chief Constable, Since you ought to have this report soonest, I am sending it by hand of messenger. Further analysis of the material submitted to us will, of course, be necessary, but I feel you should have the results of our preliminary examination at once so that you may decide what steps ought to be taken in the light of the information disclosed."

With one eye on the clock, Laporte dropped the letter, grabbed the report and started to race through the opening paragraphs.

"Since we had not been informed that the results of the examination were needed urgently, it was dealt with in normal rotation—"

Naturally, no one had told them it was urgent. No one had known.

"It was unfortunate that the contents of the stomach and the esophagus were not available to us. We should have supposed that it would have been the usual practice—"

Skip that bit.

"Sections of the liver and kidneys were macerated, extracted with chloroform and analyzed by thin-layer chromatography."

Bottom of page. Turn over.

Laporte read the next few lines, put down the report, leafed through the telephone directory and dialed a number.

After what seemed an intolerable pause, a polite voice said, "This is the South Melset Crematorium. Can I help you?"

Laporte said, "Chief Constable here. You had a cremation fixed for midday. If it hasn't taken place, it must be stopped."

"The cremation has had to be postponed," said the polite

voice. "Apparently Dr. McHarg was unwilling to sign the death certificate."

Laporte said, "Thank you." He picked up the internal telephone and dialed Superintendent Bracher's number. He found that he was sweating.

While he was waiting for Bracher to arrive, his eye fell on the letter from Rosa Pilcher. He had put it into a tray labeled FILING. NO FURTHER ACTION. He took it out and dropped it into another tray labeled FOLLOW UP.

Fifteen

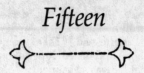

"W<small>ELL</small>," said <small>LEO SANDEMAN</small>, "and what are we supposed to make of that? Cremation postponed. Inquest next Thursday."

Driffield said, "There are all sorts of rumors floating round. The police are supposed to be prosecuting inquiries. But no one seems to know quite what the inquiries are."

"I know what one of them is," said Grant Adey. "They're visiting chemists' shops and gardening shops. I had that from— well, as he was bound to secrecy, perhaps I won't mention his name."

"Chemists *and* gardeners," said Driffield thoughtfully.

"Suggest something to the journalistic mind?"

"A faint smell of something fishy about the Archdeacon's death? If there's any real evidence, the inquest should be worth listening to."

"Standing room only, I imagine," said Sandeman.

"Do you chaps realize," said Gloag, speaking for the first time, "that if someone—" he boggled at the word "murdered"—"if someone was responsible for the Archdeacon's death, there's a strong possibility that it was done to stop us?"

The thought had been in all their minds. Now that it was out in the open, they looked at it critically. Grant Adey said, "We see what you mean, Gerry, but if it's true—and it does seem wildly improbable—then the only person who could logically have been responsible for this is the Dean."

"In the ordinary way," said Sandeman, "one could hardly contemplate such an idea. But the Dean isn't an ordinary man."

"I did manage to have a quick word with Bracher," said Driffield, "but he was playing his cards close to his chest."

"You won't get anything out of Bert," said Adey. "If you're

looking for news, why not go to the fountainhead? Not just the purveyor of news. You might say the creator of it. Sweet Rosa Pilcher."

Driffield said, "I think you might have something there, Grant."

James had planned to go back to London at the end of that week. Since it was now clear that he might be called to give evidence at the inquest on the following Thursday, he had decided to extend his stay for a further week. The Medical Registrar, when consulted on the telephone, had encouraged him to do so. He said, "I hope you're not working, James. It's meant to be a holiday, remember."

James had answered evasively and had made his way around to the school. He found Julia in the drawing room and explained what he had in mind. He said, "It looks as if I may be hanging around here for another ten days waiting for the inquest. Peter was telling me that Alan's ankle still isn't strong enough for him to take walks or games and I wondered if I could lend a hand."

"I'm sure that'd be helpful," said Julia and after a pause, "I suppose you have to give evidence if they call you."

James thought that she sounded worried. Or perhaps worried was too strong a word. But her mind was clearly on other things than school routine.

"I'm afraid so," he said. "I was with the Archdeacon when he died. I imagine they're bound to ask me about that."

"I suppose that's right." A distant bell sounded. Julia said, with evident relief, "That's first break. Lawrence will be here in a moment."

An uncomfortable silence ensued. To break it, James wandered over to the triangular corner cupboard and inspected a pair of cups and saucers. He said, "I didn't know you were a collector. Henry Brookes has a pair of bowls which might be part of the same set."

"It's Lawrence. He's always had a thing about *famille rose*." She seemed to welcome the change of subject. "I know the bowls you mean. They were in Burtonshaw's window for a week and every day I was plucking up courage to go in and ask how much they'd cost. I guessed the price would be fairly steep, because they were a perfect pair, but it was going to be a special

141

present for Lawrence's fortieth birthday. The very day I made up my mind to take the plunge, they were gone. Henry had nipped in ahead of me."

"That's life," said James. At this moment Lawrence came bustling in. He received James' offer with enthusiasm. He said, "I'd been relying on Len Masters helping us out. He's done so in the past when Cathedral duties permitted. But now it seems that he's leaving us."

"That's news," said Julia sharply. "Where's he going? And why?"

"He's been offered a job, dear. As junior cricket professional at Worcester. Apparently they've been after him for some time. Why he should suddenly have decided to take the job, I don't know. Unless all these police inquiries have upset him."

Julia started to say, "I didn't know he'd been—" and then changed her mind. She said, "Anyway, it'll be a step up for him. I'm certain the Chapter was underpaying him."

James, remembering the sad episode of the silver cups, agreed that finance might be one of the reasons for Masters' decision. But he had a feeling that there might have been other considerations involved. Something was going on that he did not understand.

As he was walking down the passage on his way out, a door opened, Penny appeared, grabbed him by the arm and pulled him into an empty classroom. She said, "Now who was right?"

James said, "I've no idea what you're talking about."

"Don't try to get out of it. I told you the Archdeacon had been poisoned and you scoffed."

"Did I scoff?"

"Certainly you scoffed. Loudly."

"If I remember rightly, what you said was that the boys were saying that the Dean had poisoned him."

"Right."

"And what makes you think that there's any more truth in that absurd idea now than there was before?"

"If there isn't any truth in it, why are the police questioning people who were in the marquee that afternoon?"

"Oh. I see."

"Stop making enigmatic remarks. *What* do you see?"

"I see why your mother was thinking of other things when I was talking to her just now. Have the police been at her?"

"She was grilled," said Penny, putting as much heartless relish into the word as if she had been an English soldier describing the fate of Joan of Arc.

"Why her particularly?"

"Don't you remember? She was one of the people serving out the coffee. She and Amanda and Dora Brookes."

"But that's absurd," said James. "What earthly reason could your mother have for poisoning the Archdeacon?"

"To be fair," said Penny, "I don't think they thought she did it. But they thought she'd have been well placed to spot the person who did. It's interesting, isn't it?"

"It's not interesting," said James angrily. "It's disgusting."

"Well, if you think that, you shouldn't have started it."

"What do you mean?"

"Everyone says that if it hadn't been for you, whoever did it would have got away with it."

"My dear," said Lady Fallingford. "Tell me everything."

"I did say I wouldn't discuss it with anyone," said Mrs. Henn-Christie miserably.

"I'm not just anyone."

"If you promise not to tell anyone else."

"My lips are sealed."

To show how sealed they were, Lady Fallingford pressed her lips together tightly.

"Well, it was this policeman."

"The nasty one with frizzy hair?"

"No. A younger one. A sergeant, I think. He arrived just after lunch and stayed for hours—well, it seemed like hours."

"Doing what?"

"Asking questions and writing down all the answers. I told him I didn't know anything. It was no use. He just went on asking and writing."

"Asking *what?*" said Lady Fallingford. She spoke bracingly because she saw that her old friend was really upset.

"About that lunch in the tent last Saturday."

"You mean when we were in the Deanery garden."

"That's right. He wanted to know all about it. Who was there and where they were standing and what they ate and drank."

"And of course you couldn't tell him. You've always had a rotten memory."

"That's just what I told him. I said I've got a very bad memory and anyway I'm not a noticing sort of person."

"But it didn't stop him?"

"My dear, it was like water off a duck's back. He simply went on and on. The thing he seemed particularly interested in was the coffee. He wanted to know who'd been serving it and who'd been handing it out and things like that. I said I'd got my back to the coffee table and was talking to the Dean. If he wanted to know about it, why didn't he ask the Dean? He didn't take a blind bit of notice."

"The man's impossible."

"When I'd told him six times over that I couldn't tell him anything and he'd written it down six times, I lost my temper. I said, 'You've got no right to pester me, and if there's any more of it, I'm going straight to the Dean to complain.' He didn't like that. He muttered something about only doing his duty and stumped off."

"Do you think he'll be after me next?"

"Certain to be."

"I shan't be able to tell him much more than you did." Lady Fallingford seemed to be reflecting. "Actually, I wasn't near the table where they were serving the coffee out and I was listening to Canon Maude's mother. She was talking about his roses. There's been a lot of black spot in all our gardens this year." She was a shrewd old lady and a lot more practical than her friend. She said, "It's beginning to look as if they thought someone put something in the Archdeacon's coffee, isn't it?"

"Don't, Constantia," said Mrs. Henn-Christie faintly.

The little car had been driven off the road, down a track that led to the riverbank. The coming of darkness had added an agreeable sense of intimacy to the boy and girl who were sitting together on the back seat. Philip had his right arm round Lucy Pomfret and his hand was lying passively on her right breast. She had her head tilted up toward him and he could see, in the dim light reflected off the river, that her eyes were wet.

"He's a beast," she said. "An utter beast. Why did he have to do such a beastly thing?"

"It was really silly," said Philip. "Just because I happened to be in the Lion that Sunday evening with Bill and Peter and that young doctor, and Gloag came in with Sandeman, and there was a bit of a turn-up which nearly ended in a fight. I suppose he assumed I was one of their gang, and the next thing I knew was I'd got the boot."

"How *could* he?"

"It did seem a pretty bloody thing to do."

"And it means you'll have to go away."

"I've been offered this job up in London. A chap I was at school with wangled it. It seemed the only thing to do."

Philip tightened his arm around the girl and they sat for a bit, locked together, thinking about the unfairness of life. Lucy said, "Isn't there *anything* you can do to get back at him? He's so horrible."

"Horrible to you?"

"Not to me. Goodness, no. If there was anything like that, I wouldn't stop there for a moment, I can tell you. Just nasty. I'm sure he's the sort of man who has books of dirty photographs hidden away and takes them out and gloats over them when everyone else has gone home and—ugh."

"That's a thought," said Philip. "Let's get hold of them and give them to Bill and he can publish some of them in the *Journal*. Artistic works discovered in the desk of one of our leading estate agents."

"He wouldn't keep them in the desk. They'd be in his private safe. The one he keeps all his fiddles in."

"Fiddles?"

"Tax fiddles. Swindles. Dirty tricks."

"They might be even more interesting than dirty pictures," said Philip thoughtfully. "The trouble is I'm no good at picking locks."

"You wouldn't have to pick the lock. I know where he keeps the key."

"You do?" Philip sat up. "Where? How did you find out?"

"There's a secret drawer in his desk. And I found out because he left it a wee bit open one morning and I spotted it. And when he was away I fiddled about with it and found out how it

145

worked. There are wooden roses above the pillars on each side of the space at the back of the desk. If you turn the one on the right, you can pull out the whole pillar. It's a sort of upright drawer, if you see what I mean."

"I see exactly what you mean," said Philip. He sounded interested. "But you'd have to open the desk first."

"No difficulty. The lock doesn't catch. You just have to give the lid a tug and it comes open. Would you like me to have a look?"

"No," said Philip firmly. "If anyone's going to burgle Gerry Gloag's safe, it's going to be me. I'm in trouble anyway. You're not. But I'll have a word with Bill first."

He lay back again and Lucy lay back with him. The thought that they might be able to do something disagreeable to Gloag had excited them both.

Bill Williams listened to what Philip had to say. They were alone in the private bar of the Black Lion.

He said, "I take it you'd have no difficulty in getting into the office after hours."

"None at all. Most of us have got our own keys to the side door."

"Would Gloag's office be locked?"

"Yes. But Lucy will lend me her key. She's got one in case she gets there first in the morning. Couldn't be easier, really, could it?"

Bill took a long pull at his beer before answering. He said, "Gloag's a vindictive beast. If you got caught, he'd run you in for burglary."

"'Tisn't burglary. I'm not stealing anything. Just looking at some papers."

"Breaking and entering, then."

"I may be entering, but I'm certainly not breaking. Not if I use my own keys."

"I'm not sure about that. I'd better have a word with Mac—mentioning no names."

"Anyway, suppose someone did see me going in or coming out, I've got a perfect right to be there. Keen young executive working overtime."

"I'm not trying to discourage you," said Bill. "Just quieting

146

my own conscience. I'm as anxious as you are to take a look at what's in that safe. I'm not all that interested in tax fiddles. Everyone goes in for them. It's information about the supermarket deal. The things I'm after are bank accounts, paying-in books and check stubs. They're the giveaway where money's concerned. They say there are two things you can't hide: the spilling of blood and the passage of money."

"Well, I don't anticipate spilling any blood."

"I hope you're right," said Bill as he finished his beer. "But, for God's sake, don't get caught. You realize that if you did, you'd have to carry the can. I simply can't afford to get involved. Bracher's after my scalp already. He'd like nothing better than to make trouble for me and for the *Journal*."

"If I get into a mess," said Philip with dignity, "it'll be my fault. And my funeral."

Sixteen

James was feeling hard done by.

If, as he told himself repeatedly, he had done anything wrong, anything blameworthy, anything illegal, immoral or unethical, then he would at least have had the satisfaction of knowing that he deserved his fate. In fact, as he assured himself, he had behaved with complete correctness.

There was, he supposed, no actual need for him to have suggested to Dr. Barkworth that certain sections and samples be taken, but no pathologist worth his salt would have omitted so obvious a precaution. He could, he supposed, have refused point blank to discuss the question of symptoms with Dr. McHarg. But that would have amounted to a deliberate concealing of facts, a sin against the most sacred tenet in the scientists' creed.

And what was the result of this absolutely proper, not to say praiseworthy and public-spirited conduct?

The result was that the girl he wanted to marry now disliked and despised him. True, she had not actually said so. In fact, he had had no opportunity in the last two days to speak to her. He had glimpsed her distantly, going in and out of the Close, and had seen her once in the town, hurrying past on the opposite pavement. He had considered calling at the Deanery, but pride had stopped him. After all, *he* wasn't the one who was in the wrong, was he?

Damn, damn and damn.

Peter, noting his depression, had suggested the obvious remedy, but James had no wish to go out and get drunk. All he wanted to do was to kick the furniture; and if it had been his furniture, he would probably have done this, but he could hardly take it out on the Chapter Clerk's chairs and tables.

At this point, when he was beginning to turn over in his mind some of the painless methods of committing suicide which were available to him as a doctor, the telephone rang in the hall.

It was the Dean. He said, "Dr. Scotland? I hoped I might find you in. If you happened to be free, I wondered if you'd walk round. There was something I wanted to discuss with you. There's no urgency about it, but—"

"I'll be right with you," said James.

The Dean was in his study, surrounded by books and papers. He waved James to a chair, but remained standing himself. "Good of you to come. I've been wanting to have a word with you. Anything I say to you is, of course, in confidence. I am treating you as though you were my own doctor and I could speak quite freely."

"Yes," said James uneasily. It seemed to him that too many people in the Close were treating him as their own doctor.

"A number of our people have complained to me in the last few days of harassment by the police. It started as soon as we learned that the cremation of the Archdeacon had been postponed. Was I right to deduce a connection between these two occurrences?"

James said, "Yes," again.

"You agree with me? Good. The next point I had to consider was the reason for the precise questions which were being put to—let me see—so far Openshaw, Julia Consett, Leonard Masters and Mrs. Henn-Christie. There may have been others who have not reported the matter to me. The police appear to be interested in our luncheon party which preceded the Cathedral service for the Friends. And more specifically interested, judging by the people questioned, in the coffee which was served at the end of the meal. Can you think of any reason for that?"

"The only reason I can think of is that they suppose that the coffee the Archdeacon drank was in some way responsible for his death."

"Exactly my own conclusion. I am glad you confirm it. The next question is, what substance could there have been in the coffee which would cause death within an hour?"

James said, "You must understand that I am not in the confidence of the police and have no inside information. But the point you make had already puzzled me. There are poisons, like cyanide and prussic acid, which act almost instantaneously. There are others, such as arsenic and antimony, which may cause distressing symptoms within an hour or so, but in which death does not normally take place for a considerable period, often for a matter of several days."

"But if the original diagnosis of Dr. Barkworth had been correct, then the timing would be normal."

"Then you knew what Dr. Barkworth's report said?"

"I think you may assume," said the Dean, "that everyone knows about it. These things have a habit of spreading."

"I see. Well, you are quite right. There have been a number of cases of virus influenza in which death has taken place in less than two hours."

"Then, judged from the symptoms alone, Dr. Barkworth's diagnosis is perfectly feasible."

James had the feeling, which he had sometimes experienced in court, that an astute counsel for the defense was leading him into making damaging admissions. He said, "Judged solely by the symptoms, yes. But one must assume that the police have got hold of some further evidence."

"Which they have not seen fit to disclose."

"Not yet."

"And until they do, we, as members of the public, have only guesswork to go on."

"I suppose that's right."

"You confirm my view. It reinforces my decision. I shall forbid anyone in the Close to give any further information to the police."

James stared at him.

"That is to say, I shall forbid anyone over whom I have direct jurisdiction. The others I shall advise. In most cases—" the Dean smiled grimly—"I think they will take my advice."

"Is that wise?"

"You think it inadvisable?"

"Well," said James, trying to express his feelings tactfully, "won't it really amount to this, that you are setting yourself up as an alternative authority to the State?"

"Interesting that you should put it in that way. Because in every country in which I have been involved in missionary work, my first task was always to assert the authority of the Church. Not always against the State. There were other contestants. In some cases, the existing religious hierarchy. In other cases, the Communist Party."

"Yes," said James thoughtfully, "I can imagine that the ruling clique would normally be hostile to missionaries."

"Hostile, yes. But not often violent. Missionaries are more often expelled than actually maltreated. It is some time—" the Dean allowed himself a further smile—"since one of them has been eaten. The last case, I understand, was the Reverend Tomkins, who was consumed by South Sea islanders in 1901."

James was aware that he was being skillfully side-tracked. He said, "In some primitive communities the struggle between Church and State may still be open, but in the Western World the result, surely, has long been decided in favor of the State."

"By no means." The Dean drew himself up to his full and impressive height. "What people are always looking for is strong leadership. They won't find it among the politicians today. There's a power vacuum. A renascent, self-confident Church could fill it."

James wondered whether the Dean could possibly be serious. If he was, James foresaw no end of trouble. Before he could say anything, the Dean continued. "Ah, yes. I knew there was one other point I wanted to mention. I believe you have become attached to my daughter."

This time James really was speechless.

"Perhaps I am wrong. If I am, I must apologize for having made a tactless observation."

"You're not wrong," said James thickly. "In the short time I have known her, I have become much attached to her."

"These things develop quickly," said the Dean. He might have been talking of measles or whooping cough. "I imagine that my daughter reciprocates your feelings?"

"I used to think she did. Not now, I'm afraid."

"Oh. Has there been some rupture?"

"She seems to think that I'm overconscientious."

"In what way?"

James hesitated for a moment and then decided to take the

plunge. He said, "When I attended the post-mortem on the Archdeacon, the South Wessex pathologist, Brian Barkworth, having diagnosed virus influenza, seemed inclined to leave it at that."

"He had reasons, no doubt."

"Certainly. There was massive edema. That is, fluid in the lungs, which is a symptom of influenza. I suggested that certain sections ought to be taken—just as a routine precaution, you understand—and sent to the laboratory."

"Yes. I see. So that is why we are being subjected to persecution by the police."

This was not said in a way which suggested that he blamed James. Rather it was a dispassionate examination of cause and effect.

"I'm afraid that's right."

"My dear boy, you mustn't take these things personally. No one can be blamed for searching out the truth."

"Canon Lister didn't think so."

"Ah, but Tom was a limited rationalist. I can't claim to think more deeply than he did, but I can claim to have seen more of life. If it has taught me anything, it has taught me this: Never stop halfway. The Bible instructs us. Having once put your hand to the plow, turn not back. Don't listen to half-hearted counsels. Ignore opposition. Press on to the end."

The Dean paused for a moment and added, "Mind you, I m talking about your scientific researches. Not about your project of marrying my daughter, or have I assumed too much? You were planning to marry her, I assume?"

"I want to marry her as soon as I possibly can."

"Then I should counsel extreme caution. We're a dangerous family."

That afternoon James went for a long walk. He needed time to think. When he got back to the Chapter Clerk's house, he put a call through to the Medical Registrar at Guy's. "Dr. Gadney?" said the Registrar. "The doctor in charge at Aldermaston. Very sound man, Bill Gadney. Trained at Guy's, of course."

"I thought I remembered the name. Did you know him, by any chance?"

"Certainly I knew him. We played in the second row of the scrum together."

"That's splendid. Because I want an introduction to him."

"An introduction?"

"I mean, could you ring him and tell him that I'll be getting in touch with him and—oh, well, you know what I mean."

He heard the Registrar chuckle. "Tell him that you're a serious pathologist?"

"Tell him that if it hadn't been for me, he wouldn't have got the results of the Pawle post-mortem."

"He's probably guessed that already."

"Well, put in a good word. I want him to do me a favor."

"I thought you were meant to be on holiday."

"Things haven't quite panned out that way."

"I've no idea what you're up to, but I could have a word with Bill. I've got his home number somewhere. I'll give him a ring after he gets home this evening. He'll be more relaxed then."

"Bless you," said James.

The next morning he telephoned Aldermaston. The Registrar had done his stuff. Dr. Gadney was genial and co-operative. He said, "I'd be very happy for you to come up here and have a further look at those sections. A second opinion is always useful. But I've had a better idea. I believe you know Dan Leigh at New Cross."

"I worked under him for a year."

"Did you know that they'd just installed a beautiful new chromatographic analyzer? An American model. God knows how they got the money to pay for it. Sheer favoritism."

"No. I didn't know."

"It can be tuned up to analyze very small quantities. If there's anything we've failed to spot, it will pick it up easily enough. What I could do is this. Just let me look at my diary for a moment. Yes. Today's Tuesday. I've got to be up in London anyway on Thursday. I'm giving a talk to the medico-legal people that evening. If I brought up the samples with me, we could run them through the machine at New Cross on Thursday afternoon."

James had been thinking, too. He said, "There's only one

snag. The inquest opens on Thursday and I've been warned that I shall be called."

"That's all right. I've already had a word with your Coroner, Andrew Rolfe. He's going to start with the formal evidence on Thursday and take all the doctors together on Friday. Sensible idea, really. If he's got four or five doctors to deal with, he can take them in sequence and we can all contradict each other to our hearts' content. Incidentally, I'm planning to have lunch with Bunny on Thursday. Why don't you join us?"

James gathered that Bunny must be the Registrar, although he had never heard him called that before. He said he would be delighted to join them.

"Splendid. We'll run those samples through the super box of tricks at New Cross and see what comes out."

"We have a choice," said the Chief Constable. "And it's not an easy one. We could tell the Coroner that the inquiries we have been making have now reached a point where a charge is likely to be made. He'd take evidence of identification and adjourn the inquest. That would be the normal course."

"But would it help us?" said Superintendent Bracher.

"You don't think it would?"

"I think it would make things even more difficult."

"Why?"

"We seem to be up against a conspiracy of silence."

"Do you mean that people are refusing to answer questions?"

"What they say is, 'What are you asking all these questions for? What's it all about? Everyone knows the Archdeacon died of flu. What are you stirring things up for?'"

"Yes. I see. And you think if we show our hand, it will help your inquiries."

"People will at least know the score."

"So we put some of our cards on the table. That will mean calling people who were at the lunch party."

"Adey and Sandeman were both there."

"Not Sandeman. Everyone knows he dislikes the Dean. The jury would discount anything he said. All right, we call Adey. Then you'll have to give evidence yourself, of course."

"To explain how we located Miss Lovelock."

"Miss Lovelock. Yes. That was a creditable piece of work."

Laporte consulted the list that he and Bracher were compiling with all the anxiety of a football manager selecting a team for a needle match. "Grant Adey will be an excellent witness. A very convincing man. The trouble is, he wasn't really near the coffee table."

"What about Rosa?"

"Rosa," said Bracher and sighed. "I've given a lot of thought to Rosa. On balance, I think it would be better to keep her in reserve."

"Rosa won't like that. She doesn't want to be a reserve. She's keen. She wants to be center forward."

"That's the trouble," said Laporte. "She's too bloody keen."

"You would have thought," said Driffield, "that they might have had more consideration than to start the inquest on a Thursday. It's likely to run for at least two days. That'll mean that we can only report the first day in our Friday issue and we'll have to wait for a whole week before we can report the second day. And my guess would be that it's the second day, when the doctors get going, that's going to be the interesting one."

The lady reporter to whom he was talking agreed that it was inconsiderate. With the prospect of the most exciting inquest for years, they might, she thought, have considered the convenience of the local press.

At the time this conversation took place, Edwin Fisher was saying to Bill Williams, "You'd better get there in good time. They're using the council chamber, which is a reasonable-sized room, but the national press are just beginning to get in on the act. My guess is that it'll be standing room only for late-comers."

"I'll be there at crack of dawn," said Bill. "I wouldn't miss a word of it."

"It really is rather curious," said Dr. Leigh. He was a tall thin man with a giraffe-like neck and a sinister smile.

"Unexpected," agreed Dr. Gadney, who still contrived to look like the formidable rugby player he had once been.

"I wonder what it means," said young Dr. Scotland.

The three doctors were examining a strip of graph paper down the center of which ran a black line. It was like the crest of a mountain range, roughly level, but with occasional peaks.

"That's the N-propanol standard," said Dr. Gadney to James, indicating the largest of these peaks. "It's inserted, as I expect you remember, as a measurement norm when making the routine checks for alcohol. Which in this case were entirely negative. But I must confess that until we had the assistance of your excellent machine—" he smiled at Dr. Leigh—"I had not attached importance to *that* one."

He indicated a deviation in the line, little more than a wrinkle on the surface.

"This machine is particularly good with volatile substances," agreed Dr. Leigh complacently.

"What is it?" said James.

"We'll soon find out," said Dr. Gadney.

Seventeen

THE CORONER IGNORED the crowded press bench and the even more crowded public benches and addressed himself directly to the five men and four women in the jury box. He said, "Before we begin, I would like to emphasize one point. This is not a trial. It is an inquiry. You have been called here, primarily, to answer one question: How did Raymond Pawle, Archdeacon of this Cathedral, come by his death? Of course, there may be supplementary questions. For instance, if you found that his death was the result of an accident, you might wish to add a rider on the question of negligence. Such verdicts can be useful in preventing further accidents. On the other hand—" the Coroner was speaking more slowly now, as though he was approaching the heart of the matter—"if you think that the evidence indicates the possibility of the unlawful taking of life, it will be your duty to say so. But bear this in mind: You are under no obligation to go any further. It is unnecessary for you to name the person or persons you feel to have been responsible. In almost every case it is preferable, in my view, for you to return an open verdict. This leaves the question of guilt to be decided by the proper tribunal. That is to say, by a court of law. I hope that is understood. Very well, I will now outline the story for you."

The Coroner rearranged his papers into an orderly pile. Dr. McHarg, who was sitting at the back of the court, reflected what a salutary change of the law it had been to insist that coroners should have legal as well as medical qualifications. He remembered old Dr. Maxwell, thirty years before, who had bumbled his way into a number of quite implausible situations.

"Archdeacon Pawle died just before a quarter to four on Saturday, September 28, in the vestry of this Cathedral. Two doctors were present at the moment when he died: Dr. Hamish McHarg, his own medical man, and a Dr. James Scotland, who happened to be in the Cathedral when the Archdeacon was taken ill and went to his assistance. Both of them will be giving evidence to you tomorrow. A post-mortem examination was held at the South Wessex Hospital. It was conducted by Dr. Brian Barkworth, the resident pathologist. You will be hearing from him also, but I will tell you now that his first diagnosis, based both on the state of the deceased's lungs and on the fact that there had already been an outbreak in the docks area, was that the Archdeacon had died of virus influenza, and certain precautions were taken to prevent the spread of what can be a very serious epidemic."

At this point the Coroner reached the end of one page of his notes. As he turned the page, he seemed to his hearers to be moving to a new chapter.

"At the post-mortem, as a routine precaution, certain organs were removed and sent to the Home Office Research Establishment at Aldermaston. The matter was not considered to be one of great urgency and it was not until the following Monday, October 7, that the Chief Constable received their report. It was written by the director, Dr. William Gadney, who considered it to be of such importance that he sent it by hand to the Chief Constable. I have asked Dr. Gadney to make himself available to answer questions on his report. He has agreed to do so."

"If he doesn't tell us soon what was in that bloody report," said Amanda to Penny, who was squashed in beside her, "I shall burst." The expression on the faces around her suggested that she was not alone in this feeling.

"However," continued the Coroner smoothly, "in order to justify the actions which the police felt obliged to take, and to set the evidence of the other witnesses into a proper context, I will read you the relevant passages. If you find some of the technical expressions confusing, I will gladly leave it to Dr. Gadney to explain them to you tomorrow. Very well. He says, 'Sections of the liver and kidneys were macerated, extracted with chloroform and analyzed by thin-layer chromatography. This demonstrated the presence in them of a substantial quantity of nicotine.'"

Nicotine? A communal sigh, like the passage of wind among trees, passed through the crowded room.

"'In order to measure the nicotine, the liver extracts were then subjected to ultra-violet spectrophotometry. This gave an amount, in the liver, of five milligrams. A calculation based on this would suggest a total intake of at least sixty milligrams, which would be consistent with a fatal dose.'"

Nicotine. Chemists' shops. Gardeners' shops. It began to add up.

"The police placed an inquiry with the Poisons Unit at New Cross. They wished to find out how long it would take for a dose of this size to cause death. I understand that the head of the unit, Dr. Daniel Leigh, may also be available to give evidence tomorrow if required. For the moment, I will summarize his answers. He said that in the case of a non-smoker, like the Archdeacon, the time might be as short as forty-five minutes. In other cases, as long as an hour and a half. If an average time was required, it could safely be taken as an hour, or perhaps an hour and a quarter."

Died at three forty-five. Subtract seventy-five minutes. Everyone was doing the sums.

"It has, of course, been established that on that particular Saturday the Archdeacon, along with a great number of other people, was partaking of a buffet luncheon prior to the annual service and meeting of the Friends of the Cathedral. This suggested two further lines of inquiry: first, of people who were present at that luncheon; secondly, of persons who might be purveyors of nicotine in one form or another. These are the witnesses who will be called, and I ask you to listen very carefully to what they have to tell you."

An unnecessary instruction, thought Bill Williams, easing his writing arm and flipping over a page in his notebook. They had started late and it was a quarter to twelve already. He hoped the old boy had civilized ideas about lunch intervals.

The first witness was Grant Adey. In answer to questions from the Coroner, he agreed that he was chairman of the Melchester Borough Council, that he was a member of the committee of the Friends of the Cathedral and that he had been present at the luncheon on the day in question.

"You will understand," said the Coroner, "that we are concerned to find out what the Archdeacon ate or drank in the period immediately prior to his death. Could you tell us who was at this function and how things were organized?"

"It's not too easy to say exactly who was there. It was very hot. The side curtains of the marquee were rolled up and a lot of people preferred to stand about outside."

"You were expected to serve yourselves, then?"

"Right. It was a sort of up-market bun fight."

Amanda snorted and this made Penny giggle.

"Could you tell us about the food and drink?"

"It was laid out on tables at one end of the marquee. There was a very nice cold soup. You grabbed a bowl and helped yourself out of one of the tureens. Then there were sandwiches and pies and cold meat and things like that. And trifles and jellies to follow. Most people piled stuff up on a plate, and some of them, as I said, moved out onto the lawn with it. Actually, I managed to find a chair near one of the tables. I'm a bit too old to enjoy eating standing up with a plate in one hand and a glass in the other."

"It requires considerable dexterity," agreed the Coroner. "What was there to drink?"

"Wine cup and cider cup and some orange squash too, I think. They were in jugs. You helped yourself."

"Did you happen to observe what the Archdeacon ate and drank?"

"Not really. He was up at the far end, near the coffee table."

"When you say the far end—?"

"I mean the end near the house. There was a covered way leading, I imagine, to the Deanery kitchen. That was the way fresh supplies came out from time to time."

"And you didn't, yourself, speak to the Archdeacon?"

"No. He seemed to be talking to one or other of the Cathedral clergy most of the time, I think. One of them was a Vicar Choral. A young man. I don't know his name."

The Coroner looked at his list and said, "I fancy that must be the Reverend Openshaw. We shall be hearing from him next."

When Adey stepped down, he was replaced by Anthony Openshaw, who agreed that he had spent much of the luncheon in conversation with the Archdeacon. He said, "You see, I've been put in temporary charge of the Theological College. When Canon Lister died, it came under the jurisdiction of the Archdeacon. So we had a lot to discuss."

"I quite understand," said the Coroner. He thought that the young clergyman looked worried and upset. More worried than was justified by having to answer a few routine questions. He wondered if he had, perhaps, been one of the few people who had been genuinely fond of the Archdeacon. He said, "Then you will be able to tell us what he ate and drank?"

"Certainly. He had some soup. He helped himself to that. And I brought him a plate of sandwiches. They were rather good sandwiches. We each ate a number of them. Then, I remember, I was silly enough to put the plate down on one of the low tables behind me and that was the last we saw of them."

"You mean someone else took them?"

"Not someone. It was Bouncer. These were liver-sausage sandwiches and apparently he's very partial to them. He scoffed the lot."

"Bouncer is, I imagine, a dog?"

"My dog," said Lady Fallingford, who was seated near the front.

The Coroner looked at her over his glasses, recognized her and said, "I hope he suffered no ill-effects?"

"Sick in a flower bed. Greedy little beast."

"But no permanent ill-effects?"

"Right as rain by teatime."

"In that case," said the Coroner, who seemed unworried by the informal nature of this evidence, "I think we can acquit the sandwiches." He returned to Openshaw. "Which of the drinks did the Archdeacon take? Wine cup, or cider cup, or orange squash?"

"It would have been against his principles to take anything alcoholic immediately before divine service. I fetched a jug of orange squash and we both drank some of it while we were talking."

"Where did the glasses come from?"

"There were a number of empty glasses on the table. The Archdeacon secured two of them and I filled them. I also poured some out for two of the students who were standing near us."

"And that was all that the Archdeacon had to eat or drink?"

"I think so. Yes."

"He didn't have any of the other meats, or the trifles or jellies?"

"I don't think so."

"Nothing else?"

"Well, I imagine he had a cup of coffee. We all did. But I'd moved away by then."

"Yes," said the Coroner thoughtfully. "Yes, we shall be coming to the coffee. That is all you can tell us from your own observation?"

"Yes, sir."

"If I might—?" said a small round man who was seated between Mr. and Mrs. Fairbrass in the front row.

"Yes, Mr. Meiklejohn. You represent the family, I take it."

"I have that honor, sir. Might I ask the witness a few questions?"

The Coroner nodded. The matter was in his discretion. Unlike some coroners, he believed in letting everyone have their say, within reasonable limits.

"I just wanted to be clear about the sandwiches. I take it you handed the plate to the Archdeacon and he selected the ones he wanted?"

Openshaw looked surprised. He said, "You mean, did I pick the sandwiches off the plate in my own fingers and give them to him? Of course I didn't."

"I thought it unlikely," said Mr. Meiklejohn smoothly. "I just wanted to be certain. And he himself selected the glasses from which you both drank? I think you said it was orange squash."

"Yes."

Mr. Meiklejohn said, "Thank you," and sat down.

Arthur Driffield replaced Openshaw and was duly sworn. He said, "I arrived early because I wanted to have a word with the Archdeacon about certain questions of Close politics that my paper was interested in. Perhaps I should explain about that—"

"I think we had better stick to the luncheon for the moment."

"If you wish. Well, I found it difficult to get near the Archdeacon. At first he had a crowd of students round him and then he was talking to Openshaw. I wasn't able to speak to him myself until nearly the end of the meal."

"But you were in a position to observe him?"

"Certainly."

"I will read over to you the last witness' account of what the Archdeacon ate and drank. Do you substantiate what he told us?"

"Yes."

"And that is really all you can tell us?"

"About the lunch party, yes. But I can give you a good deal of information about the unfortunate dispute which had arisen between the Archdeacon and—well—certain other members of the Chapter."

The Coroner considered this, in silence, for a long ten seconds. Then he said, "Unless this evidence is directly connected with the Archdeacon's death, I would not want to trouble the jury with it."

When Driffield had volunteered to give evidence, it had been in order to expatiate on this aspect of the matter, as a basis for the article which he was already drafting for the next day's edition of his paper.

But *directly* connected?

It was a difficult question.

In the end he said, rather sulkily, "I don't know that you could say that it was directly connected."

"Well, then. Oh! Mr. Meiklejohn has a question for you."

"You told us, Mr. Driffield, that you arrived early at this luncheon. About what time would that have been?"

"A little before one o'clock, I suppose."

"And since you had your eye on the Archdeacon, you would have been able to see if he had anything to eat or drink."

"I told you. He had some soup and a few sandwiches."

"Yes. But nothing before that?"

"No. He was talking to people, not eating."

Mr. Meiklejohn looked at the Coroner and said, "In view of the medical evidence about time limits, I thought it well to establish—"

"Your point is taken. Mrs. Henn-Christie, please."

"Poor old cluck," said Penny. "If anyone says a rough word to her, she'll burst into tears."

Fortunately, the Coroner knew Mrs. Henn-Christie and was able to calm her with a few formal and harmless preliminary questions. Then he said, "I believe you were talking to Dean Forrest while coffee was being served at the end of the meal."

"I—yes—that's right. Yes. I was near the coffee table, but I had my back to it."

"And did you or the Dean take coffee?"

"I did. He doesn't drink coffee, I believe. Not usually."

"Who handed you your coffee?"

"Do you know, when that policeman was asking me questions, I told him I couldn't remember, but, thinking it over afterward, I do recollect that it was our organist, Mr. Wren."

"Thank you. Who else was handing round cups? Can you remember?"

"I think—yes—there were two of the boys. Andrew and David. I'm afraid I don't know their other names. And Mr. Brookes, our Chapter Clerk, and Masters. He's the junior verger. There may have been others. It isn't easy to remember things like that."

"I think you've done very well to remember all those," said the Coroner. "You told us that when you were talking to the Dean, you had your back to the serving table, so you wouldn't have been able to see what was going on there. However, the Dean was facing it and he ought to be able to help us. And there seem to have been a number of other people engaged in serving coffee or handing it round. But, as far as I can see, the only one who has been asked to give evidence—" he cast an eye down at his list—"is Mrs. Consett." The look which he directed at Superintendent Bracher clearly involved a question.

The Superintendent rose and said, speaking carefully, "We have met with some difficulty there, sir. A number of people have proved reluctant to answer our questions."

The Coroner thought about it. Police investigations into a crime were not his province. If some action was necessary, it was better left to the proper authorities. He said, "Well, let us see what Mrs. Consett can tell us."

Julia was clearly unhappy. The police had got hold of her before the Dean's interdict had gone out, and she was trying to remember exactly what she *had* said.

"Stick to facts and avoid fancies," her husband had advised her. Excellent advice in theory, no doubt.

She said, "There were three of us serving coffee. It was made

164

in a very large brand-new coffee machine which had been installed in the Deanery kitchen. I believe there had been some complaints last year about the quality of the coffee. Supplies of it were brought out in a big jug by Miss Pilcher and poured into smaller jugs, which we used to fill the cups."

"When you say 'we,' Mrs. Consett?"

"There were three of us. Myself, Mrs. Brookes and Miss Forrest."

"Since they are not to give evidence, it might be helpful to the jury if you identified them for us."

"Certainly. Mrs. Brookes is the wife of our Chapter Clerk, Henry Brookes. Miss Amanda Forrest is the daughter of the Dean."

There was a noticeable turning of heads to the place where Amanda was sitting and a murmur of comment, like a very soft background note of music. The Coroner looked up. When the room was silent again, he said, "So the coffee was distributed into three jugs."

"Four, actually. There was a spare one which Rosa—that is, Miss Pilcher—used."

"Don't bother about too much formality," said the Coroner kindly. "If it helps you to call these people by their Christian names, please do so. We'll soon pick up who was who. So there were four of you filling up cups. Now what about handers-out?"

"There were quite a lot of them. I remember Paul Wren, our organist, and Henry Brookes. And two of the choristers, Andrew and David, were particularly helpful. But some people just came up to the table and helped themselves, and they may have passed cups to other people. It was all pretty confused."

"I quite understand," said the Coroner. He seemed to be drawing a plan on the paper in front of him and blocking in names around it. He added, almost as though it was an afterthought, "Did you happen to notice who handed the coffee to the Archdeacon?"

"I'm afraid not."

"Thank you."

Mr. Meiklejohn seemed to be hesitating. Then he bobbed to his feet and said, "Realizing the importance of this point, can you give no indication of which of your helpers you've mentioned might have taken the coffee to the Archdeacon?"

"It mightn't have been one of the people I mentioned at all. It might have been anyone." She added, with a touch of impatience, "If you're filling thirty or forty coffee cups in a hurry, you haven't much time to notice things like that."

"I think that's an entirely reasonable answer," said the Coroner, in a tone of voice which indicated to Mr. Meiklejohn, who was no fool, that if he asked any more questions, he was going to be sat on. "Thank you, Mrs. Consett. I see from my list that we are now entering a rather different field of inquiry and I think it is an appropriate moment to adjourn for luncheon. We'll then take the police evidence. Back at half past two, please. And a word of warning to you." He turned to the jury. "There's no objection, of course, to your discussing this among yourselves, but you're not to talk to anyone else. I'm sure you understand the reason for that."

Over a beer at the Lion, Philip Rosewarn said to Bill Williams, "I took time off to be there. As I'm getting the sack anyway, it didn't seem to matter. A bit slow so far, but it all seems to be pointing in one direction."

"Rolfe's very sound," said Bill. "He won't let anyone talk out of turn. He's playing for an open verdict."

"But he can't actually stop the jury from naming someone."

"You can never stop a jury from making fools of themselves," agreed Bill. "Do you think we've got time for the second pint?"

"Now, Superintendent," said the Coroner. "What can you tell us about this matter?"

"Not as much as I should like to," said Bracher. "We understood from our experts that the only probable time and place that the deceased could have taken this fatal dose was at the lunch party, and it soon became clear also that the most vital item, so far as he was concerned, was the coffee."

"I think that follows from what we have heard."

"Yes, sir. Unfortunately, it transpired that all the people who happened to be near the coffee table, or actually assisting in the service of the coffee, were residents of the Close."

"Why do you say 'unfortunately,' Superintendent?"

Bracher hesitated. He was, as he knew, on treacherous ground. But there were things which had to be said.

"It was like this, sir. To start with, we did get some co-operation. Mr. Openshaw, Mrs. Henn-Christie and Mrs. Consett all answered our questions. And one witness gave us some information, but subsequently withdrew it."

"Could we have names, please?"

"This was the junior verger, Leonard Masters."

"Why did he wish to withdraw his evidence?"

"He said that when he spoke to us, he had not been aware of the Dean's instructions."

The Coroner paused in his note-taking for a long moment and said, "You'll have to explain that."

"I was told, sir—but this is, of course, at second hand—that the Dean had issued some general advice, or instruction, to the Cathedral employees and to residents in the Close that they were not to answer inquiries by the police."

"You say second hand. Has the Dean confirmed this?"

"No, sir. He has not made himself available for questioning."

"But he was not, of course, aware of the laboratory findings."

Bracher said, quite sharply, "I don't think that was any excuse."

"I'm not prepared to comment on that. Perhaps you'd let us know what further steps you took."

"I gave instructions that inquiries should be made at all chemists' shops in Melchester and at all gardening shops which sold nicotine-based sprays and weed-killers. I wished to ascertain whether anyone who had been present at the lunch party had recently made such a purchase."

"And were you successful?"

A momentary pause.

"Not at first, sir. It seems that pure nicotine is very rarely purchased by members of the public. Pharmacists use it for some of their own purposes. So far as nicotine-based weed-killer is concerned, there were three shops that stock it, but none of them could give us any precise evidence of recent purchasers. It is true that where any preparation contains a significant amount of a substance which is on the Poisons Index, the attendant is supposed to make the purchaser sign for it, but I'm afraid this rule is not always strictly observed."

"Then your inquiries were unsuccessful?"

"In Melchester, yes. We then extended them to Salisbury, Worcester and Winchester."

"With what results?"

"Perhaps, sir, you could take Miss Lovelock now."

"Very well," said the Coroner.

Miss Lovelock turned out to be a nervous girl in her early twenties who gave her evidence in a strangled whisper. It did not take her long to reach the point. She was an assistant in Homegrowers of Winchester. It was a gardening shop. She had been questioned by a man who said he was a detective sergeant. She thought the name was Telford. Yes, it might have been Telfer. He had asked her about people who had bought certain sorts of weed-killer and if any of them had come from Melchester.

"How would you be expected to know that?"

Miss Lovelock explained that she came from Melchester herself. She had worked, until quite recently, as a maid at the Theological College. That was how she had been able to tell the Sergeant that Miss Forrest had bought some of that sort of weed-killer from her.

The name slipped out so casually that it took a few seconds for it to sink in. Then every head in the room started to turn. The Coroner said, in a voice sharp enough to override any comment, "Since this particular preparation contained a listed poison, I understand that it was your duty to get the purchaser to sign a register which you kept for the purpose."

Miss Lovelock looked upset. She whispered, "Yes, sir."

"You *did* get her to sign it?"

"No, sir. I meant yes, I knew I should have done, but it was a very busy morning. I was alone in the shop, you see. And there was a crowd of people all waiting to be served."

"Then we have only your recollection that it was Miss Forrest who made this particular purchase. That's not very satisfactory—" He broke off as the coroner's officer whispered something to him. He paused for a moment. The crowded room was completely silent, but charged with the electricity which can be produced by an unexpected crisis.

Finally he said, "I understand that Miss Forrest is present. She should, of course, have been properly notified if her evidence was wanted—" he looked at Superintendent Bracher, who avoided his eye—"but if she is prepared to assist us, then this point could perhaps be set at rest."

"Of course," said Amanda. She seemed completely cool. "Would you like me to do it now?"

"I think it would be best. If you would stand here—" As Miss Lovelock left the witness box, Amanda gave her a friendly smile and took the oath without a tremor in her voice.

"Magnificent," said Bill Williams. "What a girl."

The Coroner said, "You heard Miss Lovelock's evidence. All that I would like to ask you, at this point, is whether she was correct in her recollection."

"Perfectly correct, sir."

"Thank you."

"If I might?" said Mr. Meiklejohn.

The Coroner thought about it. He was well aware of the implications of what he had heard. He was equally aware of the danger that the jury could be influenced by improper cross-examination. In the end he said, with a smile, "I think you have had your ration, Mr. Meiklejohn. But I will allow you one question."

"I have only one question to ask, sir." He turned to Amanda. "We have heard from the Superintendent that there was plenty of this particular sort of weed-killer available in Melchester. Why did you go all the way to Winchester to buy it?"

Amanda said, "I'm afraid you are putting matters in the wrong order. I didn't go to Winchester to buy weed-killer. I went, as I have done once a week since we came here, to visit Mrs. Hawkes. She has an apartment in the King Alfred Almshouse. I should explain, perhaps—" she made a half-turn toward the jury—"that she is nearly ninety-five and was my father's nanny." One of the women on the jury smiled sympathetically. "On one of these visits—I think it was about three weeks ago—I happened to pass Homegrowers shop and noticed a can of this preparation in the window and bought it. That was all there was to it."

The Coroner said, "Thank you, Miss Forrest." He was glad that Mr. Meiklejohn's intervention had given Amanda a chance of offering a plausible explanation of what might otherwise have been a damaging matter. He was about to speak when he was interrupted. Rosa Pilcher, who had been simmering quietly in a

169

seat next to Mr. Fairbrass, jerked suddenly upright. Her hair had worked itself into a tangle and her face was scarlet with a white circle around her mouth. She said, "If she can give evidence, why am I being stopped from speaking? Tell me that. I know more about it than anyone. I was there. I saw what she did."

Mr. Fairbrass put a hand on her arm and tried to pull her down. She shook him off. Her voice, which had started high, had risen until it was almost a shriek. "It was the coffee. She poured out a cup and told one of those boys to take it to the Archdeacon. Now you know the truth."

During the whole of this outburst Amanda had been looking steadily at Rosa. Mr. Fairbrass again got hold of her arm and said, in tones of unexpected authority, "Sit down, woman."

Rosa subsided. The Coroner waited until the room was again quite silent. Then he said, "In view of that totally irregular interruption, I shall have to consider whether it is my duty to impanel a new jury. I will think it over. For the moment, this hearing will stand adjourned."

"All rise," said the coroner's officer.

Eighteen

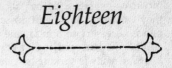

PEOPLE WHO GOT COPIES of both the local papers on their breakfast tables on Friday morning must have been struck by the different ways in which the *Times* and the *Journal* treated the inquest.

Both papers, naturally, reported at length the evidence which had been given. At that point the *Journal* concluded with a brief comment that an improper intervention by a member of the public had caused the Coroner to consider the advisability of discharging the jury.

Arthur Driffield had exercised no such restraint.

He had been prevented by the Coroner from publicizing the state of affairs in the Close. Very well. That was the Coroner's privilege. He was master in his own court. But he was not master of the *Melset Times*.

Under a subheading, QUESTIONS WHICH DEMAND AN ANSWER, he said, "There were a number of curious points about the hearing which must have struck a disinterested spectator. Why did the Coroner seem anxious to hush up the dissensions which had divided the Close into two warring camps? As this paper has reported, the burning question was whether or not to accept a very favorable offer for the land on the other side of the river known as Fletcher's Piece. We are reliably informed that the Chapter was equally divided. The Dean and one Canon were opposed to the project. The Archdeacon and one Canon were in favor of it. The Archdeacon was determined to put the matter to the Greater Chapter. His death has pre-empted this decision.

"A second point was surely significant. According to Superintendent Bracher, his inquiries have been deliberately obstructed by the Dean, who had forbidden members of the Close community to co-operate with the police. But for this it seems likely that they would by now be in possession of the final pieces of evidence necessary to bring home a charge of murder—"

When he had read as far as this, Grant Adey said to his wife, "Arthur really is sticking his neck out. He's implying, as clearly as possible, that the Dean and Amanda planned the job between them."

His wife said, "I should have thought that was pretty obvious by now. She brewed up the stuff out of that weed-killer she'd bought and put it into a cup and told one of the boys to take it to the Archdeacon."

"That may have been what happened," said Adey, "but it hasn't been proved yet. And I'm not sure this isn't contempt of court."

"I don't think you can be contemptuous of a Coroner's Court," said his wife. She had read law before marrying Grant and he frequently consulted her on matters of this sort.

The first and natural reaction of the reporters who attended the inquest from London had been to get a statement from the Dean. This had proved unexpectedly difficult. Since the Deanery was not on the telephone, they had been denied one favored method of approach, which was to ring their victim up and obtain incautious but reportable comments. Direct access proved equally difficult. Those who got as far as the Deanery gate were met by Mullins, with young Ernie in support. Young Ernie was Sam Courthope's assistant. He was a large youth who attended Judo classes in his spare time and seemed anxious to demonstrate his technique on anyone attempting entry by force.

In fact, had they succeeded in by-passing Ernie, their enterprise would have been profitless. The Dean had already left the house early that morning by the wicket gate in the garden wall and a private path across Lady Fallingford's garden.

By ten past ten every seat in the court was full. Amanda was there with Penny. She must have been aware that people in the room were looking at her and talking about her, but she gave no sign of it. One person conspicuously missing was Rosa. The Coroner had been firm about that. If Rosa was allowed in, he would adjourn the court. At ten twenty-five the jury filed in through a door beside the rostrum and took their seats. It was felt to be significant by people expert in such matters that they refrained from looking at Amanda. Phil Rosewarn whispered to Bill Williams, "I think they've made their minds up, don't you?" Bill nodded.

At this point, when everyone was expecting the appearance of the Coroner, the public door opened and the Dean appeared, leaning on his stick. He advanced slowly along the front row of seats. Penny got up. The Dean said, "Thank you, Penny," and took her seat. Penny retired to stand at the back of the room.

"Good theater," said Rosewarn. "He doesn't seem to be any more worried than Amanda is."

"It'd take more than this to worry *him*," said Bill. "Here comes the Coroner."

Everyone rose and sank back again into their seats.

The Coroner said, "I have given anxious thought to my duty in this matter. As those of you who were here yesterday will be aware, toward the close of the proceedings an entirely irregular statement, by someone who was not on oath, was made from the body of the hall. It was no doubt intended to influence the minds of the jury. I can only trust that it has not done so."

The jury looked pointedly at the ground.

"In any event, what was said has no doubt been so widely repeated that it seemed to me that no purpose would be served by impaneling a fresh jury, and I have therefore decided to let the hearing proceed. Dr. Barkworth, please."

Dr. Barkworth's evidence did not amount to much. He explained how he had come to make his original diagnosis of influenza and why he had made it, and after ten minutes of this was followed by Dr. McHarg.

The Coroner said, "There are one or two points you can clear up for us, Doctor. First, have you any comment to make on the original diagnosis?"

"Certainly. In the same caircumstances, I should probably have made the same diagnosis as Dr. Barkworth."

"Could you tell us why?"

"Because none of the normal processes of pathological examination would have detected the presence of nicotine. It required laboratory analysis to establish that."

"Thank you, Doctor. In view of certain unfounded criticisms

which have been made, I thought it as well to have that point publicly established."

"The brotherhood of medicine," murmured Bill Williams.

"Another point on which you may be able to enlighten us, Doctor. I presume that nicotine has an unpleasant taste."

"Certainly. Though not as unpleasant as most other toxic substances."

"But coffee would disguise the taste?"

"Yes. Particularly black coffee, or coffee heavily sweetened with sugar."

"I meant to ask about that. The coffee on this occasion was served black?"

"Yes. There was milk and sugar on the tables if you wanted them."

After one or two further questions the Coroner indicated that he had finished with Dr. McHarg, but the jury had not. A small juryman with a gnomelike face and pebble glasses, who seemed to have constituted himself an unofficial foreman, held up his hand and said, "Are we allowed to ask questions?"

"Certainly. Mr. Kinloch, isn't it?"

"That's right. What we'd like to know is why Dr. McHarg changed his mind."

"Did he?"

"We heard that he was going to give a death certificate, but changed his mind at the last moment."

"I can answer that," said Dr. McHarg. "I changed my mind when I haird from Dr. Scotland exactly what symptoms he had obsairved during the closing moments of the Archdeacon's life."

"And those were the symptoms of nicotine poisoning?"

"They were consistent with it."

"Then wasn't it Dr. Scotland's duty to report this to the police immediately?"

"I don't think we can criticize Dr. Scotland in his absence," said the Coroner. "He should be with us soon."

It was already nearly half past eleven and he was wondering whether the missing experts might have overslept.

They had not overslept. The three of them had started in very good time, in Dr. Leigh's aged Humber, and had soon been deep in medical shop. Crossing Blackwater Common, in the

174

middle of an interesting discussion on some recent theories about the circulation of the blood, they had suddenly realized that there was something very wrong with the circulation of their car. It had given a number of deep coughs—"Very like an asthmatic patient I once had," said Dr. Gadney—and had come to a halt.

Fortunately, the delay had not been long. An A.A. patrol had come past and had got to work with an air pump, observed by the doctors with the close interest of professionals watching another professional at work.

"A pity you couldn't deal with your patient like that," said Dr. Leigh. "We shall be a bit late, but I expect they'll wait for us."

They arrived at the exact moment that Dr. McHarg was quitting the stand. Dr. Gadney stepped into his place and was introduced to the jury, who looked gratified at meeting such an eminent medical authority.

"We have your report," said the Coroner. "It is a rather technical document and the jury might like a clarification of some points in it. Also we thought that you might want to elaborate on it."

"Thank you, sir," said Dr. Gadney. "I would welcome the opportunity of adding something to my report. Particularly since, with the kind assistance of Dr. Leigh from the Poisons Unit at New Cross, we have been able to make a further examination of the samples supplied to us and have some additional information which you may consider relevant."

James, who knew what was coming, was reminded of an expert diver poised on the high board, calculating the precise parabola of his flight, the exact moment to launch himself.

But Dr. Gadney was not quite ready to jump. First he explained, in simple terms, how the chromatograph worked, throwing up different peaks on the graph which could then be identified by spectrometry. The jury seemed to be following it all right.

"We were puzzled," he said, "by a small peak which eluted— I'm sorry—I mean, which appeared toward the end of the trace. It was only the exceptional capability of Dr. Leigh's new apparatus which showed it at all. However, having spotted it, we were able to identify it without too much difficulty. It was menthol."

There was a long pause. Then the Coroner said, "That was a curious thing to find, Dr. Gadney. What did you make of it?"

"It was a real puzzler. You appreciate, sir, that if the nicotine had come from a pharmacist, or even from some chemical compound like a weed-killer, it certainly would *not* have been mixed with menthol. So one was forced to look for some other source for the nicotine. It then occurred to us that it might have been obtained by mashing and distilling a number of what are called menthol cigarettes. This seemed quite a promising theory. When we looked into the matter further and succeeded in isolating traces of coteinine and nitrites, both indicating the presence of tobacco, the theory seemed not only possible but very probable indeed."

"That is a very interesting idea, Doctor. I have, of course, seen so-called menthol cigarettes advertised. Do they actually contain menthol?"

"Yes, sir. We were able to consult a colleague who is associated with one of the big tobacco groups. He told us that the menthol is either in the wrapping or in the filter. Less often in the tobacco itself. The manufacturers are careful to avoid any medical claims for their product. They simply describe the cigarettes as 'menthol cool.' But it became widely believed that they alleviated catarrh and other afflictions of the throat. Singers and speakers liked them for that reason. Also an idea got about that they were less likely to cause lung cancer than normal cigarettes. I do not know whether there was any truth in that, but it no doubt assisted their sales. They were particularly popular with women."

The Coroner thought about this. He said, "You spoke of distilling, Doctor. Would that be a very complex process?"

"Not in the least. You could do it, at a pinch, with ordinary kitchen equipment. In fact, I believe they sell simple distilling sets to schoolboys. You'd just boil the tobacco mash and distill off the vapor. Nothing to it. You'd get about two milligrams of nicotine from each cigarette. A lethal dose is usually calculated to be between forty and sixty milligrams. So, say twenty to thirty cigarettes."

James was observing the reactions of the jury. They looked disappointed and, he thought, resentful. It was as though they had imagined they were being presented with one problem to which they could see a straightforward and satisfactory answer and were suddenly faced with a different problem altogether.

The Coroner said, "Is that all that you wished to tell us, Doctor?"

"That is all that we have been able to detect, for the moment, from the samples submitted to us. We are still examining them."

The Coroner turned to Superintendent Bracher.

"In the light of what we have learned this morning, I imagine that the police would like a chance to conduct further inquiries."

Bracher nodded bleakly.

"In that case, I will adjourn the hearing for fifteen days." He looked at his calendar. "No. That will bring us to a Saturday. I had better say, until Monday fortnight. If the police require more time, we can always have a further adjournment. And, members of the jury, I think you agree that what we have heard demonstrates the advisability of all of us keeping open minds until the *whole* of the evidence is in front of us."

"All rise," said the coroner's officer.

Nineteen

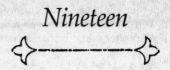

"Well," said Laporte sourly, "so where do we go from here?" It was Monday morning and he was feeling in a Monday-morning mood.

Superintendent Bracher said, "These damn doctors. You can't trust them. First they say one thing, then they say something different."

He had dumped down a loose-leaf binder on the Chief Constable's desk. It contained copies of reports and notes of interviews. It was already over a hundred pages thick.

He said, "I got a list from the secretary of the Friends—the people who were invited to that lunch do. Nearly two hundred. I pushed it round all the tobacconists in the area and got some names of people on the list they remembered who'd bought menthol cigarettes off 'em. Mostly women, like the doctor said. Mrs. Consett, Mrs. Henn-Christie, Lady Fallingford, Rosa Pilcher and the organist—what's his name?—Paul Wren. They're all from the Close. Then there's Mrs. Maggs, Mrs. Truelove, Mrs. Fisher and Mrs. Gilborne."

"Who the hell are they?"

"Just people. I know old Maggs. He owns the big ironmonger's shop in the Market Square. Mrs. Fisher's the wife of Edwin Fisher."

"The chap who runs the *Journal?*"

"Right. And Mrs. Gilborne . . . " Bracher paused for a moment. "You remember Gilborne, sir?"

"I think I do. Isn't he the solicitor who nearly got into trouble over some Cathedral funds he was handling? It was the Archdeacon who showed him up."

The two men stared at the list. Laporte said, "It doesn't get us much further, does it?"

Bracher said, "I'm told that Dean Forrest and his daughter are both non-smokers. Of course, that doesn't prove anything. I suppose that either of them could have gone up to London and bought menthol cigarettes there."

"It's possible," said Laporte. But he didn't sound as though he believed it.

"If you ask me, sir, we shan't get anywhere until people are prepared to start talking. Someone who was there *must* have seen something."

"Some of them did," said Laporte. "You never want to underestimate the strength of the S.P.A.C."

"That's a new one on me, sir."

"The S.P.A.C.," said Laporte, "is the Society for the Protection of Angelic Choristers. I imagine that every cathedral has one. Ours was in particularly good form over the weekend. I've had *fourteen* letters sent to me personally. Here's a list of the people who sent them. You can add them to your file. They all say more or less the same thing. They were served with coffee by one or other of those two boys. They add that they themselves were standing in a group, nowhere near the Archdeacon. Between them they had the boys under their eye the whole time and would be prepared one and all to go into the witness box and repeat, on oath, what they've spelled out in those letters. Now, what do you make of *that*?"

Bracher cast an eye down the list. Some of the names were very well known to him indeed. He said, "Put that crowd in the box, sir, and no one's going to believe a word of Rosa's little story."

"It goes a bit further than that, doesn't it? They aren't the sort of people who are going to commit perjury."

"No."

"Then that means that what they say is true and that Rosa wasn't just mistaken. She was lying. Lying publicly. Rather a dangerous thing to do, don't you think?"

"She was trying to shift the blame onto young Amanda. She loathes her and her father."

"Agreed," said Laporte. "But who was she shifting it *from*?"

While Bracher was thinking about this, he went on, "I've heard a lot of ideas lately about why different people would want to kill the Archdeacon. There's Driffield's theory. He's got a bee in his bonnet about disputes in the Chapter. And there's young Len Masters and that business of the silver cups—we know all about that. And I did hear there was some story about the organist, Wren, and the Archdeacon trying to sack him. But in my book none of these add up to a real motive for murder."

Bracher said, "I'd agree about Wren and Masters. And if it was anyone but Dean Forrest, I'd agree about that, too. But with a man like him you can't be sure. He's—well, sometimes he's hardly human."

"But I can think of a real motive for murder," said Laporte gently. "What about forty thousand pounds?"

Bracher said, "Yes." And, after a pause, again, "Yes."

"It's obvious when you come to think of it. Rosa had the motive. And the means. She was one of the people who bought menthol cigarettes. She had the run of the Archdeacon's kitchen to brew the stuff up. And she was in charge of the coffee. I was puzzled when I heard about that fourth jug on the serving table. If there were three servers, why did they want four jugs?"

"Answer being, I suppose, that Rosa had fixed it that way so that she could organize a special cup for the Archdeacon." Bracher was thinking it out slowly, visualizing, as policemen tended to do, how it would appear to a jury. He said, "If we could find someone who actually *saw* her handing the cup to the Archdeacon—"

"Or handing it to someone to hand to him."

"Right. Then I think we'd be justified in pulling her in. We must get the people who were near that table to start talking. It's only the Dean who's stopping them."

"I'm arranging to have a word with the legal boys in London about that," said Laporte. "I don't want to start a shooting war with the Church, but if that's the only way to get at the truth, then, by God, that's the way we'll have to do it."

"It was fantastic," said Amanda. "It was gorgeous. It was terrific. Poor old Bert Bracher. Did you see his face?"

"He took it hard," said James.

"I thought he was going to burst into tears. He had the whole
180

thing sewn up and it exploded right in his face. And now he doesn't know what to do next. I hear they've been round all the tobacconists asking who buys menthol cigarettes. Dozens of people, I should think. There was a great craze for them, I remember, about the time we first got here. And another thing, that nasty little plan of Rosa's has backfired. A lot of people, I know, have told the police those boys didn't go near the Archdeacon. They were dishing out coffee right over on the other side of the tent. Well, I could have told them that myself."

"I suppose," said James cautiously, "that you haven't got any idea—I mean, you were fairly well placed to see what was going on."

"You're forgetting what a scrum it was. Look—when did you last go to a tea party?"

"The last tea party I went to . . . That must have been at Lady Fallingford's, soon after I arrived."

"Were there a lot of people there?"

"No. Ten at the most."

"And can you remember who handed Mrs. Henn-Christie her cup of tea?"

"Well—no. I don't think I can."

"There you are, then. We were dishing out coffee to a couple of hundred people and trying to do it in about five minutes flat."

"All the same, I should have thought *someone* would have remembered. If they're all questioned—"

"They won't answer questions."

"Because of your father?"

"That's right."

"He won't get away with it. It's a direct challenge to the authority of the State."

"So what can they do?"

"I'm not sure. But no one fights dirtier than the establishment when it's up against it."

"If it comes to dirty fighting," said Amanda happily, "I guess Daddy can teach them a thing or two."

They were on their way, in Amanda's car, to play squash. James thought he had never seen Amanda so happy. She was bubbling over with high spirits. Part of it was relief, no doubt. But another part of it was the simple pleasure of seeing the civil authority make a fool of itself.

He said, "Anyway, it proves that I was right and you were wrong."

"About what?"

"Surely you can't have forgotten. What you said when we were on that walk. About scientists prying into matters they ought to leave alone and coming up with the wrong answers. They came up with the right answer this time."

This was rash of him. Amanda said, "You've got it all wrong, Buster. What I said was that scientists never know when they've reached the place where they ought to stop. Well, you've reached it now, haven't you?"

"I doubt if there's much more information to be extracted from those samples."

"Right. So you stop."

"Your father wouldn't agree with you. He said, 'When once you have put your hand to the plow, turn not back.'"

"Exactly," said Amanda triumphantly. "But when you've reached the end of the last furrow, you've got to stop. You don't want to start plowing up the road."

"Have it your own way," said James amicably.

When they got onto the court, the standard of their squash was found to have declined. They were neither of them thinking about the game. They were thinking about each other. After twenty minutes of indecisive play, James gave it up. He dropped his racquet and put one arm round Amanda. He could feel her body excitingly warm under the thin cotton singlet. Amanda said, "Ouch." Not in an offended sort of way, but as though she had put a hand on something unexpectedly hot or cold.

The next moment they were on the floor.

"I've never been so surprised in my life," said Major Mortleman. "I was up in the gallery and I came along to see if the court was empty and there they were, damn it, rolling about on the floor like a couple of copulating grass-snakes."

"Do you mean," said Brigadier Anstruther, "that they were actually—"

"No. I don't think they were actually—"

"Oh, well, then, I suppose it's not too bad."

"It's a bloody disgrace. Isn't her father a dean or something?"

"That's right. Rather an unusual man."

"Rather an unusual girl, I should say. You simply can't do things like that in a squash court."

James had managed to get both arms around Amanda and this was making driving difficult. She said, "It's no good, my sweet. Let's wait until we're married and can do it properly in bed."

"Nowadays people don't bother to wait until they're married. That's old-fashioned."

"I'm an old-fashioned girl," said Amanda. "By the way, did you notice, when we were in the court—I thought I saw a face looking down at us."

"Imagination," said James.

As they were approaching Brookes' gate, he said, "Oughtn't we to tell your father?"

"Of course. But not right now. He's been in rather an odd mood since the inquest."

"I should have thought he was deeply relieved."

"You can never tell with Daddy. He was a bit—I don't know—a bit like he was after that business with the Gangas."

James thought about this, but could make nothing of it. His mind was on the future, not the past. When, after a prolonged goodbye, he got into the drawing room, he sank back into one of the Chapter Clerk's old armchairs and allowed his eye to wander around the comfortable well-lived-in room. He and Amanda would put together such a room. There would be old furniture and pictures in heavy gold frames on the walls and china in cabinets. It would be some time before he could afford anything as fine as the *famille rose* bowls on the mantel shelf.

He remembered admiring them before and got up to examine them. They were the same pattern as Julia Consett's cups and saucers. Almost certainly they had once been part of the same set. No wonder she had wanted the bowls. A true collector's instinct.

James found his mind wandering down strange tracks. He remembered what he had said to Tom Lister in that conversation in the garden on the night the Canon had died. It was the analogy of the scientist moving down obscure weed-encumbered paths in his unending search for the truth.

When Dora Brookes came in and switched on the light, she said, "Goodness. I'd no idea you were here. You must have gone to sleep."

"I think I did doze off."

"Supper will be ready in ten minutes."

"Not for me, I'm afraid," said James. "I've got to go out."

This was literally true. He had got to go out. The thought of sitting still and making conversation was suddenly intolerable. He needed to think. He had got to be alone and he had got to be on the move.

If he had been asked afterward, he could not have said where his walk took him. Certainly he went a good way out of the town. At one moment he found himself on a bridge over the railway and sat on the stone coping, swinging his legs. Far away down the line he could hear the noise of trucks shunting, and he guessed from this that the fine weather was ending and that rain was on its way.

Some time later he walked back into the town. As he was crossing one of the streets in the business section, a car slid up behind him and a spotlight turned on. The voice of Superintendent Bracher said, "It's Dr. Scotland."

"Certainly it's me," said James irritably. "Am I breaking the law or something?"

"Not that I know of," said Bracher.

"Then stop shining that bloody light on me."

After a moment the light flicked off. He now saw that there was another police car at the far end of the street and there were two uniformed policemen further up the pavement. He wondered what the trouble had been. He concluded that it was nothing to do with him. As it happened, he was wrong about this.

Earlier that evening Philip Rosewarn had let himself into the offices of his employers, Maxwell Gloag and Partners, by a side door. It was his first essay in crime. His mouth was dry and his heart was thumping. Gerald Gloag's room was the largest in the building and fronted the street. He opened the door with the key Lucy had given him. He had brought a torch with him, but there was no need to use it. There was a streetlamp almost immediately outside the window which filled the room with diffused light.

He turned to the desk. This was the critical moment. Just give the front a good tug and it will come open, Lucy had said. He tried it, and at the second attempt the front swung up, revealing a clutter of papers and books and two sections of drawers, one on each side of a space in the middle, which housed account books and was flanked by two pillars, each topped by an ornamental wooden rose.

"All according to the book," said Philip. He grabbed the right-hand rose, which turned with a satisfactory click, and pulled. The pillar slid out, bringing with it a narrow vertical drawer. In the drawer was a ring with two keys on it. One was large and was clearly a safe key. The other looked as though it might be the key to a drawer or a small cupboard.

At this moment Philip heard footsteps coming along the pavement outside. The street, being in the business quarter, was little used at that time of night. Philip sank down into the desk chair. It was an unnecessary precaution, since the lower half of the window was covered with the fine wire mesh much favored by old-fashioned professional firms. However, he sat tight until the footsteps had died away. Then he got up, went over to the safe, put in the big key, turned it and pulled open the heavy door.

The front of the safe had another pile of account books in it. More interesting was a steel drawer at the back. Philip tried the smaller key on it, without success. He then reflected that since the drawer was inside the safe, there would have been no point in locking it. He tugged it and, sure enough, it was unlocked. He lifted it clear of the safe and laid it down on Gloag's desk to examine the contents at leisure.

He remembered that Bill had particularly wanted bank documents, paying-in books and check stubs. There were one or two envelopes with the name Barclays Bank on them, which struck him as odd, since the firm kept all its accounts with National-Westminster. Then it occurred to him that this must be Gloag's private account. There were also two clips of used checkbooks, held together by a rubber band.

He had got as far as this when he heard the car coming. It was coming fast. And it sounded like trouble.

He had very little time to think. He crammed the old check-books into his coat pocket, jumped for the door and raced along the passage. As he arrived at the top of the stairs, he could hear someone hammering on the front door.

He had reached the bottom of the stairs and was on the point of making for the side door he had come in by, when his mind started to work. Why should that policeman be *hammering* at the front door? He could hardly be expecting anyone to open it and, anyway, he was no doubt equipped with a key. Philip had done enough rabbiting in his youth to understand the technique. You put a ferret down the entrance to the warren and a net over the exit.

He swung away from the side door and raced back into the hall. There was a cupboard just inside the front door, used for coats and hats. It was shallow and the space at the back was full of old files, but he managed to insert his slender body into it and pull the door shut. As he did so, the hammering on the front door stopped. He heard the click of a key as the door opened and heavy footsteps, two men at least, coming down the hall and passing within a few inches of him. He waited until he was certain they were on their way upstairs, then opened the cupboard door and slipped out into the hall.

The front door had been left ajar. No time for finesse. He jumped down the three shallow steps outside and belted off up the pavement. The driver in the police car saw him and shouted. Then he started up the car and came after him. This was a mistake. There was a passage on the right of the road which was too narrow for motor traffic.

Philip dived down it and pursued a zigzag path through the side roads and passages which lay behind the business quarter. When he stopped to listen, he could hear nothing but the drumming of his own heart. His breathing steadied gradually. There was no sound of pursuit.

He thought that, with luck, he had not been recognized. He had disguised himself to the extent of wearing a pair of dark glasses and an old cap to cover his noticeable shock of light hair. The driver of the police car could hardly have seen more than his back as he ran up the street.

He removed the glasses, rolled up the cap and put it into his pocket and made tracks for the Black Lion, where he found Bill Williams alone in the private bar. Bill said, "Hello, Phil," and then, "What have you been up to?"

"Do I look as though I've been up to something?"

"You look as though you've had the fright of your young life. Put a comb through your hair, straighten your tie and have a drink. Not beer. What you want is a stiff whiskey. Right? Now—tell me all about it."

When Philip had told him, Bill said, "We might have thought of that. The cunning old bastard must have had his safe fixed with an alarm which went off in the police station. Do you think they recognized you?"

"I don't think they can have done."

"All's well that ends well, then. Let's have a look at what you've got. Not here, though. Better come round to my place."

Back in Bill's sitting room, Philip spread the loot on the table. He said, "I'm afraid these two lots of old checkbooks were all I could grab."

"Don't apologize," said Bill. "You did very well."

He was examining the check stubs, paying particular attention to their dates. He said, "The supermarket opened in Easter week the year before last. That's about eighteen months ago. But the site must have been bought at least six months earlier. Maybe even a year before. If it's here at all, it must be in one of these books."

"What exactly are we looking for?"

"What we're looking for is the pay-out. Gloag was fronting the deal, so the money would have been paid to him in the first place. Right? But the people who were behind him weren't the sort who'd want their share in grubby banknotes. They'd want a check. So—"

Bill's fingers had stopped moving through the check stubs.

"So?" said Philip.

"So . . ." said Bill softly. "Didn't I once tell you that the spilling of blood and the passage of money were two things that could never be entirely hidden?"

"I can't see much," said Philip, who was peering over his shoulder. "What are they? Four checks for twenty thousand pounds."

"Four checks, drawn on the same day, almost exactly two years ago. And four sets of initials. G.A. That would be Grant Adey, I imagine. L.D.S. Who other than Leo Derek Sandeman? A.B.D. That's Arthur Balfour Driffield and, finally, a gorgeous bonus. H.C.B. None other than Herbert Charles Bracher. The Council, the press *and* the police. What a gang. What a lovely little thieves' kitchen."

"What are you going to do about it?"

"I'm going to blow them up. There's the powder and the detonator." He patted the checkbook fondly.

"You won't be able to say how you got hold of them."

"You don't understand the workings of the press, my lad. A fact is a wedge. The press is the hammer that drives it in. Suppose we suggest that these four men and Gloag used their position and official information to make themselves a hundred thousand pounds for a paltry ten-thousand-pound stake, what can they do? They can fluff and bluster, but if they took us to court, they'd have to stand up and deny, on oath, that they were paid twenty thousand pounds each on a certain day by their fellow conspirator, Gloag. Well, they can't do it. Because it's now a cold, provable *fact*."

"How are you going to work it?"

"I'll have to think about it. We'll start with the easy bit. Show how little the gang had to pay for the site. Dr. Scotland's our main witness there. I'll have a word with him first."

A telephone call to the Chapter Clerk's house produced the information that Dr. Scotland was not there.

"He walked out, just before supper," said Dora Brookes. "I don't know where he went. Someone from London has been trying to get hold of him, too."

She sounded worried.

"It's quite all right," said Williams. "This is nothing urgent. Tell him I'll look him up tomorrow."

Mrs. Brookes promised to do this. She said to her husband, who had been listening to the conversation, "Why don't you go to bed? You look all in."

"It's the weather," said Brookes. "I always feel like this when it's building up for a storm."

"I'll wait up for him," said his wife. "You go on up."

She had not long to wait. It was about half past ten when

James came back. He said, "I felt the first drops of rain as I came up the path. I think the weather's broken at last."

Dora gave him the telephone messages. She said, "Williams didn't sound too urgent. But the other message was from Dr. Leigh. He wondered if you could come up to London as soon as possible."

"Dr. Leigh from the Poisons Unit?"

"That's right. The man who was at the inquest. Not the one who gave evidence. The tall doctor who was with him. He said he'd found something that would interest you."

"Did he say what it was?"

"No. He just said it was something interesting. I expect he didn't try to explain it to me because he knew I wouldn't understand it. You *will* go, won't you?"

"Yes," said James. Curiously, the possibility of saying "no" never crossed his mind.

Twenty

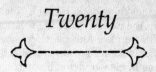

WHEN JAMES GOT TO BED, he was very tired, but sleep evaded him. Every time he approached the verge, some cut-out mechanism seemed to operate. It was as though he was unwilling to trust his subconscious, being afraid of where it might lead him when he could no longer control it.

At last, when the approach of dawn was turning the windows gray, he did drop into a deep sleep, to be awakened by a hand on his shoulder. It was Dora Brookes. She said, "I do apologize for bursting in on you like this, Doctor, but I knocked two or three times and didn't get as much as a grunt out of you. If you're planning to catch the nine-o'clock train, you won't have much time for breakfast."

"A cup of coffee will be all I'll want," said James. He looked blear-eyed at his watch and discovered that it was already five past eight. When he had thrown his clothes on and got down to the dining room, he found that only one place was laid.

Dora said, "Henry's not himself this morning. I'm giving him his breakfast in bed. He gets these migraines. Some of it's the weather and some of it's worry."

"It's been a worrying time for everybody," agreed James. "And as for the weather, I don't think I've ever seen anything quite like it."

He had been conscious, as he lay awake, of the relentless drumming of the rain on the roof. It had stopped for the moment, but a solid bank of black clouds, mounting with ominous slowness behind the Cathedral, gave promise of more and worse to come.

"It's something to do with the winds," said Dora. "Tom Lister once tried to explain it to me. There's one wind brings the rain in from the sea and there's a different one off the escarpment that prevents it from going away again. The last time it happened, about twenty years ago, it rained for two whole days and nights without stopping and the river flooded and the chairs in the Cathedral went floating down the aisle. He showed me a photograph of it."

"As long as I can get to the station without being drowned," said James.

"I'll lend you one of Henry's umbrellas. If you get a move on, you ought to be all right."

James had a call to make on his way to the station. He hoped it would not hold him up too long, and there he was lucky. As he was passing the front of the school, Penny spotted him from the window and waved. He waved back, and for Penny this was a sufficient invitation. She came bouncing down the path, dodging in and out of the puddles.

"And where is the promising young pathologist off to?"

This was a description of James which had appeared in the press when reporting the inquest and had been following James around ever since.

"I'm catching a train," said James. "And I'm in a hurry, so cut out the cross-talk. There's something I want to know and you can tell me."

"Carry on, Sherlock."

"Exactly how old is your father and when is his birthday?"

Penny started to say, "Why on earth—?" but the look in James' eye stopped her. She said, "He's coming up to forty-two, and if you want to give him a present, you're just in time. His birthday's next Monday."

"Thank you," said James.

He looked, thought Penny, as though what she had told him was bad news, but that he had been expecting it. She said, "What's it all about, James?"

"Can't stop, or I'll miss the train."

He loped off, half running, half walking. Penny watched him go. She wondered whether she ought to say something about it to her mother and decided not to.

James caught his train with two minutes to spare and had time to buy a selection of the morning papers. It was when he reached the center page of the *Guardian* that the headlines of the second leading article hit him.

BECKET AT MELCHESTER, it said, with the subheading, CHURCH AGAINST STATE.

The writer had evidently been at the inquest, had been intrigued by what he had heard, and had snooped around the town a bit.

"The inquiry into the death of Archdeacon Pawle, who died at Melchester three weeks ago last Saturday, has reached a point at which the authorities must be wishing they could call on a quartet of knights and say to them, 'Who will rid me of this turbulent priest?' Unfortunately, such rough remedies are no longer available, and it seems that in this Cathedral city, with its ancient buildings and its medieval traditions, the Church is held in greater respect than the State. Dean Matthew Forrest has forbidden the inhabitants of the Close to co-operate with the police. They are to answer no questions and give them no assistance. 'Render unto Caesar the things that are Caesar's,' appears to be his attitude, 'but to God the things that are God's.' Inside the Close it is the Dean, as God's regent, who lays down the guidelines. This has resulted in a deadlock which the police seem powerless to break. . . . "

"And that's not going to please them," thought James.

Dr. Leigh was waiting for him in his office at New Cross. He greeted him warmly and said, "I apologize for dragging you all the way up from Melchester. Actually, I had two reasons. I'll tell you about the second one later. It was Bill Gadney who suggested to me that we might tackle the very far end of the spectrum. I think he really wanted to see if our gas-chromatograph was all we had cracked it up to be."

"At the *very* far end? Wouldn't there be a good deal of distortion?"

"That's what Bill thought, I don't doubt. And it wasn't an easy operation. We had to make dozens of micro-readings and compare the results."

"Average them?"

"You could call it that, I suppose. It really meant rejecting the freaks and concentrating on anything that looked at all consistent. My principal assistant—do you remember Ron Highway?"

James laughed, for the first time on that dismal day. "Certainly I remember Ron. We used to call him the Armadillo. An armor-plated exterior and a long inquiring nose."

Dr. Leigh laughed too. He said, "Well, he got so keen on the job that I couldn't drag him away from it. I should think he spent more than thirty working hours glued to that machine. And he did get some very interesting results." Dr. Leigh looked serious again. "Our results will have to go to the police, of course. I telephoned Bill last night and he suggested that I ought to have a word with you first. He'd have come down here himself, only he's got involved with that mass food-poisoning scare at Leamington. Here's a summary of our findings. Acetone, butyl alcohol, iso-propyl alcohol and butyric acid. I needn't tell you what that means."

As James moved around to look at the paper on the desk, he became aware of two things. The first was that his legs felt curiously weak. The second was that he might be going to pass out.

Dr. Leigh must have observed something, because he said, "What's up, James? Are you feeling rotten? Sit down and take it easy."

"Stupid of me," said James. "I'll be all right in a moment. The fact is, I had rather a bad night and I skipped breakfast."

Dr. Leigh opened a cupboard, extracted a squat unlabeled bottle, poured a generous quantity from it into a glass and said, "Put that down. It'll warm your stomach and clear your head. No heel taps. There now. Is that better?"

"Much better," said James, when he had got his breath back. "What is it?"

"Secret recipe of the Poisons Unit. We call it the corpse-galvanizer. Before we do any more talking, we must get some food into you. I've booked a table for three at a little place round the corner. Bunny's joining us there. It's not far, but I think we'll take my car. It looks as if we're going to get a spot of rain before long."

"You'll be lucky if it's only a spot," said James. He explained that a sort of stationary cloudburst seemed to have settled over Melchester. "I think perhaps that was one of the things that upset me."

The little place around the corner turned out to be a wine

193

lodge, with a back room which had half a dozen tables in it. The Medical Registrar was already in possession of one of them.

"I told you there were two reasons for dragging you up to town," said Dr. Leigh. "Bunny's the second one. He's got some news for you."

"I hope you'll think it good news," said the Registrar. "I certainly do. You probably know that I've been badgering the Governors for some time to let me have a proper Number Two. I've always wanted you for the job. Originally they jibbed at the idea of appointing a pathologist. I told them being a pathologist didn't mean that you couldn't do an administrative job as well. Anyway, I convinced them. It'll mean more money, of course, quite a lot more. And there's a flat goes with the job. I hope you'll say yes."

"I won't only say yes," said James breathlessly, "I'll say thank you very much. It's terrific news." He thought for a moment. "When you said a flat—would it be big enough for two?"

Both men looked at him. Then Dr. Leigh waved an imperious hand and said to the waiter, who came scurrying up, "I see we're going to need a bottle of champagne. Don't bother about putting it on ice. Just bring it along with three glasses. Who is she?"

"As a matter of fact, it's Amanda Forrest."

"The Dean's daughter? The one they were making a dead set against at that inquest?"

"Until you and Bill Gadney came and stood them all on their heads."

"You ought to have been there, Bunny," said Dr. Leigh. "By God, there's not been anything like it since St. George killed the dragon and rescued the beautiful damsel."

"Was the Coroner being difficult?"

"No. Let's be fair. He was all right. But it was a hanging jury if ever I saw one."

The champagne arrived and Amanda's health was drunk.

"I only wish Bill could have been here," said Dr. Leigh. "That would have made it perfect."

James was feeling extraordinarily warm and happy. Part of it, no doubt, was reaction from the gloom of the morning, but there was more to it than that. These were not only friends, they were colleagues. They were the sort of people he liked dealing

194

with. Adult people who thought professionally and didn't allow sentiment to cloud their judgment. This was his real life. The other life, the life he had become involved in when he had stepped into Melchester Close a month ago, was a fantasy. A world peopled by men and women motivated by childish animosities and raw emotions. The whole thing could easily have been a dream. The only real character in it was Amanda, and he proposed to extract her from it as soon as he possibly could.

"You've said nothing for three minutes," said the Registrar. "I hope your thoughts were happy ones."

"Most of them," said James apologetically. "There's one piece of business I've got to clear up. It's not going to be agreeable, but it's got to be done. I'm afraid you must have thought I was a bit stupid when you were talking about Ron Highway's work, but I did understand what it meant."

"It's answered your immediate problem, has it?"

"Yes," said James sadly. "I'm afraid it has."

At three o'clock that afternoon Valentine Laporte summoned a council of war.

Present were Chief Superintendent Terry, head of the uniformed branch; his deputy, Superintendent March; Bracher, representing the C.I.D.; and Grant Adey in his capacity as chairman of the Watch Committee of the Borough.

They had all read the article in the *Guardian* and they were all angry.

"Any help you want from the Council," said Adey, "I'll guarantee you get it. The man's making a laughingstock of all of us. It's got to stop."

There was a rumble of assent.

Laporte said, "I've taken advice from our legal people. They say the position's clear enough. Anyone can refuse to answer questions. We know that. But if you can prove that someone is trying to prevent other people from answering questions, that's obstructing the police in the execution of their duty. He can be taken in and charged. And what's more, he can be refused bail."

"Kept inside, you mean," said Adey.

"Until he gives suitable undertakings. Yes."

"But you've got to be able to prove obstruction."

"Do we need any more proof than that?" He pointed to a

piece of paper on the table. "Everyone in the Close got one of those last night."

The document, which had apparently been typed and then photocopied, said:

> As you will know, one of the possible reasons which was put forward to account for the sudden death of Archdeacon Pawle was that he had contracted virus pneumonia. This is a very dangerous and highly contagious disease. Since there is a possibility that this infection may have been passed on to other members of our Close community, I have decided, in the general interest, to declare the Close an area of possible contagion. Until further notice, no members of the public will be admitted on any pretext whatsoever. You will, no doubt, have to go out, but you are advised to keep your contacts with the town to a minimum.
>
> SIGNED: Matthew Forrest. Dean.

"Is he enforcing this?" said Adey.

"He certainly is," said Bracher. "All gates except the High Street Gate have been locked, and Mullins or one of his assistants is on duty the whole time."

"I suppose it's medical nonsense," said Terry.

"Complete nonsense," said Laporte. "I've spoken to Dr. McHarg. The Archdeacon had been down in the docks area three or four days before he died. That's what gave some color to the original theory that he might have caught the disease. The maximum reinfection period is six days. The Archdeacon died— for God's sake—more than three *weeks* ago. Twenty-four days, to be precise. Of course it's nonsense."

"That's clear enough, then," said Terry. "Pull him in."

There was a moment of silence. Everyone was thinking of Dean Forrest locked up in a cell below the police station. The idea thus suddenly presented was so inappropriate as to be almost outrageous.

Adey said, "Might it just be worth making one last effort to induce him to see sense? If he knew what was going to happen if he refused—"

"How are we going to talk to him when he won't come out and won't let us in? He's not even on the telephone."

"I was thinking about that. One man he might listen to is his own Chapter Clerk. Henry Brookes is quite a sensible bloke. I had a lot of dealings with him when he was an estate agent in the town. And he hasn't been in that Close long enough to get infected with the ecclesiastical bug."

"How do we get hold of him?"

"Telephone him. Say that I suggested it. I think he'll come."

The others considered it. They were none of them enthusiastic about the idea of imprisoning a leading churchman. At the back of their minds were old ideas of sanctuary and clerical immunity. The shadow of the Cathedral loomed over them.

"If we do see Brookes," said Laporte, "we shall have to tell him most of the truth. That this evidence we're looking for is the last link in the chain. To put the matter bluntly, that by preventing us from getting it, the Dean is protecting a particularly unpleasant and unscrupulous murderer."

"Name her, you mean?"

"I don't think we can go as far as that. But, short of putting a name to the suspect, we'll have to put our cards on the table. Then he can take back a message to the Dean which he can't misunderstand: Either he helps us or we pull him in."

"I agree with that," said Adey. "But what if he says no?"

The Chief Constable looked at his watch. He said, "This has got to be finished tonight. The weather will be a help. There won't be too many people about. We'll reconvene at eight o'clock, gentlemen."

The down train reached Melchester at six o'clock, fifty minutes late and spouting water like a whale. What might have been a tedious journey had been enlivened for James by the presence of Lady Fallingford, who had also been up to London. She had a copy of the Dean's circular. She had approved of it strongly and had said so.

"It'll keep that nasty creature Brasher or Brayford or whatever he calls himself away from darlings like Claribel Henn-Christie, who couldn't say boo to a goose. It's lucky for him he hasn't tried his third-degree tactics on *me*."

James said, "He can't keep the police out forever."

"Not forever. But for a good long time. Then everyone will be able to say, 'Oh, that's so long ago, I've forgotten all about it.'"

"I hope you're right. It was a pretty risky step."

Lady Fallingford gave a throaty chuckle and said, "He's a man who likes taking risks. From what I've heard, he's spent most of his life taking them."

When the train drew into Melchester, there was a rush for the ticket hall, led by two men in dirty raincoats. The ones who were first out grabbed the three taxis which serviced the station. Almost everyone else decided to wait for their return. Only a few brave spirits fancied stepping out into the unrelenting downpour. James and Lady Fallingford took their places on the end of the long bench in the ticket hall. Counting the numbers ahead of them, he reckoned that they might have to wait for a third or fourth relay.

The taxis had come back once and picked up a second load of passengers when Bill Williams arrived on his motorcycle. He had defied the weather in a complete suit of black rubber and came in off the forecourt dripping water, like a diver emerging from the sea.

He said, "James! Just the man I wanted." He gestured toward the door of the inner waiting room. James got up and followed him, shutting the door behind him. There was no one else there.

Bill said, "Just when I needed you, you have to go gallivanting up to the metropolis. Things have been moving down here, I can tell you. And they're coming to a head tonight. That article in the *Guardian* was the last straw."

"I didn't think the authorities would like it."

"They're hopping mad. They're going to present the Dean with an ultimatum: Either he lifts his ban or they pull him in."

"Arrest him?"

"Right."

"On what charge?"

"Obstruction, or something of the sort."

"Because of that circular he sent round? Lady Fallingford showed it to me in the train. A bit drastic, but not entirely unreasonable."

"They're prepared to argue about that in court. If it gets that far. They don't think it will. They think that when it comes to the point, he'll give in. Though, personally, I rather doubt it."

James thought about it. He said, "How do you know about all this?"

Bill said, "If I tell you, in strict confidence, that one of our girls has got a bosom friend—and, incidentally, what a bosom, but never mind about that—who's a typist at the police station, you can imagine that we're kept pretty well in the picture."

"I often wondered how the press got its information. But there's still one thing I don't see. You said, just when you needed *me*. How do I come into this?"

Bill got up, opened the door and looked out. He said, "It'll be ten minutes before you can move. I can see that I started at the wrong place." He shut the door, came back and sat down. "The fact is, old Fisher's promised me a Wednesday extra."

"A Wednesday extra?"

"Just a double sheet. To come out tomorrow. It's not something we do very often. It's too damned expensive. Overtime for the printers and no advertising. But we make it up in goodwill and publicity. The first time we did it, I'm told, was when the Kaiser's War was thoughtless enough to start itself on a Tuesday."

"And this one is going to be about the Dean's arrest?"

"That would be part of it. But it wouldn't be worth an extra by itself. For one thing, we couldn't beat the national press on it. There were men from the *Mirror* and the *Express* on the train with you."

"Were they the two men who trod on everyone's toes getting to the door and grabbed the first taxis?"

"That sounds like them," said Bill with a grin. "Pushful lads. No doubt they'll pick up the story and it will be in their papers tomorrow. So we've got to do better than that. *And we can.* Because we've got the other half of the story and they haven't. But if I'm going to write it, I've got to be on the spot tonight, and that's where you can help me."

James was going to say that he didn't see why he should involve himself, but changed his mind at the last moment. This new development had opened up a number of possibilities, some of them disturbing.

He said, "Help you? How?"

"I expect I can get into the Close. Though it's not going to be too easy. The river's over its banks already. But once I'm there, I'll have to have somewhere to work from. I've written a lot of the story—the background and that sort of stuff—but the part that matters will have to be dictated directly from the battlefront. I could base myself on the school cottage, all right. Alan and Peter wouldn't have objected to that, I'm sure. But it hasn't got a telephone. So I had this idea. You're staying with Henry Brookes. He's a broad-minded sort of chap. Why couldn't I do the whole thing from his house?"

James was now not only alarmed, he was angry. He said, "I see no reason why Brookes should help you to crucify the Dean in your bloody paper."

Bill looked astonished and hurt. He said, "I'm not explaining this very well. We're not going to crucify the Dean. We're on his side. We're going to help him."

"You think publicity is going to help him?"

"The right sort of publicity."

"Are you serious?"

"No fooling. Totally serious. What we're going to suggest is that the police are taking this outrageous step in order to discredit the Dean *before he discredits them*. A typical fascist ploy. If someone's in a position to hurt you, blacken his character first. Then no one will believe anything he says."

"And how exactly is the Dean going to discredit the police?"

"By publishing the fact that a leading policeman, Detective Superintendent Bracher, was one of the parties to the supermarket swindle."

"Can he do that?"

Bill looked a bit embarrassed. He said, "He can't, not at the moment. But *we* can. And once the truth's out, it'll be easy enough to suggest that the Dean knew about it all along."

"I see," said James. He knew enough about newspaper tactics to realize that what Bill had said was plausible. He said, "You'll have to have some definite proof."

Bill had been unzipping the front of his waterproof jacket. Now he brought out a pouch, opened it and laid four pieces of paper on the table. James could see that they were blown-up photographs of what looked like check stubs.

"The originals are safely locked in the bank," said Bill. "But these will show you that we mean business. Four payments of twenty thousand pounds each, made two years ago by Gloag to his partners in crime. Because the supermarket deal *was* a crime. Aren't they beautiful? Two members of the Council, both with inside knowledge of the new ring road. The press represented by Arthur Driffield of the *Melset Times*—I think that was what finally persuaded my boss to go ahead with the extra—and last, but by no means least, H.C.B., for Herbert Charles Bracher."

James carried the fourth photograph over to the window. He stood there for a long minute, looking at it. Then he said, "You'll have to cancel your extra. You can't use this."

"What do you mean?"

"You've made a very common mistake: You saw what you wanted to see. You knew that Bracher was a crony of the other three and you hoped he'd be involved. If you looked at this without any preconceived ideas, you'd have seen that the middle initial isn't C. It doesn't really even look like C. It's G."

Bill looked from the photograph to James and back again to the photograph. The expression on his face was one part dawning realization and two parts horror.

Lady Fallingford put her head around the door and said, "Our taxi's coming up."

"Negative," said Bracher. "Total negative."

"All right," said Laporte. "That means we go ahead. The first thing we decide is how we're going to get into the Close." He turned to Terry. "I understand we've had a bit of a setback there."

"The thing is," said Terry, "during the war the gates had to be kept open so that fire engines and rescue crews could get in if needed. Which, luckily, they weren't. However, when the war was over, we somehow forgot to give our set of keys back. Maybe we thought they'd come in useful. Of course, they're only keys to the wicket gates. The main gate's barred or bolted on the inside."

"That's all right, then," said Adey. "Go in through the wicket and open the main gate."

"It would be all right," said Terry, who came from Devonshire and liked to deploy facts slowly, "only when we tried them, they didn't work. They must have changed the locks sometime."

"Crafty," said Bracher. "I wouldn't be surprised if it wasn't the Dean did that."

"All right," said Laporte. "We go in over the river."

"Difficult," said Terry, "and dangerous. By last reports, it was two foot over its banks and running like a millrace."

Adey said, "If it's just a question of putting your men over the wall at some quiet spot, we could lend you one of those hoists. The sort of thing we use for servicing the overhead street-lamps."

Laporte thought about it. He had a sudden vision of one of his policemen poised in a metal bucket on the end of a long expanding arm. He said, "No. I'd like to keep this as simple as possible. All we need is a couple of twelve-foot ladders from the Fire Brigade."

"No difficulty," said Adey. "No need to turn out a fire engine. They can be carried on a tender."

"Right. We run the tender up to the River Gate. The road there's a dead end. Tell the driver to take the tender about twenty yards along and stop. Then one of the police cars backs in after it, blocking the entrance. The second one stands by. As soon as the cars are in position, run one of the ladders up. There's a line of barbed wire on top of the wall. You'll need wire-cutters. As soon as the wire's clear, haul the second ladder over the top and put it down inside." He looked at the plan. "That should mean that the first men over are just inside the gate. They remove the bars, undo the bolts and open it."

"Suppose they've got some sort of guard on it."

"If they try to stop you opening the gate," said Terry, "you can deal with them as you think necessary. It's only the bloody clerics we've got to handle with kid gloves."

The Chief Constable nodded. The last thing he wanted was to have anyone hurt, but he had got well past the point where he was going to stand any nonsense from people like young Ernie.

"Once the gate's open, both cars drive in. One goes up to the front door of the Deanery, the other one stays outside the gate as a rear guard."

Terry noticed that the Chief Constable had started to talk like a soldier. Normally, this irritated him, but on this occasion there was some comfort in it. What was proposed seemed more a military than a police operation.

"As soon as you've secured the Dean, drive out with him. Then reverse the process. Bolt and bar the gate, get back over the wall, remove the ladders and return to base."

"Timing?"

"The later we go, the less people will be about. But we don't want to drag the old boy out of bed. H-hour ten-thirty. That should be about right."

At ten o'clock James was sitting with Dora Brookes in the drawing room listening to the wireless. Henry had retired to his room immediately after supper. It had been a silent meal. Dora was tackling her faithful piece of embroidery, but James could tell that her mind was on other things. He had started to read, but could make no sense of the words and had given up.

"Persistent rain in the south and west," said the wireless, "has already caused serious flooding in many towns, including Salisbury, where the water is already invading the Close, and to a lesser extent in Melchester and at Romsey Abbey. Meteorological experts have pointed out that the contra-effluxion of air currents has produced conditions very similar to those that prevailed in Florence in November 1966, though it is to be hoped that the damage in this case will not be on anything approaching a similar scale."

James wondered why experts on the wireless should always say things like "the contra-effluxion of air currents" when they meant winds blowing in opposite directions. Dora bundled up her sewing and said, "I'd better go up and see if Henry wants anything."

James stood up too, switched off the wireless, then returned to his seat and sat in silence. Even the drumming of the rain was shut out by the heavy casements and the thick old-fashioned curtains.

He heard Dora's footsteps going upstairs and along the passage toward the bedroom at the far end. He knew, with the certainty of foreknowledge, what was going to happen and found himself gripping the arms of the chair he was sitting in, like a patient at a dentist's waiting to be hurt.

There was a moment of silence and then the footsteps came clattering downstairs fast. They paused, but did not turn toward the drawing room. They went away, along the downstairs passage.

James had not expected this. He got to his feet, opened the

door and looked out. Dora was coming back. Her face was white and set.

She said, "He's gone out. I'd bolted the side door, but it's unbolted now. He must have gone that way. What can he have been thinking of?"

When James did not answer, she came past him into the drawing room and said, "You were talking to him in his bedroom before dinner. Did he say anything? Did he give you any idea—?"

"I'd no idea he was planning to go out."

Dora seemed to detect the evasion in this answer. She said, "Of course I could see he was worried. It's been coming on for the last two days. At one time I thought it was the weather. Now I think it must be something else. Something worse."

Neither of them had sat down. They were standing, facing each other, like people in the presence of a sudden crisis.

He could still find nothing to say. Dora said, more sharply, with an edge of suspicion in her voice now, "You were a long time together. What *did* you talk about?"

James had opened his mouth to speak, although he had still not the least idea what he could say, when the interruption occurred. The front-door bell rang. He went quickly along the passage and opened the door.

It was Amanda. She looked like a creature of the river. Her thin summer coat was clinging to her like a skin, and her eyes peered out from a tangle of hair smeared down over her face.

She said to Dora, who had appeared behind him, "I'll stop here. If I come in, I'll ruin your carpet. It's Daddy. He seems to have disappeared."

"When?" said James.

"I don't know. I don't think he's been in all evening. I thought one of the vergers might know where he was. They've both gone too. Mrs. Grey was very worried. There's a light on in the Cathedral. Do you think they might all be there?"

"We'll go and see," said James. He was pulling on his raincoat. He said to Dora, "Don't worry. I expect we shall find Henry there too," and then he plunged out into the streaming night. The path to the west door was so slippery that it was better to go hand in hand.

They found Masters on guard inside the west door. He was

armed with a pick helve. He said, "You'd better both come in before you get drowned." He sounded more amused than excited. As he stood by the open door, he added, "Just before you came, I saw two lots of car headlights. I guess they've got the River Gate open."

Neither of them needed to ask what he was talking about.

The only lights in the Cathedral were in the Choir, where the Dean was standing in front of the altar. He, too, seemed cheerful. When they told him about the cars, he said, "So the police have arrived, have they? They'll be here as soon as they find I'm not in the house. Would you go, James, and tell Grey—you'll find him at the south door—not to try to keep them out. Amanda, tell Masters the same thing. There's to be no violence at all. Make sure they understand."

They both sped off. James found Grey standing inside the door which led out to the cloisters. He stared vacantly at James, but seemed to understand what he was saying.

When James got back to the Choir, the police were coming through the west door, four of them, led by Superintendent Bracher. They advanced steadily, their boots thumping on the stone flags of the aisle. The Dean drew himself up to his full height. James thought, "He really is playing at Becket. He'd like them to kill him at the high altar of his own cathedral. Only, of course they won't—they're not playing to the same script."

The Dean said, "What can I do for you, gentlemen?"

Bracher took a piece of paper from his pocket. He had been told what to say and he was not trusting his memory. He said, "Dean Matthew Forrest, I have been instructed to inform you that unless you undertake to stop obstructing the police of this Borough in the execution of their duty, you are to be taken into custody and detained in custody until you give acceptable undertakings to that effect."

"And suppose I refuse to go with you?"

"Then we shall have to take you, using as little force as is necessary."

"To lay hands on a clergyman, robed and in his own church, is contrary to Canon Law."

"I don't know about Canon Law," said Bracher stolidly. "I only know about the law of the land."

"He's lost," thought James. "It's not going to work." He had a picture of the Dean being half led, half carried down the aisle. It was horrible.

Footsteps came stumbling along the south transept and Grey ran up to the Dean. James thought for a moment that it was a rescue attempt. Then he saw his face.

"You've got to come." His voice was a croak of panic and distress. "It's Mr. Brookes. In the vestry."

The Dean said, "Pull yourself together, Grey. What are you trying to tell us?"

"He's dead."

"I think perhaps this is something you'd better look into, Superintendent. I shan't run away."

Bracher hesitated, then nodded to his men to stay behind, said, "You'd better come with me, Doctor," and strode off quickly. When they reached the vestry, the door was open and the lights were all on. Henry Brookes was sitting exactly as the Archdeacon had sat, slumped in the chair, his head lolling over to one side. It was only too clear that he was dead.

There were two envelopes on the vestry table. Bracher looked down at them without touching them and said, "This one's for you, Doctor. I think you'd better read it now, if you don't mind. It might give us some idea what to do next." He sounded puzzled and angry.

James picked up the envelope. As he did so, he noted that the second one was addressed to the Dean.

The note inside was in Brookes' handwriting, which betrayed something of the emotions which must have been moving him as he wrote it.

> My dear James,
>   Will you break the news to my wife. She likes you and trusts you. I've been trying to think that I'm doing this because the police were going to arrest someone else. They as good as told me so this afternoon. But it was no use. I couldn't fool myself. I'm doing it because I realize that everything you told me this evening will have to be told to the police tomorrow. I've left a full explanation for the Dean. There was some of the nicotine left, so this seemed the easiest way.

"Easy, my God," said James, looking at the signs all about him of Brookes' death agony.

Bracher read the letter slowly and then said, "Perhaps you'd better let the Dean have the other one. It may make things a bit clearer."

He seemed unwilling to touch it. James picked it up. As they went back, Bracher said to Grey, "Lock the door and give me the key."

In the Choir they found the policemen standing in a group, uncomfortably shuffling their feet. The Dean was on his knees in front of the altar. They also found Canon Humphrey, who had arrived from somewhere. James walked down with him, between the Choir stalls, until they were out of earshot and explained what had happened.

Canon Humphrey said, "Poor Henry. God rest his soul." They walked back to where Bracher was standing, undecided what to do next.

Canon Humphrey said, "I don't think I should disturb him now, Superintendent. Anything that has to be said can be better said in the morning."

Twenty-one

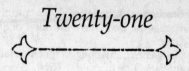

"I SET MORE STORE ON EVIDENCE than on confessions," said Bracher. "That's why I've asked you, Mr. Dean, to show me what is in that letter and you, Doctor, to explain what it was you said to Brookes yesterday evening that induced him to take his own life."

It was ten o'clock on the following morning and they were sitting in the Dean's study. The rain had stopped and a pale sun was peering ineffectively through the mist which had followed the downpour.

The Dean said, "The letter names other people. It may call for action against them."

"We can make our minds up about that when we know what's in it."

Still the Dean hesitated. Then he said, "I'm not going to hand it over to you. But I'll read you the bits that matter."

Bracher looked as though he would have liked to protest, but evidently decided to accept half a loaf, for the time being.

The Dean seemed to be skipping the opening sentences. Then he read out, "'Two years ago, I was presented with a chance of making a substantial amount of money. It came at a time when my business had failed. I had sold out to Gloag for a sum which just allowed me to pay off my business liabilities, but I was embarrassed by a number of small personal loans and debts to tradesmen. Coming at the moment it did, when I'd been offered the post of Chapter Clerk, it seemed providential. I could pay everyone off, have something in hand and start with a clean sheet. The offer, as you will have guessed, came from Gloag and his backers in the supermarket deal, Sandeman, Driffield and Grant Adey. They realized I would guess what they were up to and, unless they took me in, I'd warn off Mrs. Henn-Christie. The difficulty was that the opening stake for the five of us was £2,000 each and I simply hadn't got it. I decided to borrow the money for a few months from the Fabric Fund, which was normally under my control. I reckoned that Archdeacon Henn-Christie would never have noticed the in and out payment, particularly when the money had been restored—as it was three months later. I was equally certain that Archdeacon Pawle would notice it and question it. I had a breathing space, because his attention was first devoted to the Cathedral trusts and the school and college accounts. But my turn was coming. It wasn't pleasant waiting for the blow to fall. I was uncomfortable for another reason. Gloag and Sandeman knew I was hard up and I think they suspected where the £2,000 had come from. So I had to keep in with them. It wasn't anything very important. Things like telling them, from time to time, what happened in Chapter.'"

The Dean put the letter down and said, "So he thought that a breach of professional confidence was a small matter."

"Compared with embezzlement," said Bracher, "surely it was."

"Both were equal breaches of faith," said the Dean. He picked up the letter. "'I had read in some technical magazine about how you could distill nicotine from cigarettes and I had my brewing apparatus and the cigarettes. My Aunt Alice used to smoke them. She left a store of them in a cupboard in her bedroom. So it wasn't a difficult operation, but I was horribly careless. Dr. Scotland will tell you about that.'"

"Afterward," said James. He saw that the Dean had reached the last page of the letter.

"'About a month ago I had a note from the Archdeacon asking me to make all my accounts and records available. I knew then that I had to act. The opportunity came at the Friends luncheon. I stationed myself at the far end of the serving table, took the first available cup of coffee, put in the nicotine and carried the cup to the Archdeacon.'"

It seemed to James that there was a passage at the end of the letter which the Dean read to himself. He saw his lips moving. Bracher noticed it, too. He said, "Can I see the letter? I won't take it away."

"No," said the Dean. He had replaced the letter in the envelope and now put the envelope in his pocket. "The last bit was personal. Of no interest to anyone but myself."

Bracher would have liked to argue, but decided against it. He said to James, "I'll have to know what you told Brookes."

"I told him," said James slowly, "that a final analysis of the specimens which had been submitted to the laboratory had shown minute quantities of acetone, butyl alcohol, iso-propyl alcohol and butyric acid. That is the characteristic pattern of anerobic fermentation. It meant that the nicotine had been distilled in an apparatus which had previously been used for making wine and brandy. The evidence had been preserved because the fermentation in the tissues was stopped by the samples being preserved in formaldehyde. Otherwise it would have disappeared."

The Superintendent only understood part of this, but he recognized hard evidence when he saw it. He said, "And that was when you knew that Brookes was the guilty party."

"I first suspected it when I remembered smelling menthol in the cupboard where his aunt's things were stored. He'd destroyed the cigarettes, of course. But he'd not taken the trouble to banish the smell. He wasn't a very careful criminal. If he had been, he wouldn't have spent nine hundred pounds on a pair of *famille rose* bowls for his wife at a moment when he was supposed to be broke."

"A guilt offering to his conscience," said the Dean. He got up to indicate that the meeting was over.

Bracher followed him, but stopped when he reached the hall. He said, "There'll have to be an inquest."

"Of course."

"And the Coroner will want to see both those letters."

"I'll think about it. In fact, if he insists, I think it would be better if I read the letter out myself."

"Why?"

The Dean said, with a smile, "Because I wouldn't want it to be edited. The Coroner might feel inclined to leave out the names of the supermarket gang. If it brings that mean little swindle into the open, some good at least will have come of this horrible affair."

The Superintendent grunted and moved toward the front

door. The Dean opened it to let him out. When James would have followed, he stopped him. He said, "I think my daughter wants a word with you. She's in the dining room. She's a bit upset. You must do what you can."

James went into the dining room with a sinking heart. His worst fears were more than realized. Amanda was on her feet. Her face was white. She said, before he had taken three steps into the room, "Why the *hell* couldn't you stop when I told you to? *Why* did you have to go on and on, meddling and interfering? Everything was just perfect. The police were lost. The only thing they could think of was arresting Daddy. Which was just what he wanted. They could never have held him. They'd simply have made fools of themselves. And then you—you had to play the clever little scientist and set them onto poor old Brookes."

"Do I gather you've been eavesdropping again?"

"Certainly."

"In that case," said James, who was beginning to lose his temper as well, "you heard the truth about Brookes. The whole truth. How he not only killed the Archdeacon, in a particularly cruel and unpleasant way, but how he helped to swindle poor old Mrs. Henn-Christie. He was meant to be acting as her adviser and he *recommended* her to take a twentieth of what he knew her land was worth. I find it more difficult to forgive him for that than for the murder."

"And who the hell asked you to forgive him? Did you think you'd got some God-given right to judge people? Forgive? When I hear a meddling little doctor use words like that, it makes me squirm."

"Am I to assume from that," said James stiffly, "that any arrangements we had made are canceled?"

"Marry you, you mean? How could I marry you when I couldn't even trust you?"

"Very well," said James, in what he hoped was a dignified voice. "There's nothing more to be said, is there?" He stalked to the door and out into the hall without looking back.

The Dean was waiting by the front door and held it open for him. James felt that something must be said, but could find no words. The Dean saved him the trouble. He laid one hand on his arm and said, "When we are young, James, our lives are ahead of us. We have the three great gifts of faith and hope and love. When we grow old, when most of our hopes have proved liars and love is cold, there is still faith. I have found it to be a strong rock. I hope you will, too."

James said, "Thank you," absent-mindedly and walked off down the path to the road. What had not escaped him was that the Dean had, for the first time, addressed him as James. He wondered whether that devious man had meant anything by it. He was more interested in this than in the Dean's words. He crossed into the precinct.

After he had spoken to Dora Brookes, he had realized that he could not face her again and had packed his few belongings and left his bag at the school cottage. The next train to London was in two hours' time.

The bell for morning service had just stopped. He made his way toward the west door of the Cathedral.

The Dean watched him go. Then he closed the front door gently and made his way to the dining room.

He found his daughter in tears.

The Dean was not a man who was sympathetic to tears, particularly in his own family. He said, in a voice which had the effect of a cold douche, "Crying won't help. I assume you've stamped on the aspirations of that young man, who would, incidentally, have made you an excellent husband."

Indignation getting the better of her tears, she said, "How could I marry him? He doesn't think like a human being."

"I've heard a number of silly statements in my life, but I'm not sure that doesn't take first prize. Do you suppose that all human beings think in the same way? He's a doctor and a scientist, so naturally he thinks like one."

Amanda said, "I know, I know. But when you were talking next door, I suddenly realized what it must have been like for Henry, alone in that room. Knowing what a horrible death it was, nerving himself to do it. All right, he was guilty, but was that any reason to drive him into a corner, to condemn him to such a wretched, miserable death? Had anyone the right to do that?"

The Dean said, "I can assure you that Henry Brookes was neither wretched nor miserable when he took his own life. He was triumphant."

His daughter stared at him.

"If the Superintendent had been less intent on finding out what was in the parts of that letter that I didn't read to him and had listened more carefully to the parts I did read, he'd have realized that what Brookes said was impossible. Quite impossible. How could anyone, carrying a cup of coffee in one hand and moving through a crowd, pour poison into it without being noticed half a dozen times? The idea is ludicrous. The poison was in the cup already. Put there by his wife. She had only to cover it with coffee, hand it to her husband and tell him to take it to the Archdeacon."

"You mean she planned the whole thing?"

"Not the whole thing, no. It was her husband who brewed the poison. But he was a weak man. He'd never have brought himself to use it. When the Archdeacon asked him for his accounts, his nerve gave way altogether. He told his wife everything. About the money and about the poison. But she was the one who decided to use it. She was Lady Macbeth: 'Give me the daggers.'"

"And you saw her putting it into the cup?"

The Dean looked at his daughter curiously. He knew exactly what she meant. He said, "It would have raised a difficult question for me if I had seen her, wouldn't it? But, as a matter of fact, I saw nothing."

"Then how can you possibly know all this?"

The Dean was silent for a long time. Then he said, "I know because Dora Brookes came round early this morning and confessed to me. She wanted to know what she ought to do. I instructed her that she must say nothing to anyone. If she did say anything, the sacrifice her husband had made for her would be wasted. I realized that it would be difficult for her to keep quiet, perhaps almost intolerably difficult. That was the cross *she* must bear."

The Dean paused again. Then he said, "I have broken the seal of the confessional by telling you that much. You will, of course, say nothing to anyone. But I considered that you ought to know, so that you would not blame Dr. Scotland for what happened. Brookes realized that as soon as suspicion swung toward him, it must involve his wife. In fact, as soon as people started thinking clearly about it, they must have realized that it was her hand that put the poison in the cup. That was what he was determined to prevent. That was why he killed himself."

James had very little recollection of the service. It was taken by one of the diocesan clergy. As he was leaving, Masters shook him by the hand and said goodbye as though he was certain he would never see him again.

When he went to collect his bag, the cottage was empty. He walked past the school cottage, past Canon Maude's house, across the corner of the school playing field toward the High Street Gate.

On the heels of the rainstorm, autumn had come with a single stride. Summer had been wiped out with one ruthless stroke of the scene painter's brush. The white vapor which the storm had left behind hung so close above the sodden earth that the roof of the Cathedral was shrouded and the top of the spire was invisible. As James paused for a moment to look back, he saw the file of black-cloaked choristers emerge from the north porch, march across the precinct lawn and whisk into the school. The door banged shut behind them.

The curtain was down. The play was ended.

He turned away to walk to the station through streets that seemed unnaturally empty. Had any of the people he passed been curious enough to look closely, they would have seen a twenty-four-year-old doctor with tears in his eyes.